Orpha

Dora Lee

Chapter One

Orpha slowly opened her eyes. As the view of her surroundings came into focus, a feeling of deep dread arose. She lay enveloped in the silence that hung heavy in the old farmhouse, knowing at any moment the quiet would end with a child's voice or a stirring from one of the back rooms. Instead a cock's crow in the distance reached her ears. She held to her warm bed a bit longer, hoping to prolong the calm of early morning as she reflected on the happenings of the previous day.

The feds had a bird's-eye view from where they sat in the old apple orchard and had been watching for nearly two weeks before the raid took place. Through binoculars they saw the bottles systematically being filled then loaded on trucks that regularly came and went under the cloak of late evening. Orpha remembered noticing on occasion a tiny light flickering between the trees. But people were known to cut through the orchard headed for town or back again.

Yesterday had started out as any other. But glancing through the kitchen window Orpha thought she spotted Melissa Palmer. Drawing back the curtain, she saw the tall, thin woman charging madly up the road—her long, skinny legs flailing out from under her faded housedress, her face red with exertion. As she began cutting across the small grassy area in front of the house Orpha had called out, "Floyd, something is wrong. Melissa Palmer is coming and she's running like a bat out of hell." Orpha and Floyd rushed out to meet her. Breathlessly Melissa told of the imminent raid while clutching her chest. The feds had gotten careless with their cover as the surveillance wore on.

"Strangers all suited up buying cigarettes is something the townsfolk just ain't used to seeing," Melissa excitedly pointed out.

Melissa Palmer and her husband were the owners of the small, rundown farm on the outskirts of Vigus, Missouri, that Floyd and Orpha rented with the understanding that Floyd would work the still for the privilege of working the land. Though they were well aware that running a still was against the law (despite the fact that prohibition had ended the year before in 1933), they decided to take the chance along with the Palmers' offer.

With their two small children and Orpha's younger sister, Mary Barbara, Orpha and Floyd had moved in eleven months ago, bringing three suitcases, a number of cardboard boxes, a few sticks of furniture, and determination to better their circumstances.

It was a year ago last May that they had decided to take advantage of an offer made by President Franklin D, Roosevelt's administration called the New Deal of 1935. Anyone willing to farm would be given a voucher to purchase what was needed in order to follow through with the government's expectations. Orpha was quick to find and fill out the necessary forms in order to receive the badly need help.

With their government voucher they purchased a team of draft animals or, as it happened, one draft horse and a jackass (who learned, over a short period of time, to work well together), as well as a sow they were lucky enough to find pregnant, one cow, a few chickens, six cases of canning jars, and a large pressure cooker. When harvesting time was in full swing, canning the harvest followed close behind. Whereupon the government, in conjunction with the farming agency, sent out a canning instructor. The woman sent to teach Orpha left before the time allowed had passed, saying, "I do believe I've learned more than I've taught." Orpha let a small smile escape as she remembered how impressed the lady had been with her canned goods—something that Orpha had learned from Floyd's stepmother prior to their marriage.

Orpha was young and full of pride and no stranger to hard work. Her five-foot-two stature and slight frame did not hamper her determination. The second oldest of three girls and very different in appearance from her sisters, Orpha had dark hair, olive skin, large gray-blue eyes, and was often called striking. Although she was acutely aware, at this particular time in her life, of not having much going for her and her children.

Orpha stretched her arm out across the bed knowing all too well she would not find Floyd, and she was not really sure she cared. Without her knowledge, he had made a pact with Palmer that if they were caught running the still he alone would take the fall for the Palmers and by doing so there would be healthy payback. Orpha tugged at the quilt, bringing it up closer to her neck. Then, running her hand across her swollen belly, she thought, "Just what we need, another baby."

The thought trailed off as she heard a small voice in another part of the house. Throwing back the warmth of the quilt Orpha pulled herself from the bed with some effort into the chill of the late October morning. Picking her clothes from the nearby chair, she dressed herself, then hurried into the kitchen to the old wood-burning stove sitting off by itself near the end wall. Shivering, she quickly removed two of the round black lids, putting them aside. After crumpling several pieces of old newspaper, she dropped them in along with a few sticks of kindling. Touching a match to the paper, she watched it slowly catch, then blaze upward.

Once she had shoved the well-measured pieces of wood into the gaping iron cavities, Orpha stood for a short time staring down into the fast-building flames that were now licking at the hot, crackling logs. The pungent smell began to fill the room as she dropped the lids back into

4

their positions as the sounds of doors opening and hushed voices from the back rooms announced the day's true beginning. Approaching the small wooden table that sat beneath the window Orpha methodically dipped water from the galvanized bucket into the face pan. Scooping it up with cupped hands she splashed her face. After a brisk brushing of her teeth and a couple fast rinses that she spat into the water of the face pan, she lifted the small window and tossed the water outside. Without fuss she ran the large comb through her long, tangled hair tying it back with a strip of cloth. Her mind picked over yesterday's calamity as she made hot cereal for the kids. It was shortly after Melissa's breathless warning of a possible raid that all hell had broken loose. She was remembering how Floyd bolted to the barn where the mash was stored in two separate concrete vaults that had been poured beneath the floorboards.

Orpha knew that Floyd hoped to beat the feds to the punch by starting the motor that was connected to the hoses in the holding cells to suck the damaging evidence out into the creek. But the damn motor wouldn't turn over. And panic set in as Floyd ripped the hose from its connection, put his mouth to it, and began sucking. He'd taken no more than two or three deep pulls when the butt of an agent's gun landed with a painful thud on the side of his head. Staggering, he desperately tried to stay upright as he was cuffed then shoved to the ground and held as three cars tore down from the orchard across the yard at breakneck speed, taking high, bone-jarring jolts until they came to an abrupt stop. The agents jumped from their cars taking with them sledgehammers, ax, and crowbars.

Charging into the old barn the G-men destroyed everything they could, even hacking at the old wading boots that were used to walk through the mess created by the liquid from the still and the straw that was scattered

5

over the ill-fitting floorboards to hide the trapdoors that led down to the mash.

Orpha had stood there watching as they pushed a submissive, badly dazed Floyd into the back seat of one of the cars, slamming the door behind him.

She recalled that even at a time like that, humor found its way in. "Jesus Christ!" one of the men could be heard yelling as he tore from the barn heading in the direction of the others. Orpha knew immediately what had happened. The sow that she had been keeping in the barn had just given birth to her second large litter, making her very protective.

"That gull darn sow is the meanest, orneriest dang hog I've ever met. She could have eaten me alive. Dang thing got hold of the corner of my jacket, wouldn't turn loose of me until I found a pitchfork and ran it up its snout."

The group started laughing and razzing him about his close call with death. "Hey Max," one of the men taunted. "You know if we stuck you in there with the fumes of all that booze coming up through those floorboards and forced you to stand there day and night sucking it up into that big nose of yours, ten to one you'd be more ornery then you already are." Again, the men laughed.

"Yeah, yeah," Max responded.

"Stupid man," Orpha thought. "He should know better than to approach a sow that's nursing piglets."

As she looked back she could see Mary Barbara, in her mind's eye, becoming furious with the treatment Floyd was receiving. Orpha made the most of an opportunity given her when one of the men suggested with a wink that they might get together behind the barn and possibly it could make things go easier on Floyd. Without a moment's hesitation she had kicked him with all she had in the shin. "Shit, damn it," he swore, seeming to smother a loud yelp

6

into a moan. Grabbing his leg, he gave Orpha a shove, then limped away, obviously not wanting to risk a scene.

Another thought occurred to Orpha while banging the spoon against the edge of the pot, setting the captured glob of oatmeal free. She let the spoon fall into the steaming cereal and ran outside to the back of the house. Bending over, she searched the darkness beneath the decaying wooden porch to try to see the half dozen empty sugar sacks she had tossed there yesterday after emptying them into the creek—thinking at the time it was getting rid of more evidence. But as she fished them out with a long tree branch she could hear the one fed saying to her in an amused tone of voice, "Lady, you could have kept the sugar." "Well, anyway, that's that," she consoled herself. The sacks could be used for many things. And she knew sure as heck she wouldn't be missing the scorching smell of that sugar. It always made her sick to her stomach while burning it down in a large, heavy skillet. After which she had all she could do to lift it so it could be blended with the freshly stilled liquor to give it its rich amber color.

Walking back into the house, Orpha let the screen door bang behind her, then quickly closed the inside door to keep the stove's warmth from escaping. She dropped the sacks on the floor and lowered herself into the nearest chair.

"Mornin'," Mary Barbara chirped, as she entered the room with the two children dressed and ready for breakfast.

"Mornin'," Orpha answered despondently.

Placing each child in their respective chairs, with dishtowels tied around their necks to catch any cereal that might drop, Mary Barbara poured coffee for Orpha and herself, then waited patiently for her sister to break the silence.

By nature more optimistic than her sister and taking life one day at a time, Mary Barbara knew this morning would be different. It was time to figure out how she and her sister would survive. The arresting feds had made it clear that Floyd would be sent to St. Charles Federal Prison for at least eight months and they might as well get used to the idea.

They sat at the kitchen table quietly drinking their coffee while the children made their own kind of chatter between mouthfuls of oatmeal.

Looking about the room Orpha glanced at the dull clapboard wainscoting. Once white, it now carried yellow vein-like cracks across its surface. Her eyes fell to the kerosene lamps in the center of the table that were black with soot. In her mind, they belonged in the garbage dump.

Orpha could not help but explode in frustration, slapping her hands down hard on the surface of the table, making the kids and Mary Barbara—along with the dishes—jump. "Damn this hillbilly way of living! There are going to have to be changes!" she avowed, her voice cracking with emotion as the enormity of her situation came crushing down. "I can't wait for my life to change itself! God, how I hate this!" Once again she grew quiet. Holding her head in her hands, Orpha shielded her face. She did not want Mary Barbara and the children to see her eyes swollen with tears. A short lull ensued as the children sat looking at their mother, not knowing what to expect.

"It's okay, kids," Mary Barbara said softly. "Finish your breakfast. Then you can go out and play." With their aunt's assurance they went on with their meal but kept an eye on their mother.

Getting a grip on her emotions, Orpha lifted her head. "I guess we can . . . " she began, haltingly, "butcher the sow and pigs and hopefully someone will want the cow. God knows she's a good milker. We'll have to buy canned milk for the kids. Don't have much choice. With any luck," Orpha went on, "maybe we could work out something as far as the crops go with one of the neighbors."

"I'll do some asking around down at the post office tomorrow when I pick up the mail," Mary Barbara offered, solemnly. "We're gonna do all right, Orf, I know we will."

A light rapping on the kitchen door interrupted their conversation. "How do, missus," Joe Palmer greeted Orpha. He was a burly man whose form swallowed the opening he now stood in. His wife, Melissa, who was his total opposite —tall, thin, and frail—stood directly behind him, peering around the best she could. "Can we come in for a spell?" Joe asked, taking his hat from his head as he slowly crossed the threshold with an anxious-looking Melissa following close behind.

Joe nervously fingered the brim of his battered straw hat, then continued with what he had come to say. "We weren't sure your husband told you about our deal and so we was thinking we ought to come on by to do what we could to help youns."

Orpha felt a slight prickling at the back of her neck. "No, he didn't! If he had, things might not be as bad as we now know they're going to be. He mentioned a short time before the law got here that you two had some kind of deal and for me not to worry—that we would be taken care of properly."

"We're gonna do what we can missus," Joe continued, shifting his weight from one foot to the other. You can stay rent-free but only until he gets out. The best we can do in money is twenty-five bucks the start of each month for groceries." With that, Joe Palmer shoved the small amount of bills across the table in Orpha's direction. "Can't say as you shouldn't have more but that's how things are for us now, with losing this still and having to lay low on the other one, there's just no telling when more money will be coming. Everyone hitched to this deal is running scared." Orpha bit her tongue. She knew if she were to say what she was thinking, they could wind up with minus the twenty five dollars and a place to live for the next eight months.

Nodding her head approvingly, Orpha picked up the bills, stuffed them in her dress pocket, and moved toward the door, hoping the Palmers would follow. It was obvious they didn't want to stay any longer than Orpha wanted them to.

As the Palmers reached the doorway, Mary Barbara spoke up. "Do you know anyone that might be able to give us a hand with the crops this spring? Any help we can get will be appreciated?"

"I'll check with old man Brunega to see if he knows someone," Palmer offered.

"Thanks," Mary Barbara answered.

Once the couple had left, Orpha shut the door and leaned against it, furious with Floyd and the Palmers, but more upset with herself than anyone. "When will I learn not to believe anything that SOB tells me? He has the dependability of a one-year-old. And this is what he calls well taken care of?" At twenty-two years of age Orpha was quickly becoming wise to the fact that if you want something you may have to get it on your own. Certainly she could not count on the man she was foolish enough to marry.

After an early breakfast the following morning, Orpha and Mary Barbara and the children made their way up the hill to the orchard where the sisters cut down small trees, taking turns chopping them with a hand ax into sizes that would fit the opening of the wood-burning stove. If the farmers who met regularly down at the store were right it was going to be a very cold winter and the wood was going to have to be stacked high. The potatoes had already been dug and put in the small bin of the cellar. Apples were picked, then carried into the shed a short distance from the house where they were buried in large mounds of straw, which kept them from freezing yet left them crisp and cold to be enjoyed while a roaring fire was blazing in the stove.

Orpha was grateful she had canned more this year than last. Her larder would go a long way in stretching the little money they would have.

The day was slipping by quickly and Orpha and Mary Barbara admitted to being bone tired. The children needed to be fed and put down for their naps, so the women headed back to the house—one pulling and one pushing an old, wooden, makeshift cart piled high with logs and two giggly children sitting on the top holding on for dear life.

The warmth of the house felt good to Orpha as she pulled off the children's coats as well as her own and hung them on hooks near the door. Mary Barbara followed behind them, going directly to the cupboard from which she took a quart canning jar and scurried out the back door in the direction of the cellar to collect milk from the large dairy milk can. Returning she filled the children's glasses with milk as they were already vigorously enjoying a bowl of hot vegetable soup Orpha had set in front of them. The morning in the outdoors appeared to have made all of them hungry. Once everyone had eaten and the kids were down napping, the women busied themselves in thoughtful silence as they straightened the kitchen. After the last thing was put back in its place Orpha took the dishtowel from her shoulder that more often then not lay there in readiness. Draping the cloth on a fat nail protruding from the side of the water table she announced, "I'm gonna take a walk over to the post office while everything is quiet here and see if I can scare up some of that help we need." She threw on her coat and headed out the door looking back long enough to give her sister a weak smile as she called out, "Wish me luck."

Taking short, quick steps Orpha hurried in the direction of the orchard just across the gravel road. At the road's edge she caught sight of an old rattletrap pickup truck heading her way. As the truck came near she could see that the bouncing figure of a man was Mr. Glaze, a middle-aged man who she was told lived with his wife and four children a mile or so from her and Floyd. They had only met briefly once before—at the moment she couldn't remember where —she had a good memory for faces. Once she reached the roadside she stood waiting until the truck pulled to a stop in front of her.

Mr. Glaze leaned out the window saying, "You're Mrs. Wilkerson, ain't ya?" Orpha nodded her head. Obviously he too had a good memory for faces. Although his in particular made a lasting impression. Weather beaten, it was broad and flat with small, close-set eyes beneath dark, overhanging brows. His nose spread generously above his full lips that, when parted in speech, showcased missing teeth.

"Well, I hear you're looking to sell some livestock. Would you be interested if the price were right."

Orpha's face brightened with a smile as she asked, "Would you want to come back to the house for coffee and talk it over? I'm sure we can work something out."

"Don't sound too anxious," she thought to herself, trying to keep calm.

"Jump in! Might as well ride as walk," he offered as he reached over pushing the passenger side door open. They drove the short distance without speaking a word, and as they reached the house Orpha could see Mary Barbara peeking from behind the feed-sack curtains, and shortly thereafter meeting them at the kitchen door with a quizzical look on her face.

"Mr. Glaze is interested in the animals," Orpha beamed. "We came back to work out a deal."

"Swell," Mary Barbara smiled.

"Mr. Glaze, cream, sugar, both, or black?"

"Black," he said, settling his short, well-padded body in the chair, pulling it up to the table.

12

Quickly they got down to business with Orpha stating what livestock they had for sale and the looming problem of harvesting the crops. The man took a moment or two for thought as he scratched his chin with the tip of his thumbnail. "I'll take both the Guernsey and the mule for the flat price of fifty bucks, and if you need help planting and harvesting we can do that on shares. That's my offer, take it or leave it."

The women looked at each other, taken aback by his abruptness, but nodded their approval. At this point, any offer would have to be considered fair.

"We really could use some help with butchering," Orpha declared with a hint of desperation, "though we hate killing the litter, being they're so young and all, but we need the meat to get us through the winter."

"That I can do for the sharing of the meat. Let's say three of the litter, done?"

"Done!" Orpha answered, although not sure if she was truly getting the best of the deal.

With business taken care of Mr. Glaze rose from his chair saying he'd be in touch sometime in the next few weeks to take care of the butchering before the weather turned bad.

As Orpha handed him his coat, he caught her hand in his large, fleshy grip, holding it for a moment too long for her liking. He grinned at her now for the first time, flashing what was left of his two rows of imperfect teeth. "I'm happy to help whenever I can. What's your name, girlie?"

"Mrs. Wilkerson, Mr. Glaze," she answered, pulling her hand back and ramming it deep into her dress pocket, not offering her first name.

"Well, you girls just call me Harry," he said, grinning even wider. "Seeing we're partners and all." And with that he jerked opened the door and left.

"He gives me the willies," said Orpha.

13

"Nah, he's harmless, but he don't need to be thinking any slick thoughts when he's around here," her younger sister warned. Mary Barbara had always been very protective of her family and that's the only time Orpha would see her angry, when someone appeared to be threatening them. She recalled the time Floyd had struck her during an argument, and how Mary Barbara went flying at him screaming and ripping the shirt right off his back.

Not being a large man, Floyd decided to call a truce and somewhat muted his anger when she was with them. Not that he was afraid of her, he stated. He just wanted to keep things peaceful.

It had been a very productive day. Orpha was tired but feeling hopeful about their chances of getting over the hump. She sat watching her children playing quietly that evening, George being the oldest by eighteen months and his sister Theresa Ruth two-and-a-half-years old. The baby she now carried was already much heavier than they had been this far along in her pregnancies with them. Arrangements would have to be made before she got too close to her due date. She had it figured for late April but it seemed too far in the future to be concerned with. Nonetheless she made a mental note to take time in the oncoming week or the next time she was at the post office to use the telephone and call Dr. Defoe—who lived on the other side of town—for an appointment.

A midwife had delivered her first two babies without too much difficulty. Her mind trailed back to the night she had had Theresa Ruth, and the odd woman who had assisted her, who was strange but efficient. She had heated two bricks in the oven, wrapped them tightly in towels, and put them at the base of the bed next to Orpha's feet saying it would make the delivery easier. To this day Orpha had not found out what the thinking behind this ritual was.

But that was not the only weird happening at Theresa Ruth's birth. Orpha remembered how excited the woman became as she announced that the baby had been born with a veil covering her face and wanted to know whether Orpha wished to save it. The midwife explained that when a child comes into the world with such a veil it signifies special heavenly powers.

Orpha declined, saying as nicely as she could, "Whatever it means, we'll keep her without that."

Later, Orpha found out from her mother-in-law that the "veil" was nothing more than a membrane that had been left on the baby's face and that she ought not waste her time wondering about this old wives tale.

The next morning before anyone else had awakened Orpha wrote a note to Mary Barbara saying that she would be back soon. She was picking up the mail along with some canned milk, for what fresh milk they had was gone and, of course, the Glazes now owned their cow.

She tightened her scarf and pulled on her gloves while stepping out into the unseasonably cold weather. The wind, damp and cold, whipped about her, seeming to ignore the heavy coat she had bundled herself in. Breaking into a fast walk she steeled herself against the cutting wind by stiffening her body so tightly that after a short distance her back began aching. Shoulders hunched over and her head down she quickly hurried through the orchard. Picking up more speed, now half running, half walking, she was slowly warming from the exertion. She began cutting through the cornfield, which had been recently plowed under, making it difficult to miss the large clods left behind and occasionally turning an ankle, momentarily losing her balance. She lifted her face, which she had buried in her coat as deeply as possible, to see how much longer it would be before the town's buildings would become visible. Just as she cleared the next small hill, there it was. What a welcome sight.

A farm town of seventy families at high count, Vigus, Missouri, was easy to miss. One building housed the three main functions of the town—the grocery store, the tavern, and, of course, the post office. Farther down the street was an auto repair shop that also did emergency welding on farm equipment.

Socializing was rare but once a year a dance was held down at the tavern, and on an occasional Saturday night a few of the farmers would gather at one of the homes to play music —mostly banjo, guitar, and accordion—but if they met at Doc's house you more than likely would be treated to piano and a bit of harmonica.

Floyd played the guitar well, and most of the other instruments—all by ear. He also seemed to do most of the singing until the rest would join him after a few beers. Prior to marrying Orpha, Floyd had traveled with a small country band playing the honkytonks, and did so for his own enjoyment more than any other reason. But that's how Floyd tried to live most of his life many thought—for his own enjoyment. Just under six feet, he was handsome, with a good, strong physique. What attracted Orpha, aside from the palest blue eyes she had ever seen, was his ability to make her laugh.

Floyd accepted life for what it was and what it had to offer. Education came with just everyday living and doing what had to be done to survive. Rolling with the punches was a lesson that came early in Floyd's young life. At age ten he came storming into his home after walking the distance from school, dropped his books on the kitchen table, and yelled, "Mom!" With no answer forthcoming he tore through the house still calling for his mother. He reached the small laundry room at the back of the house and found his mother slumped over the washboard. "Mama?" he called softly as he came close. "Mama?" She did not move. Reality struck a hard blow. Fearing for his mother as well as himself he turned, sobbing, and ran as

16

fast as his young legs could take him to the neighbor's a mile or so up the road. Floyd pounded as hard as his little fist would allow on the front door yelling and crying, "My Mama needs help!" As gently as possible, the doctor confirmed the small boy's worst fear later that day as he spoke with the family. Floyd's young mother, age thirty, had died of a heart attack, as far as he could tell.

Floyd took refuge in his small bedroom, closing the door, pulling the shades, and blocking with his clothing any light that tried to seep in through the cracks around the windows and door. He refused to come out for days and ate very little of the food that was brought to him. Other then the food, he was left to heal at his own pace. One morning, without urging from anyone, he was sitting quietly at the breakfast table, when his father and brothers came down for their morning meal. Although they were pleased to see him, they said nothing and went about their chores for the day.

Floyd's father remarried two years after his mother's death. Although Floyd missed his mother deeply he truly liked this new women—a large lady who obviously enjoyed mothering, baking, and his father. Floyd had two older brothers—Paul, the oldest by three years and Fred, one year older, who was called Cotton, for the lightness of his hair.

Fred and Floyd had both dated Orpha. While she cared for Fred, she found him too serious and old for his years, so she chose Floyd. They laughed easy and often together for he was also a prankster and loved to tell tall tales. Floyd seemed generous to a fault and a perfect gentleman throughout their courtship—rarely showing his irresponsible side. In the spring of Orpha's seventeenth year, Orpha married Floyd. He was twenty-three, and thought he was ready to start a family. And she, more than any other reason, married to pull away from her mother. To have a place of her own, whatever it might be, would be better than living with her.

Floyd's stepmother, Theresa, had been a close friend and neighbor of Orpha's mother, Ruth, long before his father, George, met and married her. Ruth and her family would often be invited out to the farm for weekends. They always had good times together and the two families grew close.

Ruth and Theresa continued their friendship for a long time afterward or until shortly after Theresa Ruth was born. Orpha thought perhaps putting her mother-in-law's name first may have led to the gap between the two women—for she knew how vain her mother could be.

Orpha stepped aside as the post office door swung open and Martha Obeshon brushed by her with more of a grunt then a good morning.

"And a good morning to you, Martha!" Orpha responded, smiling at the women as she hurried off. Once inside she pulled her coat loose and tucked her gloves and scarf into the pockets of the coat.

"Any mail for us?" she asked the man behind the desk. "The name is Wilkerson."

"Oh, I know the name, Mrs. Wilkerson. We heard of the happenings over at your place. How are you girls coming along all by yourselves out there?"

"We seem to be making it just fine so far," Orpha responded. "We are ready for winter and that's the best we can do for now."

The old postal clerk turned to check for mail, and as he did so Orpha felt someone come up behind her and move in close.

"Hey, lady, if you need anything at all—and, baby, I mean anything—I'll be there and ready," a man's voice whispered close to her ear.

She spun around looking into the face of one of the men she had noticed standing in a small group upon entering the building. He smelled unclean, and his surly grin exposed nasty, yellow teeth. She pushed him back and wiped her hand on her coat—as if that would clean off what she had been forced to touch.

"Hey," another called to her, "eight months is a long time for any woman to do without her man, how about it?" The men seemed to get a big kick out of her discomfort, poking at each other and laughing like a bunch of school kids.

"Go to hell!" Orpha retorted, turning back to grab her mail, furious with these clods. She stormed off into the next room, which served as the grocery store.

The old clerk could be heard scolding in a low, muffled voice, which Orpha was sure would do no one a damn bit of good.

"Good morning," a cheerful voice called out as Orpha entered the large room. "What can we do for you this morning?" Still smarting from the encounter that took place next door she forced herself to be pleasant and smiled without much feeling, saying good morning in return.

"Don't let those galoots get at you," the woman behind the counter consoled her. "It seems they got nothing better to do than to stand around and make trouble for folks. It's early for liquor I know, but I'm willing to bet they've been next door already. Now what can I get for you, my dear?"

"I'd like six cans of milk, a couple packets of yeast, a nickel's worth of licorice, and that's it for now," Orpha said, trying to sound friendlier.

She waited, looking about as the woman went off to fill her order. Out of the corner of her eye she caught a glimpse of a figure standing in the doorway. "Oh great, it's that silly pig that was in my ear." Orpha pretended not to see him, asking the woman if she would mind adding a small sack of flour to the list.

"Be happy to. Did you know there's going to be a dance down here Saturday? I guess everyone around these

19

parts will be coming. You girls ought to try to make it if you can. We always have such a good time."

"I would love to, but with two children and one on the way it's not likely. My sister, Mary Barbara, will no doubt want to come. She's crazy about dancing. And, guess what, that's something she's been known to do on occasion all night long without taking so much as a break, would you believe that?" The two of them laughed, enjoying their exchange as Orpha paid for her supplies. Buttoning her coat and wrapping her scarf she prepared herself for the cold trek back. "See you later," she said, smiling.

She started for the door and was relieved to see that the tall, dirty-looking young man had gone. "What a jerk," she thought, pushing him from her mind.

The wind had died down, and what there was would be at her back on the way home. A sack in each arm, Orpha started out walking as quickly as she could, head down, not bothering to look about, just pushing ahead with one thought in mind—getting inside where it was warm.

She had gotten through the field and neared the end of the orchard when she took a backward glance. Startled, she began walking faster. When she took another quick look over her shoulder, her heart jumped to her throat as she gasped, "Oh my God!"

The man she had encountered at the post office was taking long strides toward her and shortening the distance between them very quickly.

Orpha dropped her packages to the ground and started running, stumbling, and catching herself before she lost her balance as she crossed the road. "Mary Barbara!" she screamed. "Mary Barbara!"

She made it as far as the shed, when she felt herself being grabbed from behind and with great force thrown to the ground. He was on top of her, his one hand around her throat and the other pulling at her clothing.

"Wait!" he shouted, stopping and raising himself off
of her. "Come on, god damn it, get up," he said, letting go
of the clothes and grabbing her by the hair, yanking her up
to where he could get his arm around her middle. He started
dragging her into the shed. "My God!" Orpha cried, "I'm
pregnant! Please, I'm pregnant!" She began swinging
wildly at him and looking toward the house, hoping her
sister might look out the window and see what was going
on.

"Hey," he said, "it won't hurt you. Be nice and
we'll both have a little fun." With that, he wrestled her to
the dirt floor of the shed straddling her. He ran his dirty
hand up inside her dress and painfully squeezed her inner
thigh, and as he reached even higher, she mustered all her
strength forward bringing her right knee up as hard as she
could, catching him in the groin. He let out a loud yelp
rolling off on to the floor holding himself.

Orpha pulled herself up and grabbed at the first
thing her hand touched and beat on him, yelling, "You
bastard, you bastard," and continued screaming and beating
him until he lay still. She tore out of the shed, crying
hysterically, running to the house calling out to Mary
Barbara, who met her at the door.

"My God, what the hell happened to you?" Mary
Barbara shrieked as Orpha's coat fell open and she could
see her dress in tatters, her face dirty and bruised, a mixture
of dirt and straw clinging to her hair.

"I think I killed a man!" she cried, pointing to the
shed. "He's in there!"

Mary Barbara finally grasped what had happened to
her sister. Anger like she had never felt arose inside of her.
"That dirty son of a bitch," she yelled. "If you didn't kill
him, I'm sure as hell going to." With that, she ran into the
house, pulling the shot gun out from its hiding place behind
a couple of loose boards in the kitchen. Grabbing the shells

from the drawer she tore past Orpha, loading up while running toward the shed.

The door was open but not enough to get a good look inside. So Mary Barbara kicked it wide open and, without taking aim, fired full blast into the small, weathered shed. She waited and listened, but heard nothing, so she cautiously went inside, ready for anything, hoping this animal would still be there, for her anger needed resolution of some kind.

"Orpha must have used this piece of pipe," she said aloud, turning it in her hand. A bit of red stain could be seen on it as she held it to the light streaming through the open doorway. "I hope the son of a bitch has a headache that never quits," Mary Barbara continued. "He better keep his distance or I'll blow his ass off and love doing it."

She left the shed and headed back to the house, grumbling all the way.

"Are you going to be okay?" Mary Barbara asked upon entering the house. "Should I call Doc?"

"No, I don't think I need a doctor. I just need a few minutes to pull myself back together. Is there any coffee left in the pot?"

"Yeah, I think so."

"Would you heat it up while I wash up and try to get a comb through my hair? Oh damn! The groceries are up at the end of the orchard where I dropped them."

Without answering, Mary Barbara left and headed for the orchard, leaving the shotgun still strapped over her shoulder in hopes of catching sight of the jerk who did this to her sister.

Once back in the house, Mary Barbara set the groceries down and started putting them away. "Maybe we should let someone know what happened. Just in case he decides to try again, with someone else. We could tell people at the post office and let them warn folks when they come for their mail."

"I think he's new around these parts or maybe just passing through," Orpha answered, still visibly shaken by what happened. "I had never seen him before yesterday."

"Had he not crawled away like the coward he is we would be picking pieces of his ass off the shed walls for a good year," Mary Barbara said, anger still apparent in her voice.

Tears now ran down Orpha's face with relief as she became fully aware of what the outcome could have been to her unborn child and herself. "Oh my God, Mary Barbara, I am now realizing how bad this could have turned out. Thank God Mama raised strong women," she continued while taking small swipes at her tears and straightening herself upright in the chair.

"Mommy, you okay?" a small voice asked.

George, who now stood alongside Orpha's chair patting her arm gently, appeared to be frightened and in need of reassurance. "Ah, sweetheart, come here," Orpha said, reaching for her young son and scooping him up in her lap. "Everything is okay, and don't you or Theresa Ruth worry about anything. Aunt Barbara and Mommy are going to be right here to love and take care of you forever and ever, all right?" Shaking his head yes George sat for a long moment, then seemed to understand there was nothing to fear and slid from his mother's lap. Once down he took hold of Theresa Ruth's hand, for she had come looking for him after he had left her alone for too long. Leading her off into the back room to play they could hear him say, "I take care of you forever and ever, okay."

"What a doll," Mary Barbara cooed as they moved into the living room. "Coffee?" Mary Barbara offered.

"Sure, thanks," Orpha replied, as her sister went to the kitchen and returned with a cup of coffee in each hand. Settling down on the old brown frieze sofa with coffee and cigarettes the women tried to recapture the calm that had been lost.

After pondering their situation and what had happened they agreed that they could still be in danger. "We will have to keep our eyes open and our guard up at least until Floyd comes home. When word gets out that women are on their own, it's open season for any jackal that wants to try his luck." Her anger and fear were now ebbing into a more cautious awareness.

"But, you know, Mary Barbara, I have to say this: If that pig was still hanging around when you kicked that shed door in and let go with that full blast, even God damn Jesse James would have crapped his pants."

A few moments of silence ensued.

"Oh, I wanted to tell you I'm thinking about taking the bus Saturday to see Floyd. Would you mind staying with the kids? If I leave early enough I should be back by late afternoon. Then you can still make the dance they're having in town if you want. Just do me a favor. If you decide to go, be sure someone brings you home."

"Yeah, maybe you're right. It might not be too fetching to go to a dance with a shotgun," Mary Barbara replied with a chuckle.

Early the next morning Orpha boarded the bus that would take her to St. Charles Federal Prison. It was a ride she didn't take too often, only when she felt she could no longer make excuses that Floyd would believe. She found the ride too long and arduous in her condition.

Choosing the seat next to the exit door in the rear of the bus, she moved in and sat down by the window. While looking out she caught her own reflection in the glass and smiled briefly, thinking not bad, for she had taken special care to look her best not so much for her husband but for her own feeling of self-worth. Well into her fifth month now she was becoming quite large and still had a way to go before the baby would be due. While mulling this over she did not pay much attention to someone taking the seat next to her.

"Going far?" a voice broke in.

"No," she answered, glancing over at the man. He was persistent with his desire to make conversation but she answered his questions with one-word responses. The man finally grew still, and Orpha returned to her thoughts. The bus was bumping along a bit too slowly it seemed to her and she really wanted to get through this day as quickly as possible. Aside from the trip being unpleasant, she knew what Floyd's request would be as soon as she arrived at the prison and she also knew she would refuse it.

A cot with a sheet suspended from the ceiling covering the bars on the front of his cell space was hardly enough privacy for sex. And Floyd being Floyd would never take into consideration the fact of her size and her possible discomfort on a small cot, so to hell with him she thought. The slowing of the bus and finally the noise from the brakes brought her back and she could see the prison from where the bus sat. The man who had been sitting next to her got up, stepped out into the aisle, and extended his hand to her.

Orpha smiled, "I can manage, thanks." He politely nodded and turned to walk forward and she followed him off the bus. "He probably meant well but you just don't know anymore," Orpha thought as they went their separate ways.

Floyd stood there with a big grin on his face as she walked in, grabbing her to him tightly as soon as she was close enough.

"Hey doll, you look great! Good enough to eat. Come to Daddy! Let's see what you brought me." His hand unabashedly went up the side of her skirt and down across her stomach, searching.

"For God's sake, Floyd!" she said pushing him away from her. "You don't have to act like a starving dog after a bone, and there are other people in here."

"Yeah," he said, "and some of them are getting what I'm supposed to be getting." He was losing patience now and putting pressure on her to come across with what he felt was his for the asking.

Orpha looked him in the eye and said in a sweet sarcastic voice, "If you think for one minute I'm going to screw you or you me on that damn tiny cot and have everyone within earshot listen to the sounds you enjoy making, not today or any other."

Not pleased with the results of his efforts, Floyd nonetheless settled down in conversation. They spoke of where they might move when he was released and what their money situation was and would be. Orpha said nothing about the attack made on her, not for the reason of sparing Floyd worry, for she doubted he would suffer much anxiety over it. It was simply that she wanted to forget it and not have to rehash it. She let him know how well the Palmers took care of them and that if he ever made such a harebrained deal again without her knowing, she and the kids would be gone.

"Hey, I thought he was a man of his word, a swell guy. You can count on me to kick his ass when I get out of here, for playing me for such a chump." Orpha knew hot air when she heard it and went on to other things—changing the subject. She reminded him that the baby she was now carrying would probably be born before he returned home. She felt he or she would be larger than the other two and was nervous about the delivery. This brought a smile to Floyd's face. "Good stock, that's what it is," he crowed, smugly. "I'll try to hold back a little next time," he laughed, seeming quite pleased with himself as he reached over and grabbed Orpha's knee, squeezing it. She gently brushed

Floyd's hand away and began talking about their situation and what arrangements had been made with Harry Glaze.

"Times up!" one of the guards yelled out into the large, hollow room. Low mumblings of private conversations and the occasional laugh were now replaced by the sound of chairs scraping across the floor as visitors rose to say their goodbyes.

Floyd reached for Orpha, looking intently into her eyes as he sadly shook his head. "You poor kid. I wouldn't blame you if you did leave me, but whether you believe this or not, I do love you!"

Orpha felt a surge of warmth pass through her, but it was short-lived, for she knew from the past that his words would be quickly forgotten and things would probably remain the same and would only change if she took steps to change them.

Floyd kissed her long and hard until she pushed him back. "I've got to get going," she told him. "I'm going to miss my bus."

Chapter Two

Mary Barbara had never known a stranger, and a smile
came easy to her face, which was framed by thick,
unkempt, dishwater blonde hair cropped just below the ears
that did nothing for her strong, angular features. Her
personal grooming habits left a bit to be desired. Although
she bathed often, she had a habit of donning the same
rumpled dress she had just shed prior to her bathing—a
habit that annoyed and perplexed her mother and sisters.
"Why do you put dirty clothes on a clean body?" they
would ask. Her standard lighthearted answer was, "Come
on, now, you know there are a few spots on here I've
missed. I'm just giving myself a second chance." Humor
that was lost on her family tickled her. Unbelievably as a
baby she had been so tiny that a small dresser drawer had
served as a crib for such a long period of time, so the story
went, that her mother became concerned that she would
never grow. "But once I started growing," she enjoyed
saying, "I liked it and didn't want to stop." At the age of
thirteen her hand was as large as the average adult male's.
At nineteen she was taller and much larger than Orpha and
most women they knew and worked easily alongside any
man. And she knew not to quit until the chore was done.

Mary Barbara was looking forward to the dance in
town tonight and decided she was going to have one hell of
a good time. But right now she would start working at
looking her best. Taking the large face pan from beneath
the cupboards she filled it full of water, placing it on the
stove to heat. She then began tearing small strips of cloth
from an old rag to wrap her hair around making curls,
which was a style she seldom wore. Selecting one of the
three dresses from the closet that badly needed pressing
was not difficult using the eeny meeny miny moe method.
Dropping the printed cotton across the ironing board that

was always left standing, she reached for the flat iron, placing it alongside the pan of water that by now was producing a light steam.

"Someone is going to get hurt, slow down," Mary Barbara called out to the children, as they chased each other around the kitchen table and back through the house laughing and making growling sounds. "Oh well. I guess it's better they're noisy and playing than fussing at each other," she thought out loud. Taking the pan of water from the stove, she placed it on the table and proceeded to wash her hair and then herself. Once finished with her sponge bath she pitched the water out the back door and went to rolling her hair on the small pieces of rag that she pulled from the stringy pile on the kitchen table.

The door opened and Mary Barbara looked up. Seeing her sister she gave her a smile. "Well, how did it go?"

"Oh, pretty much the same as it always goes with him." Exhausted, Orpha dropped in the chair closest to the door still wearing her coat and scarf, needing to rest after the long trek from town.

While sitting Orpha noticed the pains Mary Barbara was taking to fix her hair. "Anyone special you have in mind? Or are you just thinking the prettier you look the larger your selection?"

"Something like that. Hadn't really thought that deep on it," Mary Barbara laughingly replied.

Rising from her chair with the intention of shedding her wrap Orpha was met by two small children who came barreling at her as fast as they could, yelling, "Mommy, Mommy!" She grabbed them both to her and threw the coat she was wearing about them saying, "Aunt Mary Barbara, have you seen Georgy or Theresa Ruth?"

"Nope, haven't seen 'em. They're probably gone."

"We're here, we're here," they said, playing the game and peeking out from underneath.

29

"Oh well, I guess if we can't find them. We won't be able to give them a licorice stick."

With that, both children came out from their hiding place, standing directly in front of their mother so she would have to see them. Orpha looked over their heads, saying, "Where could they be?"

Tugging at her coat, Georgy and Theresa Ruth called to her, "Mommy, down here."

She looked down at them smiling and said, "I found them! I found them!" Hugging them both she then gave them the candy they came out of hiding for, and sent them off to play.

"What time were you planning on leaving?" Orpha asked while shedding her wrap and dropping it on a hook.

"Well, maybe I should think about going before it starts getting too dark, so I can see where I'm walking and who might be coming at me. Not that I wouldn't be willing to give that creep a shot, but might as well give myself every break I can. Although I doubt he or anyone else is standing out in that freezing cold in hopes I'll be coming down the pike. And if that's the case they are really nuts and should be feared," Mary Barbara laughed, finding the idea of anyone wanting her that badly ridiculous. Orpha was quick to let her know that there were plenty of men that would give their eyeteeth to be with her.

"Yeah? Name one!" Mary Barbara dared her with a smile on her face. "Men are scarce in these parts unless they are married, and I don't need those kinds of problems. But I'll go to the dance anyway. Who knows? There may be a good-looking single Joe visiting one of his relatives. Or maybe one of the ladies wouldn't mind sharing her husband for a dance or two. We shall see." She pulled the ironing board over nearer the stove to make it easier to reach the flat iron and continued taking fast swipes as she finished pressing her dress.

"Guess I'd better get dinner started. It's getting late," Orpha announced. "You are planning on eating before you leave?"

"Sure, I'll need something to keep me going other than booze tonight," she quipped over her shoulder as she left the room to dress. Moments later she returned, taking a spin about the room asking and hoping for approval. "Do I look like someone's dancing partner?"

"You look swell! You really do! You won't have any trouble finding a partner, believe me!"

"Thanks! Just what I wanted to hear," Mary Barbara said, tickled with the answer.

In the midst of their meal, the sound of someone pulling up to the house caught their attention. Mary Barbara pushed her chair back from the table and hurried to the door, just as Martha Obeshon was stepping down from the running board of their truck. The Obeshons lived a distance from them, so they only saw them occasionally in town or maybe at one of the very few social functions. Nice sorts— both Martha and her husband Heinz—most people thought. Quiet, easygoing, hardworking, but once they started drinking and having a good time—especially with Martha—you never knew what was going to happen.

"We heard you might be going to the dance," Martha called out to Mary Barbara, so we stopped to see if you wanted a ride? If so, shake a leg. We want to get there early enough to nab a good spot." Mary Barbara waved her arm with one finger extended, letting them know she'd be there in a flash, tore back into the house, grabbed her coat, and said, "I've got a ride, see you later."

"Well, don't you look real special," Martha teased, as Mary Barbara climbed in the front with them, "curls and all."

Mary Barbara blushed with embarrassment. "Thanks for stopping for me," she said, hoping to quickly change the conversation. That something else was still gnawing at her. "Have you heard anything about a drifter being in town lately?" she asked.

Heinz leaned forward enough to see past Martha and said, "No, why? Something going on we should know about?"

Mary Barbara explained what had taken place a few days ago, and that she still would like to get a piece of this animal, who as far as she was concerned should be strung up by the apples. Bad enough he should try raping any woman but a pregnant one to boot she protested. As her anger started to build, Mary Barbara kept in mind that she didn't want to ruin the evening by dwelling on it for too long, although she needed to know if he was still hanging around.

Martha shook her head slowly, saying, "My, my, my." Looking directly at Mary Barbara she asked," Your sister is all right? I mean he didn't hurt her did he?"

"She's okay other than having the living shit scared out of her," Mary Barbara answered.

Then as if struck by a revelation, Heinz spoke up. "I'll bet he's the same fella Doc stitched up some days back. He said a young man staggered into his waiting room with his skull split wide open, mumbling something about getting into a fight and a beer bottle being used on him. Doc said he stitched him up, and the last he heard he was seen the next day getting on a bus headed for St. Louis. I guess he figured he had better high tail it out of here while the gittin' was still good.

Slow to give up the idea of getting revenge for her sister, Mary Barbara had to finally admit to herself this was more than likely the same creep. "Well, I hope he's not so in love with dying that he'd take a chance in coming back, for I would hate to burn for such a piece of trash."

"Let it go, girl, let it go," Heinz advised. "Don't let it eat you up! Anyways it sounds to me like your sister pretty well took care of the varmint."

As they drove into town Martha made notice of hardly seeing a soul but once they saw the building where the dance was to be held they understood why. "Every truck and car within a twenty-five-mile radius must be here tonight," Heinz said with a big grin on his face. "Yep, looks like a big time heading straight for us."

Once the truck came to a complete stop, Mary Barbara flung open the door and jumped down—great expectation and excitement now surging through her.

She became acutely aware of the sounds and smells that seemed to intensify her enthusiasm for the evening as she entered the spacious, well-lit room. Loud talking, laughing, and the musicians tuning their instruments gave her cause to scan the room quickly, searching for her first dancing partner. She had come for a good time, and wasting one moment was not in her plans.

"Over here, Mary Barbara," Martha called from across the room, waving her arm madly in the air. "We have a table."

Making her way through the ever-growing crowd, Mary Barbara joined her friends but did not yet sit, as she still hadn't seen anyone that didn't seem attached to someone else.

"Looks like they're going to have to open those doors to the post office to catch some of this overspill. Whew, what a turn out!" Martha commented.

As if on cue, the large doors that separated the two rooms were thrown open. Extra seating was quickly created by covering wooden crates with wide boards that served as benches along the walls.

"Here we go," one of the men said loudly from the makeshift bandstand. Music with a quick beat filled the rooms. Martha and Heinz were one of the first couples to hit the dance floor. Mary Barbara, still anxiously looking about, finally settled her attention on a good-looking man standing at the bar—seemingly alone.

She moved toward, then hesitantly up to him. "Say, would you mind being my first victim?" She smiled her best smile, hoping it would get her the right answer.

"If I said yes you would be the victim," he laughingly replied. I don't dance too good."

"I'm not bad," another voice spoke up from behind her. Turning, she looked up at a tall, thin, homely older man, whose smile seemed to make up for what else he might be lacking.

"Sure, why not?" she replied. "A dance is a dance, and that's what I came for," she thought. He took Mary Barbara's hand, leading her out onto the crowded dance floor. "My name is Frank. What's yours?" he asked, leaning down and closer to her.

"Mary Barbara," she answered, beaming up into his face.

They left the dance floor only twice that night for quick drinks and brief rests. Mary Barbara commented that she hadn't had this much fun in a very long time.

"Frank wasn't much to look at, but he was one hell of a swell guy and a great dancer," she thought. "How lucky for me he decided to come tonight!"

"Ladies and gentlemen, we're taking a short break but we'll be back in a jigger," the guitar player announced. Mary Barbara and Frank found their way back to the table where the Obeshons were already sitting and laughing and cutting up; they were more than a little drunk. They hadn't been there for more than a couple of minutes when a very loud angry woman, pushed her way over to their table loudly calling Martha a slut and accusing her of dancing suggestively with her husband. She continued yelling at Martha as she poked at her shoulder with a rigid finger. She went on to say she didn't like it one damn bit and that she had better keep her distance if she wanted to keep her face where it was. The woman turned in a huff to leave, but Martha wasn't ready for her to go. With one fast move,

Martha was on the back of the woman—one hand in her hair and her other arm locked around her throat, dragging her to the floor. By now everyone had stopped what they were doing to see what the ruckus was about and stood watching the two women rolling around on the floor beating the hell out of each other. Heinz finally pulled himself up from his chair and—with the help of another man—broke it up, scolding his wife as he brought her back to the table and made her take her seat.

"She called me a slut. You heard her," she said loudly. I'm not taking that from anyone." Her hand came up above the table, still in a tight fist that was holding a large hunk of the other woman's hair.

Before Heinz could grab her, Martha took off across the room, finding the owner of the hair, which she dramatically threw at her, saying, "I think your missing this." Turning on her heel with head held high, she projected a picture of the victorious warrior as she made her way laughingly back to her husband, who by now was losing his patience. "You'll sit down, okay, Liebchen?" he requested firmly. Martha brushed herself off, and after straightening her now-soiled and torn dress, she plopped down on her chair, brooding while she ran a comb through her long, dark, badly tangled hair.

They all sat quietly for a short time with no one really knowing what to say. Martha broke the uncomfortable silence with, "I think maybe we should go home. I don't feel so good." Heinz, in full agreement, went to get their coats.

"Sorry," she muttered, "but I guess it's just as well. Morning comes early and the work waits to be done." Heinz returned and began helping his wife into her coat. With a knowing grin, he asked if Mary Barbara would be coming along or if she had a ride with someone.

"I'll see her home," Frank said with a broad smile. "We still have a dance or two we would like to finish. With that, the Obeshons left, and slow-dance music began.

Frank motioned to Mary Barbara, asking if she cared to dance. Without hesitation she took his hand and let him lead her once again to the dance floor.

As their bodies moved to the tempo of the music Frank tightened his arm around her waist and brought her in closer to him. Mary Barbara sucked in a small gasp of air, as he placed his mouth alongside her ear and asked how she felt about him seeing her home.

She looked up at the tall man, and with a smile replied, "I would like that very much." They moved in even closer and she could feel his body tightening and pushing gently against her. It was nice to be dancing with someone she was attracted to who was taller than herself.

The music ended and the announcement made, "That's it folks, a good night to you all." Mary Barbara looked about and became aware that they were one of four couples left on the floor. Most of the crowd had left; they and a few stragglers sitting about were the only ones there now.

"Oh gosh! I didn't notice so many leaving. I must really be having a good time!"

"That's swell," Frank answered, giving her a good squeeze. "You should enjoy yourself. You're young, beautiful, and deserve a good time." Mary Barbara was startled by such a statement, for she could not remember anyone ever referring to her as beautiful. And she doubted the sincerity of such a compliment, even coming from this kind man.

"Should we take the time and have one for the road or would you rather make tracks for home?" Frank inquired, his arm still around her waist as he led her back to where they had been sitting. It didn't take any coaxing for Mary Barbara to decide to stay a bit longer, for she had thoroughly enjoyed his company throughout the evening, and hated to see it come to an end.

Once seated she watched Frank return to the bar for their last drink. The homeliness she had noticed earlier seeming to recede beneath the quality of his personality, and she now found him quite attractive. Returning, he placed the drink in front of her as he whispered softly in her ear, "I think you're a very special young lady, and I would really like to see you again."

Mary Barbara found herself uneasy with his flattery and not knowing how to respond she shook her head yes, saying, "Sure, why not? Sounds swell."

Reaching into his shirt pocket, he pulled a pack of cigarettes out, offering her one, lighting it, then lighting one for himself.

After blowing a cloud of smoke toward the ceiling he went on telling her a little about himself—his full name, Frank Wierzynski, and that he was a close friend of Doc Defoe. In town for a short visit while getting some work done on his car, the charges were more to his liking than what he would pay in the city. As to whether he was or is or ever will be married, he wasn't, isn't, and has no plans in the near future, unless, he teased, she would consider his proposal.

Mary Barbara had never met such a charming man before, and really was at a loss for words. But a few of his polite questions about her and her family relaxed her as they finished their drinks. Finding their coats, they left the all-but-deserted rooms that just a short while ago had been filled with sounds, the clinking of glasses, loud happy voices, and feet keeping time with the music on an old wooden floor. It seemed almost sad Mary Barbara thought to herself, that such a good time had to end so soon.

The ride home was very quiet and she could feel the tenseness of anticipation between them. Frank drove with his one hand on the steering wheel, and held her hand in the other. As they were about to pull into the area behind the house, Frank turned out the headlights and killed the engine, as not to waken Orpha or the children.

Nothing had to be said. They reached for each other, as though a great thirst had to be satisfied, and in their embrace and deep passionate kisses, they lost all connection with the world.

"Frank," Mary Barbara, whispered.

"Hum?" he responded.

"This is my first time."

He pulled back from her, took her face gently between his two large hands, brushed his lips across her mouth, and promised he would be extremely considerate.

Taking off his coat, he formed it into a pillow, laying it up against the door on Mary Barbara's side of the car, then slowly and gently pushed her back until her head was resting on it. He ceremoniously began opening the buttons of her dress. Her firm breasts had no need for a brassiere, and the night's soft light lit the way. He pushed the dress aside and while admiring what had been exposed, slid his hand down the front of her panties and into a very warm, moist and now welcoming place, for she was pressing up against his searching hand. Her deepening wetness made soft noises as it kissed his fingertips. Then leaning over he kissed her first on the mouth, then flicked each protruding pink nipple with the tip of his tongue, leaving the moisture to coolly evaporate.

"You truly are beautiful," he murmured, his mouth now sucking lovingly on her breast and still gently caressing and fingering her below.

Mary Barbara thought to herself, "My God, this is painfully wonderful." The intensity of her feelings were almost frightening to her.

"Would you like to try? Do you think you're ready for me?" he asked as he kissed her gently about the face.

" Yes," Mary Barbara whispered. "I think so."
Frank moved to the center of the seat at the same time
helping Mary Barbara up and onto him. "Ever so slowly,"
he said, guiding himself into her. She hesitated for a
moment, and then lowered herself the rest of the way. They
moved together rhythmically for a short time, until, with a
small moan, her surroundings blurred. "Oh my God!" she
breathed, as her short prayer was followed by an intense
shudder. Mary Barbara went limp, resting briefly, then
slowly pulled herself back onto the seat while quietly
adjusting her clothing, not knowing what to say for the
moment. Frank reached over. Cupping her chin in his hand,
he turned her head so he could see into her eyes. He kissed
her lightly on the mouth, as he spoke softly, "Sweetheart,
you'll never know how wonderful you were or how much I
enjoyed being with you." "Me too, Frank," she said,
smiling. "Me too."

The weak light of the chilly early morning seemed
to strain against the night's darkness, while barely
silhouetting the trees against the now gray sky behind the
orchard. Mary Barbara waved goodbye to Frank, then
leaned heavily on the back door while turning the doorknob
to keep it from making noise as she opened and closed it.
Tiptoeing past Orpha's room and into the privacy of her
own, she quickly undressed, as an afterthought fished her
underwear from her coat pocket, dropped everything into a
heap on the floor, and with great relish fell into bed too
exhausted to even think.

Chapter Three

For Orpha the winter months seemed to drag on forever. Although some cold weather was still with them, spring was just around the corner as the saying goes and would be bringing up the young shoots of crocus along with other early spring bulbs that others before them had planted about the house. Once the ground dried and warmed up enough, the sowing of the crops would begin. Orpha was really looking forward to the sunny, mild weather that the changing of the season would bring.

Being very large and quite heavy with her baby, Orpha was forced to fashion a sling for herself to lessen the stress and discomfort that she now carried. Folding the material from an old sheet into a long broad piece, she brought it up under her pregnant belly tying it behind her neck. Catching her reflection in the dresser mirror she cringed at what she saw. "Oh my God," she gasped as she came close to breaking into tears. "I look like a freak from one of those circus sideshows." Fear of the delivery that, up to this point, Orpha had stubbornly pushed to the back of her mind now surfaced. "I hope I can do this," she said out loud with a quiver in her voice. "Baby, you had better come soon or I'm going to bust." Turning from her image she pulled her large sacklike dress back over her head, tugging it down over her enormous stomach.

Mary Barbara had been a great help these last few months. She all but took over the chores and the children and refused to let Orpha do much of anything.

Although Orpha protested that she was not a cripple, she was grateful to her sister. At the end of the day, she was exhausted from the little bit she did do, and from carrying her unborn child.

Orpha had noticed that Mary Barbara seemed to be singing and almost giddy much of the time lately. She wondered if her sister might be getting too involved with that long drink of water from St. Louis, Frank Wierzynski, who had been out to the house almost every weekend since the dance early last fall. He is nice enough and he certainly appears to be crazy about her, Orpha thought, but she would talk to Mary Barbara about him next chance she got. Maybe when she returns from town.

Mary Barbara came bursting through the back door tossing some of what mail she had on the kitchen table but still grasping one small envelope. Upon hanging her wrap, she gleefully began waving the envelope about with such delight that it appeared she might be about to start dancing a jig. "I know something you don't know," she said in a teasing voice grinning from ear to ear. "Guess who's coming to visit?"

"Who?" Orpha inquired.

"Guess!"

Aw, come on Mary Barbara. I don't feel like guessing."

"Mama, that's who!" Mary Barbara exclaimed as she laid the letter down in front of her. "I didn't think you'd care if I opened it. I recognized her writing and couldn't wait to see what it was about."

Orpha began reading her mother's letter, which said that she would be stopping in for just a short visit, on her way to Mercy Porter's home, with whom she had been a close friend for years.

Mercy had moved to a town not all that far from Vigus, and she figured she would kill two birds with one stone. She should be arriving around four o'clock on the eleventh of March via the bus, and would be leaving on the thirteenth.

Orpha was pleased about her mother's visit, yet grateful it was to be brief. She had enough to contend with without the strained feelings that might occur if she and her mother spent too much time together.

Her mind began sifting through the past, which still vividly lived with her. The fact that she and her two sisters were placed in Catholic orphanages shortly after their father left their mother was not the thing that she felt resentment for. Her mother had no choice and was lucky to have had an in with the mother superior, Sister Louise.

What she could not get past, were the infrequent visits. The free tuition that had been offered for a college education through the home and flatly refused by her mother, who said, "I have done without long enough. It's time they do for me!" The beatings with the broom handle when she was late getting home from her job downtown. That the train was off schedule wasn't a good enough reason—or as far as her mother was concerned a good enough excuse. She would have severe panic attacks on the way home knowing her mother would be waiting for her.

She tried to run away at age thirteen with three other girls and met up with two boys the same age. They hadn't gotten far from the home before they were caught. She and the other two girls were taken to a girl's detention home at the request of her mother where she was then examined to see if any sexual activity had taken place. Of course, they found nothing, as she kept trying to tell her mother through her tears. Orpha remembered what a horrible, scary place it was, and begged and cried to go home, but her mother said she deserved to at least spend the night for what she had done. Enough time had passed that she was able to understand why her mother might be the way she was, but she still couldn't let go of the hurt.

As a child she had learned by example that expressing or showing emotion was considered a character flaw—unless of course the emotion was anger. Spoken love and loving acts were saved for infants or for the bedroom. Touching others was, it seemed to Orpha, always a little strained. Marrying Floyd had not changed things much. For sex was just that, nothing more. Orpha had never discussed her feelings about her mother or such things with anyone, not even Mary Barbara. For she felt Mary Barbara harbored ill feelings for no one. She accepted people mostly for the good in them, unless of course they meant to do her loved ones harm.

"Well," Mary Barbara began, breaking into Orpha's thoughts, "anything special we should do before Mama gets here? She can have my bed. I'll even iron the sheets. You know how fussy she can be." Her younger sister, as far as Orpha could tell, didn't seem even a little offended at her mother's constant needling about her appearance and attitude toward life. She would respond with, "Oh, that's just Mama," if Orpha would refer to any critical remark their mother might make.

Mary Barbara waited no longer for her sister's answer as to what must be done in preparation. Dragging a chair to the window she began taking the kitchen curtains down to be washed. Remember when we were living on Wild Horse Creek Road, Orf? And Mama came to visit that winter. It was so cold one of the pillow slips you hung out on the line broke in half in the wind. I would have never believed such a thing if I hadn't seen it with my own eyes," Mary Barbara chattered on. "But for days afterward your hands were swollen from rubbing so much laundry on the board. I remember how Mama sat and massaged them for you with warmed oil. She was really worried."

"Yes, she seemed to be," Orpha answered, thinking to herself that that was one of the very few times her mother had demonstrated she cared at all. She often wondered whether her father's leaving was because of her mother's aloofness or whether his abandoning them made her that way. He and his brother disappeared about the same time. It was reasoned that they had left together. Orpha could remember her mother and her Aunt Annie discussing their husbands when they thought they were alone. How little they had seen of them due to the fact that they were both actors. And between barnstorming and odd jobs, there wasn't much time for family life. Her father had been a child actor, and in fact her mother still had a photograph of him in his costume as Little Lord Fauntleroy. It had been said that his theatrical group, which included his two aunts known as the Leslie Sisters, had indeed given a command performance of this play for Britain's royal family. "Their claim to fame," she thought, and smiled to herself. Neither her mother nor her aunt ever heard from their husbands again and, to this day, neither has any idea whether they are still among the living. But one thing Orpha did know for sure: they never rose to the top of the profession they had left their families for, unless they chose to leave the country and work the theaters of Europe. "That's a wild thought," she told herself, as she grabbed the edge of the kitchen table, pulling herself up from the chair. Adjusting her sling, she walked toward the door, taking a sweater from the hook saying, "I'll check for eggs."

She went out the back door, and as she headed in the direction of the chicken coop she could hear Mary Barbara yelling, "You kids get back in here."

"I must have left the door ajar," she thought.

The very next moment, a loud commotion caught her attention, and it seemed to be coming from the hen house.

Orpha hurried as best she could, but before entering, she peeked through the small window on the side and could barely see what was taking place due to the thick coating of dirt. So with her hand she rubbed a small circle clear. She could see well enough now, spotting a very large king snake that had gotten in and seemed to be having his fill. At his mercy were the baby chicks, for the hens had taken refuge in the rafters.

Picking up a hand ax and rake that were left leaning against the outside wall, Orpha opened the door slowly. Taking short, hesitant steps toward the snake, and in a move that proved to be fast enough, she pinned the culprit with the rake and then in one pass of the ax behind his head declared, "Dinner is over!" She forced not only four chicks out of the opening where his large head had once been, but a few eggs as well. With the prongs of the rake, she picked up the snake and his now-useless meal, tossing them outside in the nearby field. Gathering what eggs were left, she started for the house. Back inside, Mary Barbara, with excited energy, continued bustling about as she hummed a tune.

"You know I just killed the biggest damn snake in the hen house. He had four chicks along with enough eggs to make breakfast for everyone, and was still eating when I got him."

Taking the eggs she had collected from the skirt of her dress she carefully put them in a bowl.

"Mary Barbara, did you hear what I just said?"

"Yep, I did. Those snakes can be real pigs, can't they?" she snickered, obviously in a happy frame of mind and amused at her own wit.

"Did you know you're a nut?" Orpha asked, smiling as she shook her head.

"I know. Ain't that great?" She stopped long enough at what she was doing to face her sister and give her a bright, exaggerated grin.

"Okay that's it, this place shines like a new penny," Mary Barbara declared, obviously pleased with the results of two days of scouring and polishing. "I'll put out a few fresh doilies and we'll be all set," she said, dusting her hands against each other.

"It really looks very nice. You knocked yourself out. I'm sorry I wasn't much help, but maybe in a few more weeks I'll be able to carry my fair share of the load a little better. With any kind of luck the baby might just decide to come early. God knows he's big enough to make it on his own.

"Anyone home?" a voice called from outside the kitchen door. The women looked at each other in disbelief.

"Mama?" they said to each other. Mary Barbara hurried to the door, yanked it open to find their mother, Ruth, on the other side.

"Mama, what are you doing here? I mean how did you get here? Your bus isn't due until four."

"Mary Barbara, would you please let me come in?" her mother pleaded impatiently. "These bags are getting heavy!"

"Oh sure, Mama," she said, stepping aside, and at the same time taking her luggage. I'll just put these in the bedroom that we fixed up for you. Even ironed your sheets! We know how you like that."

"Thank you, dear. I'm pleased to know you haven't forgotten the little things that make me happy," Ruth called out to her daughter as she left the room.

"You look wonderful, Mama," Orpha declared, "but then you always do." Here stands a woman close to her forties, and yet she could be strong competition for most women in their late twenties, Orpha decided, while looking at her mother.

Vain and self-centered, Ruth took care of her needs first and, if at all possible, in a first-class manner.

Her clothing, although not top quality, she wore exceptionally well, and always knew what styles and fabrics showed off her slim body. Orpha's large blue eyes were the only characteristic that resembled her mother. Ruth was a tall, well-proportioned strawberry blond with legs that had modeled silk stockings for a living, and she did not mind showing them off whenever the opportunity presented itself. "She can still make heads turn," Orpha thought.

"You needn't get up, Orpha. I can see from the size of you it would be too much trouble. Mary Barbara, please take my coat," Ruth asked as she slid from it.

46

"My God, girl, you are huge! Are you carrying twins? And how do you get around? Have you seen a doctor?"

"No, Mama. As far as we know it's just one baby, and it's not easy getting around as you can't help but see. Yeah, I've seen a doctor who promised to be here when it's time."

"Speaking of babies, you have not asked about the children, Mama. Would you like to see them?" Orpha inquired, putting Ruth on the spot.

"Of course, where are they?" she said, not quite convincingly.

"Mary Barbara, would you mind fetching the kids for their grandmother?" Orpha asked.

Without responding, Mary Barbara left the room briefly and on her return walked George and Theresa Ruth over to where Ruth was sitting on the sofa. The children stood awkwardly before their grandmother.

"Give Gramma a hug," Orpha instructed.

Obediently George reached toward Ruth, but before he could touch her she took his small hands in hers saying, "That's all right, sweetheart, you don't have to hug me. As little as you two see me, I know I'm a stranger to you."

By this time Theresa Ruth had found her way next to her mother and was watching the exchange between her brother and grandmother. Ruth smiled one of her lackluster smiles and she dismissed the children with, "The two of you can run along now. Gramma will see you later." With one last light squeeze of her small grandson's hands she released him.

"Come on, Theresa," George said softly as he waved his younger sister to follow him. They were more than willing to be excused and tore off in the direction of the back room to play.

Orpha was not at all surprised at what had just taken place. Ruth had never been receptive around children let alone her grandchildren. Not that long ago, Arline had told a story of Ruth's complaining of Arline's two little boys, Donald and Raymond. While visiting with her she accused them of stealing candy from her candy dish and when Arline asked how she knew, she said, "Because I counted the pieces before they got here." Orpha was shocked when she heard the story and just thinking of it now made her sad.

Ruth's concern lasted moments more after which she returned to her favorite subject. "Whew! What a trip! I swear that bus stopped at every jerkwater town from here to St. Louis." Pulling a chair away from the table Ruth slowly sank down on it and continued. "It made very good time. I arrived in Vigus about twenty minutes early and decided to join a fellow passenger for a quick refreshment in town. Maybe you know him? I think he said he was related to your doctor or a friend of his, a Frank somebody. All I know is he was good enough to run me out here, and for that I'm grateful."

"Was he very tall and thin?" Orpha questioned.

"Yes, a beanpole. His name was Frank Zinski or something on that order. Some very Polish-sounding name. Nice man, but, God forbid, homely as a mud fence."

"I think he's the same man Mary Barbara is dating and has been since last fall. His name is Frank Wierzynski. He's from the city. Strange he didn't come in with you."

"Who are you talking about?" Mary Barbara asked as she joined them.

"Mary Barbara, you shouldn't break into other people's conversations like that. It's bad manners. Please try to remember that dear," Ruth lightly scolded. "We are talking about this friend of yours who rode out with me on the bus. During our visit he had mentioned that his car was ready to be picked up from the repair shop. He offered a ride and a drink, and, needless to say, I accepted both. He's quite a bit older than you isn't he?"

"Yes, but we have a great time together. He even asked me to marry him you know."

"No, we didn't know! When did this happen? What was your answer?" Orpha probed.

"He asked me last weekend, and I said maybe, but not right away. He seemed okay with that so it was left there. I'm not sure I want to be married to him though, even as good as he is to me."

"Well, if you have doubts, don't do it. It's as simple as that," her mother instructed. And I do hope you're not doing anything that you might have to pay for later."

"That's right, Mama," Orpha thought, "always think the worst." Mary Barbara's face showed her embarrassment as she tried changing the subject. "Anyone for a cup of coffee or bite to eat?"

"Coffee will do just fine," Ruth replied as she gave her youngest a good looking over. "I mean it, Mary Barbara, you had better be very careful with what you do or you will pay, not him. A man never seems to pay. He can just leave when the fun is over. Love them as little as possible. Trust them even less."

"Which reminds me," Ruth continued, "Mercy's daughter, Roberta, would like you to come and stay, whenever you can for as long as you care to. The request was made through her mother's letter to me. You two always seemed to get along during the time we were neighbors. It was probably because neither one of you ever had a serious thought in your head," she added with a scoff. "Make sure you do think about it," Ruth instructed. "Change your surroundings and the course you seem to be taking. God knows you would be in good hands."

"I'll think on it, Mama, but not until Orpha has the baby, okay?"

Later that evening, as the women sat talking about recent happenings, as well as the happenings of years ago, a knock at the door made Mary Barbara bolt from her seat in the sitting room and race for the back door. "It's most likely Frank. He said he'd stop by," she declared.

"Mary Barbara, do you always have to run? Can't you walk like a young lady?" Ruth called out.

Hesitating at the door for a moment, trying not to appear too anxious, Mary Barbara slowly turned the knob and pulled open the door. "Hello Angel," Frank said with a big grin on his face. "Miss me?"

"Well, of course," she laughed. "How could I not miss you?"

"That's true," he said leaning in to lay a quick peck on her cheek.

"Come on in. I want you to meet my mother."

Taking his hand she led him into the living room where Orpha and Ruth were waiting.

"Frank, this is my mother, Ruth Hellings," said Mary Barbara, gesturing toward her mother upon entering the room.

"We've met, and not that long ago," Ruth said in a soft, throaty voice.

"I know," Mary Barbara insisted," but not as my mother and my boyfriend."

Frank flashed his beguiling smile, bowing slightly as he respectfully offered, "Nice to meet you again."

Not too sure of her mother's response, Mary Barbara slid her hand into Frank's other hand as it hung by his side.

"Had I known you were seeing my daughter at the time, I might have allowed you to buy me another drink," Ruth beamed up at him as she extended her gracefully draped hand.

"Oh brother," Orpha chuckled to herself. "I wonder who will win this shoot-to-kill charm contest." The encounter lasted only a short period, due to Mary Barbara's suggestion that she and Frank take a ride to town, as Ruth had a way of monopolizing any man's attention

The visit from her mother was brief, and, therefore, pleasant enough. Ruth left Monday morning early, telling Orpha to let her know when the baby arrived, and that she would be writing once she got settled at Mercy's. Orpha watched as her mother and sister walked down the dirt driveway, headed for town. Mary Barbara carried both pieces of luggage, while Ruth picked her way carefully over and around the thinly iced puddles left from the storm the night before. Orpha continued watching until she could no longer see them.

She remained at the back window looking toward the sky. The sun seemed to be fighting for its right to shine as the soft gray clouds brightly edged in its light moved continuously across its face. The strong gusts of wind blowing through the yielding branches of the budding trees huffed at the muddy puddles of water scattered about the dirt, making small, disappearing ripples on the surface.

Orpha welcomed the changing weather. It had warmed considerably from a week ago, bringing a lifting of her spirits in knowing that in the very near future her baby would be born. "Oh God, make it soon," she prayed out loud, a small desperate prayer, as she turned to leave the window. The oncoming weeks were like a slow-motion dream, with each day dragging on forever.

Planting had already begun, and the canning jars that were emptied on a daily basis were washed and stored in bushel baskets in the cellar waiting to be refilled again. Orpha made the trek to the underground storeroom this morning, her apron filled with jars that clinked against each other as she walked. She added the empties to the growing glass pyramid protruding from one of the baskets, and pulled herself up the first of the broken concrete steps that led to the outside. Grabbing hold of the old wooden door that had been flung back against the ground, Orpha suddenly found it necessary to grip tightly until the strong contraction faded. Once it had subsided, she made her way into the house, urgently calling to Mary Barbara, "The baby is coming! See if you can get hold of Doc!"

"Oh my God, are you going to be okay?"

"Just go!" Orpha snapped.

"I'm on my way." Mary Barbara tore out the back door, letting it bang loudly behind her, running as fast as she could—headed for town.

Orpha's water had broken and the pains had reached intervals of every two minutes, and were very strong by the time she heard the doctor's car pull up to the house and the doors slam shut.

"We're here, Orpha!" Mary Barbara anxiously called upon entering the house. Black bag in hand, Doc Defoe hurried into the room Mary Barbara pointed to.

"Mommy's in the bedroom," Georgy told them. "Is Mommy going to die?" he asked, with obvious fear, as his little sister hung to his side, her eyes wide with worry.

"No, of course not," Mary Barbara assured him, scooping the two of them in her arms. "Your mommy will be just fine. Don't you remember? She is just having a baby, another little sister, or maybe even a baby brother for you. You two go play now," she smiled as she took her arms from about them. "And don't worry. I promise your mommy will be okay. Okay?"

"Okay," they both answered, holding hands, as Georgy tugged his sister out into the bright, warm day.

Orpha's delivery was long and hard as she suspected it might be. The baby's head had crested shortly after the doctor had arrived but his shoulders were very broad and had to be massaged and manipulated with large amounts of Vaseline to help him through the birth canal. "It's a boy, a very big little boy! Oh, Orpha, he's beautiful, and not a wrinkle anywhere on him," Mary Barbara excitedly declared, as the doctor cut the cord that had connected the mother and child. Then, in a sweeping move as he supported the infant's head, Doc took the baby by the ankles, holding him in an upside down position. But before he could smack his behind to dislodge any mucus that might silence him, the baby let it be known he was not happy with what was taking place and in a loud, lusty voice registered his angry complaint.

"He certainly sounds healthy," Doc Defoe chuckled. "And he most definitely looks healthy. Let's clean him up a little, then we'll weigh him." He worked on the infant for a short time, sponging him off and doing what was necessary, then lowered the screaming child onto the small scale he had brought. "Twelve pounds! That's a lot of baby—the largest I've ever delivered of three hundred births," the doctor proudly told Orpha, as he leaned over and placed her now-clean and snugly wrapped newborn in her arms. "It's no wonder you had such a grueling time of it. Now, Orpha, I want you to take it easy for a few days whenever possible. Although we saw to it that you didn't tear any, the birth was not easy on you."

"Thank you, Doctor," Orpha responded. "I don't know what I would have done without you."

Smiling, Dr. Defoe patted Orpha gently on the head. "You just take care of my little mother and my big baby. I'll be back to check on you both in a few days," he said, snapping his bag closed and picking up the scale. "Stay down as long as you can," he instructed, as he and Mary Barbara left the room.

Looking down into her new son's tiny face, she whispered, "Well, little man, what shall we call you?" But before she could respond to her own question, she fell— exhausted—into a deep sleep. Sometime later that evening, the door cracked open just enough for a sliver of light to come in, then a bit more, so that two small heads could fit past the doorway and peek at their new baby brother. Looking up at their aunt they wore disappointment on their faces, as they shook their heads. "No," Georgy whispered, "we can't see him."

53

"Wait here!" Mary Barbara told them, as she went back into the kitchen, picking up one of the lamps. Turning it down very low, she led them into the room and alongside the bed. As they leaned in to take a better look, Orpha opened her eyes and smiled at them, asking, "Well, what do you think? Should we keep him?"

"Can he talk?" Georgy asked.

"Not yet, but I promise you he will," his mother replied.

"Okay," Georgy said, "let's keep him."

"Can I touch him?" Theresa Ruth wanted to know.

"Very gently touch his face with your finger," her mother told her.

"He's soft," the little girl said. "Yes," her mother answered. "Say good night now. We'll see you in the morning."

"Good night, Mommy, good night, Baby," both children said together, as Mary Barbara led them from the room with the muted light of the kerosene lamp. "Goodnight, see you tomorrow," Orpha called out in a quiet voice. Now alone with Ronnie she murmured, "Well, my little son, your father could not make the big event and welcome you this day, and that is sad. But I am here and I will be here with you for as long as you need me."

Chapter Four

It was late in the month of June and the women were just finishing the morning chores. The last piece of laundry had been clipped to the clothesline, and a persistent balmy breeze made them flap themselves dry under a cloudless blue sky.

With the windows and the back door open Orpha could hear the baby crying as she approached the house. It was time for his late morning feeding and she could tell from his urgent cry that he was hungry. Hurrying to the bedroom she grabbed the sheet that had been folded back to the foot of the bed. Slinging it over her shoulder she bent down picking the baby up from his crib while speaking softly to him. "It's all right, Ronnie. Mommy is here. Shush, don't cry sweetheart, it's okay."

"Mary Barbara," Orpha called out, "the baby and I will be outside!"

Pushing the screen door open with the arm that held Ronald, she let it close with a bang behind her. Orpha settled down on the sheet beneath the swaying branches of the old willow that stood by itself at the side of the house. With her back supported against the tree she began to nurse her son.

Floyd would be coming home any day, she thought. Aside from the fact that the children would be happy to see him, the idea of them picking up where they left off gave her a feeling of hopelessness. She was not looking forward to it.

She leaned her head back on the tree looking up into the long, slender branches of delicate, green leaves gracefully moving with the warm breeze. The constant motion of the green against the deep blue of the sky was hypnotic and seemed to soothe her.

Her sister's voice brought her out of the spell of richly colored tranquility. "I thought I'd take the kids with me, if it's okay with you," Mary Barbara stated. "We need a few things from the store, and if there is any mail at the post office I could pick it up."

"If that's what you want to do it's okay with me," Orpha said, smiling at her sister. Looking across the yard she got a kick out of the preparations Mary Barbara had made for the long haul.

The old cart they used to haul logs had been covered with a well-worn quilt to soften the ride, and there were sandwiches and a big jug of lemonade. Also in place were Georgy and Theresa Ruth waving goodbye while the cart stood motionless. "They are so excited about their trip to town," Orpha thought, smiling at them as she waved back.

She watched as Mary Barbara walked back to her small, anxious passengers. Grabbing hold of the long, narrow, old board that had been attached to the cart to serve as a handle, she began pulling the cart with her as she left the yard and headed for the road. "Bye, Mommy! Bye, Mommy," the two children yelled back as they continued to wave until they could no longer see her.

Ronnie had fallen into a sound, contented sleep, satisfied by the richness of his mother's milk. Orpha remained sitting, enjoying the weather and the outdoors a bit longer, then pulled herself, the baby, and the sheet from the ground, and went into the house. Slowly and gently, so as not to wake him, Orpha laid Ronnie in his bed, then left the room, shutting the door quietly. As she turned, her heart leaped in fear and a loud yelp escaped her lips.

"Hi, doll face. Surprised to see me?"

"Floyd, for God's sake, you scared the holy hell out of me."

"Hey, that's the best you can do?" He grinned, almost leaping at her, grabbing her around her waist at the same time yanking her body into his so close that she could feel what his thoughts must have been on his way home.

"You look good and smell even better!" Floyd said, as he buried his face in her neck and fumbled impatiently with the front of her dress. Kicking the chairs out of his way, he lifted her, sitting her on the table, then with his hands on either side of her buttocks, pulled her to the table's edge.

"Baby, I have nearly gone nuts just thinking about this," he said, his voice low and a little shaky as he quickly unzipped his trousers.

Gripping her firmly, he pushed his way past her underpants and in, as he moaned out loud, "Oh God, oh God!" Orpha offered no resistance nor did she allow herself to participate or help for she knew it would be over so quickly, there would be no sense in it.

Once he had finished, Floyd backed away, adjusted his clothing, and zipped his pants. "You're still the best piece of ass around," he proclaimed, grinning from ear to ear.

Ignoring his crude compliment, she slid from the table, while buttoning her dress. Walking to the water table, she grabbed a wet cloth and the bar of Fels-Naptha soap, and proceeded to scrub the table where Floyd's one-sided sex act, as most of them were, had occurred.

"Would you like to see your son now that the important things are taken care of?" she asked.

"Yep, sure thing," he answered, following her to the bedroom. Floyd bent over, peering into the crib as he took the corner of the blanket from his new son's face. "Good-looking boy," he said, smiling, "but we knew that before he was born, didn't we? We do good work, baby," he continued, as he patted Orpha on her rear. "Now, what do you say we get back to catching up on our loving?"

"You seem to have only one thing on your mind, Floyd, and that's most of the time," she chastised him. "For

God's sake, what about the kids? Aren't you the least bit curious as to where they might be?"

"Look toots," he responded with a shameless smile on his face. "If you were a man who'd been sent to the pokey for six months with your hand as your best friend and not a woman around when you needed her you sure as hell wouldn't be asking about the kids. So, come to Papa," he said, reaching for her. "Later! Not now!" Orpha snapped. "Mary Barbara will be back any minute, so just pull your horns in."

"Okay, cookie, he reluctantly gave in, but tonight it's you, me, and the big fella." Orpha turned her back to him and began making a fresh pot of coffee and at the same time asked if he was hungry. Even though she would rather not be married to, or living with this man, she was, and, as such, she was raised with the knowledge that sex and being waited on by her were his supreme right and her wifely duty.

The two of them sat quietly for a few moments. The summer breeze picked up a little strength and could be heard whistling softly through the screen door while coffee percolating filled the room with its rich aroma.

"I don't remember if I mentioned in any of my letters that Mary Barbara had received an invitation from Mrs. Porter's daughter, Roberta, asking her to come and stay a while with them," Orpha began.

"Oh yeah?" Floyd answered, with obvious interest. "Is she going?"

Orpha thought she detected a slight touch of hope in his voice. "Yes, she wanted to make sure you would be home before she left, you know how she is about us?"

"You mean you and the kids, don't ya?"

Come on, Floyd, how about the time she nailed that truck driver with a beer bottle, when he was using you for his punching bag?"

"Yeah, that was some kind of a brawl wasn't it?" he answered, and started laughing thinking about it. "Did you catch the surprised look on that palooka's face when she nailed him? Wham! Hey, I could have handled him easy if I had seen him coming. He caught me by surprise," he said in his own defense.

"Oh, is that right?" Orpha scoffed. "Well, if there is ever a next time I'll tell her to leave it be, then she can just warn you, instead of saving your butt," Orpha suggested. They hadn't gotten off to a very good start and the nagging discomfort she was feeling was beginning to really irritate her. "He's such a jackass," she thought. "But ass or not I'm stuck—at least for the time being."

They decided to stay on in the small farmhouse, paying the Palmers rent by the month in order to take advantage of the harvesting and canning season. Shortly thereafter, in late September, they moved to St. Louis into a large second-floor apartment. Floyd found a job working in the laundry room of De Paul Hospital in the city. The pay wasn't that good but it allowed them to eke out a living. Orpha took in ironing by the basketful along with mending, which augmented Floyd's paycheck.

Chapter Five

Mary Barbara, by this time, had settled into the Porter home, sharing a large four-poster bed and enormous bedroom with Roberta. The room, as with the rest of the manor, had been dressed in a garishly ornate, almost vulgar, decor, but to Mary Barbara's untrained eye it looked almost regal.

The friendship between Mary Barbara and Roberta picked up where it had left off—as if they had never been apart. They did everything together for the first few months and had a grand time about town. Her friend bought her small gifts, treated her to lunch, and paid her way to the movie theater numerous times. Mary Barbara had begun to feel uncomfortable with Roberta's endless generosity, so much so that she began refusing to tag along, giving any plausible excuse.

Time passed quickly and she saw less and less of Roberta aside from an occasional morning meal or a Sunday dinner.

To fill time as well as attempting to pay her own way, Mary Barbara diligently set about cleaning, polishing, and doing anything needed to keep the stately old house running smoothly. Eventually, without a formal agreement, she assumed the position of housekeeper, receiving little or no resistance from any member of Roberta's family. In fact, Mercy appeared quite pleased with the arrangement, giving Mary Barbara a weekly allowance that she not only felt fair but found to be overly generous, even with the number of chores that grew steadily.

Mercy's father, who had arrived from the old country just a year back now lived with his daughter's family, keeping to his room most of the time. The old man spoke only German, and, being feeble, his daughter was given power of attorney and ran all aspects of his life.

Albert Tobeck had brought with him great savings that Mercy now controlled aside from the money she obtained from the selling of her previous home shortly after his arrival. She seemed to be swept up in a new kind of spending frenzy and was self-indulgent to a degree some said bordered on mental illness.

Mary Barbara paid no mind to the gossip. She had known this woman a long time, and knew of many selfless deeds she had performed for others.

Mercy's husband, Verne, a man of meek disposition and a good twelve years older than his wife, shared Mercy's home but not her bed, not for years according to Mama. Only one other person lived at Mercy's aside from Roberta, that being her simpleminded older brother, Willie. Pleasant and unassuming, Willie trusted most people and would give the shirt off his back if he thought it would help. But more often than not, Willie was the butt of others' jokes.

Mary Barbara remembered when Willie dropped in to see Floyd and Orpha one summer. Sitting at the kitchen table, he spotted a large wasp on the inside screen of the kitchen door. He had asked Floyd what it was. Floyd, knowing all along the danger that might be involved for Willie, responded, "Go ahead. Touch it, Willie. It's just a bug, it won't hurt you." And of course it did hurt. Willie let out a loud yelp of pain.

Floyd was still laughing when Orpha heard the commotion. And once she was made aware of what had taken place, she was furious with Floyd. "You know," she censured, "it's bad enough to inflict pain on a person that has all his faculties, but to do it to someone as slow as Willie, you should be horsewhipped! What is wrong with you?"

"He'll be okay," Floyd chortled, brushing off the scolding with a wry grin. "He wasn't hurt that bad. Things like that will help make a man out of him," said Floyd, obviously still pleased with the success of his mean prank. As far as Mary Barbara knew, that was Willie's last visit. And she couldn't blame him one bit.

The Porter home was a hub of activity, with people coming and going constantly. Two who seemed to be there a great deal of the time were the Gencola brothers— Tommy, twenty-one, the oldest of the two; and Dominick who had just turned seventeen. Mary Barbara noticed Tommy was forever hanging on Mercy and looking at her with big lovesick cow eyes. Apparently, she was not the only one aware of what was going on. One morning at the breakfast table, Verne uncharacteristically spoke up, saying timidly to his wife, "Mercy don't you think it's about time you told that boy to go find himself a girl and stop making a fool of himself with you?"

Her response was immediate and furious, taking everyone by surprise. "How dare you!" she screamed, pushing her chair back, assuming a position over him as though she were ready to swoop down and pluck him from his chair. "How dare you tell me what to do," she went on, her face now red with anger, "you worthless piece of trash. You had better heed my warning old man and keep your mouth off of me! Do you understand?" Verne said nothing as he bowed his head in submission, obviously regretting his provoking such a blistering attack that continued for some moments. Mercy slammed her husband with a seemingly endless barrage of scathing insults. Once she had finished her tirade, she stomped across the room and up the stairs that led to the upper floor.

Mary Barbara and Roberta were stunned as they watched Mercy disappear from the stairwell that was directly across from where they sat at the table. Willie had a silly grin on his face, appearing to be snickering at someone else's misfortune for a change, until Roberta shot him an angry look, and he, too, as Verne had earlier, bowed his head.

Tension at the Porters' mounted as the days and months slipped by. Mercy seemed agitated, and complained of not having enough money. Her, as well as Roberta's, spending habits had taken their toll. She appeared to be more relaxed when Tommy was around, whose unabashed billing and cooing with her disgusted the entire household. But she would spin off into fits of anger that more often than not were directed at the poor old man upstairs or her husband, Verne, who tried desperately to stay out of her way.

Mary Barbara had prepared breakfast this morning as she did every morning, leaving what was allotted for the others on the stove to keep warm.

Verne had been served his hot Cream of Wheat, the cereal he preferred during the cold months, for—as he had put it to her each and every time she served it—"It keeps the fire going in the old belly."

"His weak attempt at humor," she thought, as she smiled and agreed with him.

But this morning would be a morning Mary Barbara would never forget. She had helped herself to a bowl of cereal, sat in her chair across from Vern, poured milk from the quart bottle, and just as she placed it back on the table a loud crack rang out in the kitchen. She saw the milk and the bottle spread across the red and white checkered oilcloth that covered the kitchen table.

Verne had slumped over with his head resting half on the cereal bowl and half on the table in front of him. Blood from his head wound, a large gaping hole, was now mixing with the shattered glass and milk. Mary Barbara fell to the floor as she tried to flee the horrifying scene that she had now become a part of. Her mind and physical movements seemed to be working in slow motion. She pulled herself up and mouthed a scream that could only be heard in her own head.

The second one had just passed her lips and could be heard well throughout the house as the others came racing into the room.

"What the hell is going on in here?" Mercy demanded, entering the kitchen from the back bedroom located on the first floor. Her eyes looked at Mary Barbara then took in what the young woman was pointing at.

"Holy God!" she exclaimed, approaching her husband's now dead body. "Did any of you see who did this?" she asked, her voice choking with tears. "Dear sweet Verne," she mourned, using endearments that Mary Barbara was sure no one had heard Mercy use for a very long time, and her otherwise bland response made it seem hollow.

"No one," Mary Barbara answered, feeling herself shaking from the inside out.

Willie was still standing in the upstairs doorway with his eyes as big as saucers and his mouth hanging open in a state of shock and disbelief. Roberta was now sobbing uncontrollably over her father's body, crying, "Daddy, please Daddy, don't die." Mercy took her daughter firmly by the shoulders, yanked her away, and pushed her toward Willie. "Take her upstairs!" she ordered. "Now!" she shouted at the young man, bringing him out of his daze.

As they left the room, Mary Barbara mentioned she had not seen Tommy this morning. Mercy spun her very large frame around so she could look directly into Mary Barbara's eyes and said with a look that made Mary Barbara's blood run cold, "Young woman, you did not see Tommy because Tommy wasn't here—period! Do you understand? I'm sure you're aware that bad things can happen to people and those close to them if they go around trying to get certain other persons into trouble! Is my meaning clear?" Mary Barbara nodded that she quite understood the woman's meaning, for she would never subject any of her family to danger through her own lack of thinking.

What followed next was almost as unbelievable to Mary Barbara as the murder itself.

Mercy left the room and went into the hallway where the telephone was located and asked the operator in a voice close to hysteria for the police. Someone had shot her husband, she explained, and then, as if she were truly in pain, she began sobbing pitifully.

By the time the cops had arrived she was red eyed and close to passing out. As a matter of fact the smelling salts had to be passed under her nose at least a half a dozen times while she lay convincingly across the sofa, her hand spread dramatically over her forehead.

The cops bought it hook, line, and sinker. That in itself was mind-boggling. But when Mercy pointed the accusing finger at the feeble old man who was not equipped to defend himself Mary Barbara was convinced the whole thing was a very bad nightmare and in desperation gave her head one hard shake—trying to awaken herself—but the distress continued. The inspector in charge of the murder investigation went from one to the next, all of them suspects they were informed, and would be continually questioned at his will from then on until he was satisfied with the answers. The inquiry seemed to drag on forever, until finally the man in charge announced that a visit should be paid to the old gentleman upstairs, to see if some kind of sense could be made from the answers he might give. The police had been told that he spoke no English and the only one that could understand him at all was his daughter who of course was so overwrought at this time, she would be of no help to them.

"Herr Tobeck, this is the police, *kommst du bitte.* May we talk with you?" The inspector tried desperately to remember the little German he had learned during the war as he rapped loudly on the bedroom door, but there was only silence from the other side. He pushed the door open to find the old soul hiding beneath his huge feathered comforter. He would not let go as the two cops tried to tug and pull it back. He kept going further toward the foot of the bed, but with one very hard yank the two policemen ripped the old man's covering from him and found him huddled in a frail ball.

The inspector continued to try to converse with the man who kept pressing himself tighter, trying to become even smaller, but they could not get through to him. "He seems incapable of hurting anyone," the assistant commented, "but if we can't talk with him how will we ever be sure one way or the other?"

"Well, we do know that he and his son-in-law had a great dislike for each other. And according to the daughter, she heard her father threaten the deceased more than once," the inspector pointed out, "and the others did not refute her. That's hardly proof of murder, but it certainly bears looking into. Have the men check this room thoroughly and let me know what they find," the officer in charge directed as he started to leave the room.

"Inspector, I don't think we have to look any further. I found this under the sheets beneath the pillows." Dangling from the fountain pen the cop used to pick it up was a thirty-eight Smith and Wesson, and with a quick sniff he determined that it had recently been fired.

The inspector shook his head in pity at the form still rolled up in a fetal position. "Come on, let's go. It appears that we have what we need; and for God's sake give the man his blanket."

Mary Barbara had followed the two men to the top of the stairs and had been standing and waiting on the landing in hopes she might be of some help. She liked Abeck, a name the family members sometimes used in referring to him. As far as she knew in the time she had been living there he had not so much as raised his voice, let alone become violent with anyone. She watched through the open doorway as the two cops went about trying to get answers. She felt so sorry for this pathetic, frightened old man, knowing that down deep he was not the murderer.

As they were leaving the room the inspector took the weapon from his assistant, wrapping it in the handkerchief he had pulled from his pocket. Looking up, he noticed Mary Barbara and motioned her to him.

"You're the maid?" he inquired.

She hesitated for a moment, not having ever heard herself referred to that way, and answered, "Yes, you could call me that I guess."

"Would you get this man's things together?" he asked, motioning with his head in the direction of the bedroom. "Prepare him the best you can for a small trip."

Mary Barbara's heart sank, for it seemed to her that the old man was about to be charged with the murder of Verne. And because of his inability to speak clearly in his own defense, poor Abeck would wind up in some nasty, terrifying state institution for the rest of his life.

As she went about gathering Abeck's things, her thoughts went back to the session of questioning by the police and how Mercy had kept alluding to her father, calling him that crazy old man, all the while appearing close to collapse with grief. "Lies all lies," she thought. "Mercy knows something. My God, what happened to this woman to make her so heartless? She knows her father didn't do this thing. Why?" she asked herself out loud.

"Why what?" another voice spoke from the opening door.

Startled, Mary Barbara looked up quickly to see Mrs. Porter walking toward her, still dabbing at her now-swollen red eyes.

"You have questions about something that's bothering you, Mary Barbara? Please tell me, my dear. What would you like to know?"

A strange mixture of anger and fear seemed to be taking over, anger because she knew without a doubt the old man had done nothing wrong and felt she had a pretty good idea who had killed Verne.

The night before she had seen Tommy go up the stairs still wearing his coat. At the time she thought it strange. Normally he threw it onto the large, wooden coat tree at the front door. She knew he had not come down in the morning before or with everyone else, guessing that he had done the dirty work, then slipped out of one of the upstairs windows. These things were racing through her mind as she prepared Abeck for his departure. Then there was Mercy's unexplained threatening of her. For now she was convinced that there was a definite conspiracy between her mother's close friend and the woman's young lover Tommy. She also felt without any doubt that this madness could affect her loved ones. As much as she hurt and feared for the old man there could be nothing on God's green earth that would make her offer up her family members as sacrifices for him. "Well," she stammered, "I . . . feel bad about your husband. Umm, now they seem to think Mr. Tobeck had something to do with his death. I . . . just don't understand why."

Mary Barbara tried desperately to hide her true thoughts while at the same time she hoped she had given Mercy a satisfying answer.

The large, intimidating form now stood at Mary Barbara's side. Taking both of her hands from the midst of her packing, and with a firm tug, Mercy turned Mary Barbara to face the cold, dark evil exuding from those small, swollen eyes.

"You know your mother and I have been the best of friends for many years, and I have a great affection for all of you. I know this has been a terrible experience for everyone." Lowering her voice to the point that Mary Barbara strained to hear, Mercy whispered, "But we must all go on living, mustn't we?" As she spoke, she was squeezing Mary Barbara's hands harder and harder. But at the point where Mary Barbara felt the urge to lash out at her new enemy, Mercy suddenly let go, turned on her heel, and left the room.

Chapter Six

Mary Barbara moved back in with Orpha and Floyd as soon as the law allowed her to leave town. The newspapers had carried a full account of the murder, citing the deranged father-in-law—though definitive proof had not been established—as the likely suspect. The gun had been found in his possession and his grief-stricken daughter's statement that there had been great animosity between her father and her husband rendered the case all but closed. Mary Barbara was mentioned only briefly but not by name, referred to as the maid who had been on the scene at the time of the murder.

Orpha noticed that since Mary Barbara had returned, she was different somehow—edgy and unresponsive. And when she was pressed for information about what had happened at the Porters, she would become evasive, doing her best to change the subject.

"Maybe we should leave it alone for a while," Orpha suggested to her sister Arline as they chatted over a cup of coffee. Arline had come to collect her two young sons from Orpha's care. She had arrived in St. Louis a short time ago via Greyhound bus, fleeing an abusive marriage and the state of Florida. After a short stay with Orpha, she found a tiny furnished apartment some six blocks east of Orpha's. The first month's rent and a short supply of groceries had taken most of what she had squirreled away for the move. But fortunately the defense plants were running round the clock and were hiring new help almost continuously. Aside from frequent letter writing, the sisters hadn't seen much of each other over the last few years. Their paths had taken them in opposite directions—though, it appeared, along the same lines. All three knew they could count on each other when the need was there—as it often seemed to be.

Their arrangement had been working out rather well for all concerned. Arline paid what she could for her children's care; Orpha took in ironing and some mending, while Mary Barbara cleaned the homes of the wealthy. All and all things weren't too bad, and a heck of a lot better than when Floyd was in prison. It was now late afternoon and Floyd had left for work. He would be working the night shift for the next couple of weeks, which to Orpha's mind was a pleasant thought. It meant she would not have to share herself or her bed with him for the time being.

Having gone to the confectionery down the street, Mary Barbara unknowingly offered her sisters the chance to discuss her and the Porter affair at full length.

"I would bet my last dime, Orpha, that she has more to tell than she's letting on. Whenever I bring up the Porters or anything that has to do with them she denies knowing what went on or just plain won't answer me—like she didn't hear the question. Come on now, we know she was inside that house probably every day that she lived there? Shouldn't she know something more than what she says?"

"Well maybe she's telling the truth. Maybe she really doesn't know anything. It's not like her to be too scared to speak up."

"Not usually, but if it turns out she knows nothing I'll be one shocked cookie. Good riddance to that whole clan. Frankly, I'm glad she got out of there. No telling what might have happened had she stayed longer."

"But you know, Arline, I do agree with Mary Barbara on one thing that she said. It had to be someone other than the old man. What would he have to gain by killing anyone at his stage of life? According to her, he was a sweet old guy who hardly left his room. When would he see enough of Verne to build up that kind of hate? Without a doubt, it's a good thing she's here with us. And besides, we have a heck of a lot more room than we had in that small farmhouse."

The apartment rooms were quite large, and, in fact, larger than any they had seen before. The floors were covered with colorful print linoleum. Although not her choice of color, it was fairly new and pleasing enough.

Their entrance to the upper floor of the two-story flat was at the back of the building by a wooden stairway. The stairway led to a large porch where they could sit in nice weather. The windows were large, and from the kitchen you could see into the apartments next door.

The flat directly across from theirs was still empty and had been for sometime. Money was short for most people now, and landlords were renting cheap in hopes of filling vacancies. Floyd and Orpha were paying fifteen dollars a month—more than a fair price for what they were getting. And it was one of the better places—if not the best—she had lived in since her marriage to Floyd.

"Well," Orpha sighed as she rose from her chair, "guess I better get started on supper." She moved across the room to the unevenly stained wooden icebox. Bending over, she lifted the narrow-hinged door at the bottom, making sure the pan that caught the water from the melting ice block above had not overflowed. She picked up a ten-pound sack of potatoes from the floor that had been sitting alongside the icebox and put it on the kitchen table. She pulled open the table's small center drawer and took out two paring knives. "Here, have a knife my friend. You might as well stay for supper, but you have to work for it," Orpha smiled.

"Oh, thanks, don't mind if I do," Arline said.

Just then, someone began thudding up the back stairway. Nodding at the door, Arline snickered, "Mary Barbara must be back."

"Sure sounds like her dainty footsteps," Orpha agreed with a smile.

"Hi, I'm back," Mary Barbara announced, as she came through the door.

"We noticed," Arline chortled.

Mary Barbara thunked the groceries on the table, and as she looked out across the way, her face turned white.

"Isn't that Willie Camplin?" Orpha asked.

"God, don't let him see me," Mary Barbara said, anxiously, moving away from the windows. "Do you think he knows we live here?" Without waiting for a response, she quickly left the room.

"What the hell is going on with her?" Arline wanted to know. "It's not like her to let anyone scare her—especially a twit like Willie."

"I don't think it's Willie," Orpha countered. "I'm beginning to think maybe she knows a lot more about Verne's death than she's willing to say. She's scared shitless—it's obvious."

"Do you suppose someone has threatened her?" Arline conjectured. "It has to be something like that in order to spook Mary Barbara."

Nothing more was said that evening to Mary Barbara, but Orpha wondered if maybe Willie might be taking the apartment they had seen him in.

A month later she received an answer to that question. Returning home from work that morning, Floyd tossed the *St. Louis Post-Dispatch* on the center of the kitchen table. "Take a gander at that," he instructed.

"Why, what's going on?"

"Willie Camplin's been killed."

"Oh my God," Mary Barbara gasped from where she stood across the room.

Orpha grabbed the newspaper and began reading out loud. "A nude body that was identified as that of Willard Camplin has been found in East St. Louis, with a gun shot wound to the back of his head." Orpha stopped long enough to ask Mary Barbara if she was okay, for she appeared as though she might faint. Mary Barbara nodded yes, and Orpha continued.

The article went on to say they had no suspects but that the police department had some strong leads and would be making arrests in the near future.

The Porter affair and Willie's murder became the topic of conversation for many people as the facts unfolded in the papers in the coming weeks.

OLDER WOMAN, YOUNG LOVER, MURDER HER BROTHER FOR INSURANCE MONEY the headline screamed. The article reported that a thirty-seven-year-old woman named Mercedes Porter—better known as "Mercy"—had bribed the two young Gencola brothers to assist with her brother's demise with a promise of sharing the sizeable insurance policy she had purchased in her brother's name. At twenty-one years of age, Tommy was said to be Mercy's ardent lover as well as her main accomplice. With his seventeen-year-old-brother, Dominick, he had broken into the mentally challenged victim's apartment late the night before he was to be married and at gunpoint dragged him from his apartment dressed only in his underwear. They brutally shoved him down the stairway and into the back seat of his sister's spacious new Terraplane Hudson. With Mercy at the wheel, they sped off into what was to be the last night of Willie's life.

"Hey Willie, say hello to your sister," Tommy had laughed, slapping the now-crying man on his back. "Or maybe we should say, 'Willie, say goodbye to your sister.'"

Mercy had sat in the front ignoring her traumatized younger brother's pleadings. "Mercy, help me! Mercy, please, please don't. I'm your brother. Please don't," he begged, while hysterically crying for her to spare his life as they drove on to East St. Louis. But not once did she respond. She sat granite-faced and untouched by his agony. Tommy had thrown a sheet over Willie at the demand of Mrs. Porter in order to keep the bloody mess to a minimum and shot him in the back of the head, dumping the body in an uninhabited area, according to his younger brother.

Dominick told the police the insurance policy Mercy had talked Willie into taking out, which named her as beneficiary would more than likely change if he were to marry and because of that she had no choice but to do what she had to do. It was business nothing more.

The investigation turned up five bullets that appeared to have been marked for a select few. Insurance policies had also been taken out on these same individuals; both the bullets and policies were found hidden in the chimney inside the Porter home. The story went on to say that the case involving Mrs. Porter's husband's murder would be reopened for further investigation and that she had gained a generous payout at the time of his death. The article made reference to Mercy's name and the irony that a person so named could not find any in her heart for her unfortunate brother.

Mercy was arrested two months after the murder, forcibly taken from her daughter's elaborate wedding reception. Kicking up a huge fuss, she not only made a scene during the arrest but also flatly refused to cooperate during questioning. "You won't get anything out of me, coppers. If I go to the chair I'll go with my lips sealed."

The tip-off had come to the police from an anonymous caller who had overheard Dominick's bragging at a local watering hole the night after the brutal killing. The informant said the young braggart "appeared to be drowning himself with straight shots in rapid succession." His tongue loosened by drink, he spoke names and dates that were handed over to the authorities.

"Hardly a way to keep a horrible secret," Orpha thought out loud. "Mary Barbara, got a minute?" she called into the other room.

"Be right there, hang on," Mary Barbara answered.

Orpha began reading the paper aloud as her sister joined her, looking up occasionally for the reaction. It was one of visible relief. Once she had finished, Mary Barbara eagerly purged herself of the terror she had carried quietly within for sometime now. Had she divulged what she suspected took place while living in the Porter household before Mercy's arrest, bad things, without a doubt, would have befallen her family. That had been Mrs. Porter's threat months back, and Mary Barbara refused to take that chance. She also knew it to be impossible that such a sweet old man could have been in any way involved with such a cold-blooded murder. Then, convincingly, she revealed what, in her mind, had happened the morning Verne had been shot. Orpha, dumbfounded, listened—as her sister continued with a sinister tale that she had been forced to keep to herself, but now could share.

"Poor Willie. He was just starting out on his own and she couldn't allow that to happen. She deserves to fry!" Mary Barbara said, her voice edged with anger. "I'm not the least bit sorry for her. At one time, Mercy suggested that Willie and I marry, and she wanted to know if she could take out an insurance policy on me. At the time, I told her I didn't care. And what's really scary—I'll bet you anything one of the policies that the police found has my name on it." Over coffee and cigarettes, the two women continued discussing what had happened and what could have happened, resolving that Mary Barbara had gotten out in the nick of time.

The story continued to unfold in the daily papers, and the sisters expected the police would be at the door with questions. But for reasons they could not figure they heard from no one. The last they read, Mercy had been sentenced to die in the electric chair on October 23 at precisely ten o'clock in the evening; the two Gencola brothers were given life sentences instead of death for their cooperation during the investigation. The paper noted that Mercy—a woman lacking any sign of remorse seemed to be adapting well to her new surroundings. The women she now lived with seemed to have a great deal of respect for her that perhaps involved an element of fear. Not a soul in the women's reformatory could beat Mercy at pinochle, which had been bringing in a sizeable amount of pocket change for her—although she had nowhere to go with it.

"A good case in point! When money becomes your God, it rots your soul!" Ruth sermonized, while pulling a chair back from the kitchen table and at the same time dragging the ashtray to rest in front of her. She proceeded to light her cigarette inhaling deeply. With her eyes staring straight ahead she forced the smoke with a short burst from between her lips.

Ruth had entered the apartment in the midst of conversation that once again swirled about the Porter affair, and, in particular, about Mercy. Her reaction upon hearing of her old friend's incarceration and death sentence seemed cold and lacking in feeling—"too harsh even for her," Orpha thought with a shiver.

"I thought the two of you were so close," Orpha probed, while pulling the apple pies from the oven. She placed them alongside the loaves of bread and the pans of cloverleaf rolls she had made earlier that now wore clean dishtowels to help keep them warm until the rest of the meal was ready to serve.

Ruth and Arline had quickly accepted Orpha's invitation this bright September day that carried with it a little nip in the air. Inside, the sun was pouring through the large kitchen windows blanketing the linoleum floor as the room brimmed with the wonderful smells of a Sunday dinner.

Abruptly a loud racket could be heard coming from the living room—voices of the little ones fussing and yelling at each other. Much to Orpha's and Arline's surprise Ruth rose to her feet declaring, "I'll take care of it."

She could be heard scolding and was then interrupted by Donald, Arline's four-year-old son who seemed to have something to say. "She took my toy," he protested, and his younger brother by one year, Raymond, backed him with, "His toy."

"Where is this toy?" Ruth asked. Pointing at his small cousin Theresa Ruth, Donald said, "There! She has it! It's mine!"

"Well now," Ruth answered, as she gently took the toy from the little girl's hands.

"Now it's mine and all the fussing will stop all right?"

With that said a hush fell over the children. Leaving the room with the toy in hand Ruth decided to take one step back and peered in at them long enough to say, "Be good, and get along with each other, do you hear me!"

Now back in the kitchen she sat herself back in her chair, placing the toy on the table.

"There! That is that!" she announced. "So, where were we?"

Arline and Orpha glanced at each other in disbelief. Their mother had never before seemed to have an interest in correcting the children.

"All of my favorite things," Floyd announced as he came into the kitchen lifting lids and snitching samples. He came up behind Orpha as she bent over to take the pork roast from the oven. Grabbing her by the waist he tried kissing her on the neck while pushing himself into the backside of her. "And this of course is my most favorite thing of all," he said as he began crudely laughing.

"God damn it, Floyd, get the hell out of here before someone gets burnt," Orpha snapped, turning around with the roasting pan in her hands and at the same time twisting free of his grip.

"Floyd, behave yourself," Ruth chided.

"Yeah, beat it," Mary Barbara chimed in.

"Okay, okay, I'm leaving," he laughed, as he took a playful swat at Orpha's rear and left the room.

78

Ruth then preceded to tell her daughters what had occurred on her last visit with Mercy, after leaving them in Vigus.

Three days after arriving at the Porter home, her friend called out for her to come into the back bedroom.

"I could tell just by the way she called my name that something was very wrong. She sounded scared to death. I hurried in to find her on the bed lying in a pool of blood. It turns out she was about four months pregnant and had tried to rid herself of the unwanted baby by methods I won't go into right now. But because of what she did to herself, her body was trying to abort the fetus and having a nasty time of it. She was in a great deal of pain. Vernon and the rest of them had already left the house by this time in the morning, which meant I was on my own with this woman, who by now was screaming and begging for me to help her out of the hell she was in. I had no idea what I could do for her. My first reaction after handing her a full bottle of whisky, hoping she could numb the escalating pain, was, of course, to try to get hold of a doctor. But anyone I tried calling was not available. They were either out making house calls, or not expected back that day. I left messages with everyone I called to please come at once, but no one seemed to be coming.

"Mercy's screams were so loud I could hardly think. So I did the only possible thing I could think to do. I forced her knees apart, ran my hand up into her, and cleaned her out the best I could. I had remembered, as a child, seeing my father do this with a mare that was too weak to help herself.

"Mercy was out cold by the time a doctor finally got to the house, a combination of the whisky bottle being drained and pain she could no longer tolerate. He examined her, and then what I had extracted from her body. Shaking his head, he spoke softly, saying, 'She had better thank her lucky stars you did what you did. But for you, she could have had a slow and painful death.'

"On his return visit the next day, the doctor made it clear to Mercy that I had all but saved her life. She seemed grateful enough at the time and thanked me continuously during the rest of my visit. She even asked me to stay on just a bit longer until she could get some of her strength back.

"But soon after returning home I received a letter from her attorney, stating that I was being sued by her for endangering her life through practices that I had used on her, and was not legally trained for, at the time of her illness.

"I could not believe what my eyes were telling me," Ruth continued, as her face hardened with anger.

"Well I don't need to tell you I had my say with her and that's the last I heard from Mercy Porter and thank God for that."

"What was it you said to her, Mama?" Arline asked, leaning toward her mother from across the table—then taking a long drag on her cigarette and blowing the smoke off to the side.

"Yeah, I'd kind of like to hear that myself," Mary Barbara quickly agreed, as she came over and stood beside Ruth's chair, waiting to hear what her mother had to say. Orpha knew her sisters were halfway expecting to hear that their mother had put a curse on the woman, for there had been other times in the past they knew of when she became very angry, coincidence or not; at least one person had died after an encounter with her.

Such as the unfortunate cobbler who got into a screaming match with her over a pair of shoes she insisted she had brought to him to resole. And he was just as convinced that she had not.

When it seemed to her that her shoes were lost along with the battle for them, she stomped toward the door. Then, suddenly, she turned facing him, and spat her curse at him. "You'll not live long enough after today to accept another pair of shoes to repair."

The story goes that the cobbler's obituary appeared in the next day's paper. Orpha had always figured the man probably had a heart condition to start with, although he was not old.

It was said to be a known fact, by people who swore to it, that not only Ruth but her mother possessed special powers. Ruth's predictions, along with her reading of tea leaves had some convinced. And neighbors of their grandmother believed her to be a witch.

The Hellings sisters would laughingly agree with that, and not necessarily in the occult sense.

"Orpha, would you like the table set for dinner?" Ruth asked her daughter as she made a move like she might get up to do so.

"That's okay, Mama, we can do it," Mary Barbara said, as she and Arline moved from where they had been waiting for Ruth's response to Arline's question.

"It's not important what was said," Ruth continued. "What's important is that she allowed herself to be swallowed up by greed, forsaking even those closest to her, and by doing so she cursed herself, and for that she will receive her just deserts."

"Why is it so easy for Mama to see others' wrongdoings to their loved ones, but she's totally unaware of her own shortcomings for her family?" Orpha wondered. But she knew she would never know the answer.

Chapter Seven

Things appeared to be running smoother, with Orpha pinching every penny, plus walking to the hospital and accepting what was left over from the day's meals. She hated doing it—her pride suffered each time they packed her large basket. But she knew that pride would not feed her children, and for some unexplainable reason as of late, Floyd's pay envelopes, seemed to be holding less.

"Floyd, do you think someone's making a mistake with your pay? It's been short two to five dollars the last couple times," she calmly confronted him.

"No kidding? Half the time I don't count what's in it. I'll check first thing tomorrow. Can't let some shmuck get rich off me," he quipped.

Orpha's intuition nudged at her—letting her know things weren't being played on the up and up, and more than likely her husband was the culprit. She decided to let it be for the time being, but she would definitely be on top of it the following Friday.

"Floyd, damn it anyhow!" Orpha exclaimed, her voice full of irritation. "Where the hell is the rest of the money?" she demanded after the following Friday had arrived and she found that the pay envelope came up short once again.

"What money?" he shot back.

"For God's sake," she snapped. "I know how much you make and so do you. Don't you even look to make sure they've given you what you have coming?"

"How in the hell am I supposed to know what they're doing down there? I told you I would look into it. Now get the hell off my back."

"But when?" she countered. "After we're in the poor house? We have bills to pay."

"Yeah, yeah," he responded. "I'll take care of it first thing, okay?"

"Okay," she answered. "Just make sure that you do."

"Anybody home?" a voice called out from the back porch, as a rhythmic banging on the door followed.

Feeling the hopelessness of the situation, Orpha shot Floyd a look of disbelief. "I'll get it," she announced curtly.

"Is Mary Barbara here?" the handsome young man asked as he waited to be invited in.

"Hey, Lemvel!" Floyd called out. "Come on in here. You're not working tonight, huh?" Sitting down, Floyd began tying his shoelaces, preparing to leave for the nightshift.

"Nah, me and Mary Barbara thought we'd go to the picture show, then tie on the feed bag."

"I'm ready," Mary Barbara announced as she entered the room in a rush, tugging at her friend's coat sleeve. "I hate missing the first part of the movie," she went on, "so see you later."

"Oh, by the way, Orpha, this is Lemvel. Lemvel, my sister. Bye," she waved.

"Have fun," Orpha said, smiling.

"Yeah," Floyd called out, "don't do anything I wouldn't do," and laughed a knowing laugh.

"He seems to be a nice enough guy," Orpha commented. "Where do you know him from?"

"Work. He moved here from way back in the hills of the Ozarks," Floyd replied. "From what he told me he has never been to school a day in his life. It's a good thing God gave him a strong back. I think he said he's living with his aunt here in St. Louis."

"But it seems to me that I've seen him before tonight. Where was it?"

"He was in that bar that night we all went honky-tonking a while back."

"That's right," she remembered now. Pat Cooper, the woman in the downstairs apartment had agreed to keep an eye on the kids that night, including Arline's two boys, Donald and Raymond. So once the children had been safely tucked in, Orpha, Floyd, Orpha's two sisters, and her mother, Ruth, set out to do the town. Orpha would never forget how her mother had let her hair down after a few drinks, showing a side of herself, Orpha was convinced, few people had seen.

One thing in particular came to mind and she could not help letting a chuckle escape loud enough that it caught Floyd's attention. "What err you laughing at?" he asked, turning from the icebox where he was rummaging for a last-minute snack before leaving the house.

"Oh, I was just thinking about that night, and how Mama was really feeling her oats. How she had everyone singing and clapping as she danced and sang to that big fat man sitting on his barstool smoking his cigar. How did that song go? A big man from the South with a big cigar in his mouth, he just sat there grinning at her, loving all that attention I guess."

"She sure was a ball of fire," Floyd agreed. "Had a lot of laughs that night. Yep, I saw Mary Barbara sidling up to Lemvel that night, too. She was working her charms all over the poor guy."

"Floyd, why do you make everything sound so damn nasty?"

"Well, I guess I'm just a nasty man," he chuckled, slapping her across the rump as he passed by on the way out.

The evening wore on, and once the kids were down and sleeping, the dishes from the evening meal washed and put away, things became wonderfully peaceful and quiet. A time of the day Orpha appreciated with relish.

As Orpha walked slowing into the living room, a thought that had been slipping in and out of her mind all day once again returned.

Today was the twenty-eighth of January nineteen thirty-eight. And although no one living with her had mentioned it, the *Saint Louis Post-Dispatch* announced it in large print on the front page. Marie "Mercy" Porter was to be put to death in the electric chair precisely at 12:19 A.M. She had murdered her brother for a little over three thousand dollars in life insurance the night before his wedding. Orpha glanced at the small brown leather travel alarm that sat centered in a doily on the end table. She stood motionless watching the hand slowly moving toward the mark of ten. Not sure what she was feeling—perhaps regret, that a once-good person, who had lost her way, would now have her life taken from her. Then the small voice in her mind told her, an eye for an eye, for she could now look back at the scheme of things that Mercy had going, and Mary Barbara might well have been one of her unsuspecting victims.

Once the hand of the clock passed twelve, Orpha made the sign of the cross and walked away. She crossed the room and knelt on the old green sofa that sat in front of the long, low window. "Not much to see," she thought as she peered out, other than an occasional car spotted by the street lights as it passed beneath them. Splaying her fingers, she pressed her hands on the back of the sofa and pushed herself off. Feeling a sadness down deep, she entered the bathroom, put the tub's plug in place, and turned the hot water on full force.

Steam billowed from the faucet, filling the tiny room. Quickly she reached for her only bottle of perfume and let a miserly few drops hit the water and mix—the fragrance lifted by the warm steam, penetrating her nose.

Turning on the cold water, Orpha brought her bath to the perfect temperature. Then, after leaving the door open just a crack to hear the children if they cried out for her, she undressed and lowered herself into the tub slowly, enjoying the soothing feel of the sweet-smelling liquid taking in her body a little at a time until she had let herself be covered past her shoulders. She lay there with her eyes closed lost in a deliciously fragrant, warm, velvety world that let her leave momentarily the harshness of reality.

Orpha had been soaking and relaxing for some time when muffled voices from the kitchen made her sit up with a start. She quickly pulled herself from the tub while straining to identify whom the voices belonged to.

A loud giggle followed by a smack let her know Mary Barbara had come home sooner than expected.

Upon entering the room Orpha found her sister and Lemvel wrapped tightly about each other, unaware that she was present.

"Hey, you two, come up for air," she called out mockingly. They drew back from each other instantly, appearing somewhat embarrassed as Lemvel softly cleared his throat and Mary Barbara blushed faintly. "How was the movie?" Orpha continued. "We didn't go," Mary Barbara answered. "We went for a couple of beers, danced a few dances, and came home."

Lemvel once again encircled Mary Barbara's waist, giving her a short hug and a quick peck on the cheek. "I gotta git goin' darlin'. It's gettin' late. I'll call you up."

"Tomorrow?" she pressed.

"Sure thing, tomorrow," he smiled.

"See ya later," he said, passing by Orpha with Mary Barbara close behind him, grasping for, then capturing his hand, as they went out the door.

Orpha sat down at the table, lit a cigarette, and waited for her sister. After what seemed like a very long time Orpha decided she would wait no longer. Rising to her feet she stubbed out her last cigarette and was about to leave when Mary Barbara returned beaming a smile from ear to ear. It looked as though it was all she could do to keep from bursting.

"Well, now, don't you look like a Cheshire cat that swallowed a mouse?"

"Guess what he asked?" Mary Barbara said as she danced about the kitchen like a giddy little child.

"I can't," Orpha replied, somewhat annoyed, for she was really wanting to go to bed now and felt it was too late for guessing games. "What? Tell me."

"Lemvel asked me to marry him," she said, excitedly. "What do you think?"

"I'm surprised to say the least. I don't know what to think, to be honest. What did you say?"

"I said yes," she answered, all but bubbling over.

"Well then I guess I say congratulations. But just be very sure, Mary Barbara. You two haven't known each other very long. What—about two or three weeks at the most?"

"Yep, but I'm absolutely positively sure," she replied with conviction. "I'm crazy about the guy. The only thing that bothers me is he wants to get married right away and move to Arkansas. He says his folks have a huge white house on the river, and that we can move in with them until we get a place of our own. He comes from a big family. All of his relatives live there excepting his aunt and himself, but I guess he's kinda homesick. So that's where we'll be living afterward."

"So when's the big day? Or have you picked one yet?"

Orpha was asking questions of interest to her, but at the same time was not overjoyed at her sister marrying this good-looking man that no one seemed to know much about.

"As soon as we can get blood tests and a marriage license, we're off! God, it's so exciting, don't ya think?"

"I don't mean to be a crepe hanger," Orpha persisted, "but what do you know about him other than he comes from this large family and he's from Arkansas?"

"Well . . . I guess I know him good enough. I love him and that's all that counts," she snapped back.

"Okay, all right, it's your life. Just trying to look out for you. Do whatever it is that makes you happy," Orpha exclaimed, throwing her hands up in a motion of defense as she turned to leave the room. She knew she would be fighting a losing battle to press any further. Aside from all of Mary Barbara's good points, she was as stubborn as a Missouri mule once her mind was made up.

"Orpha, wait a minute, there's something else I wanna tell ya. But I'm not sure that I should. It's something Lemvel told me."

"What now?" Orpha asked as she turned back to face Mary Barbara. "Well you know how Floyd's pay envelope has been short lately?" Hesitating momentarily, she then went on. "He's been kinda treating the girls who work with him to lunches and candy bars. Lemvel says he likes playing the big shot and that the nuns allowed him to run a tab in the cafeteria, then it's subtracted from his pay before he gets it. I feel like a snitch telling you, but it also makes me damn mad to think that we've been scratching to make ends meet and he's buying goodies for those dames at work."

"Why that heel! I've been asking for leftovers from the hospital kitchen and he's trying to impress the women, that son of a bitch!"

"What are you going to do?"

"Well one thing's for sure, he's going to hear about it."

Floyd didn't come home that morning, and Orpha knew his reason would be the same as it was often lately: he had been too tired and had slept on the cot in the employee's lounge. Not that it particularly upset her.

88

Their sex life had never been anything to write home about anyway and had now reached a point of no return. Whenever he touched her, her skin would crawl. She remembered confiding this fact to Arline one muggy summer day while they were still living at the farm owned by the Palmers. Arline had stopped in for a short visit and as the two of them had passed by Orpha's bedroom Floyd had been sprawled out on the bed without a stitch on, exposing all God had blessed him with.

"Holy cow!" Arline had exclaimed. "You have to take that?!"

Orpha had philosophically replied at the time, "I hear it's not what you have, it's what you do with it." She could have sworn she detected a note of interest in her sister's voice and had wondered ever since. "Oh well, who really cares?" her thought trailed off. When Floyd finally arrived home shortly after noon, all hell broke loose as Orpha confronted him. Mary Barbara quickly bundled the children for a walk down the street to the confectionery. She hated hearing the children screaming and crying while their mother and father shouted at each other. And besides she felt somewhat responsible for what was taking place.

She walked the kids slowly up the street, taking as much time as she could, all the while talking to them, asking what kind of candy each would like once they arrived at the store.

"You know what? It's a beautiful day for a walk, right kids?"

"Right!" they answered in unison.

The two oldest children began running ahead kicking at the big red leaves that had fallen from the maples lining the street on both sides. The sky was a clear, deep blue, and a brisk wind with a slight nip in it would rise up long enough to set some of the smaller leaves in motion, rotating and spinning them rapidly in circles.

Mary Barbara loved the changing of the seasons and delighted in everything each had to offer. She would purposely step where the leaves were the heaviest so she could hear their crisp breaking sound beneath her feet then sniff at the fall air that carried in it the heavy incense of burning leaves and small twigs. More often than not she would say "thank you God" whenever her eyes took in what she considered a glorious thing to behold.

After what she considered time enough they returned to the apartment. Things were quiet as Mary Barbara ushered the children through the door. Floyd, sitting at the kitchen table, smiled weakly at them. "Good, the storm has passed," she thought, tossing the newspaper she had purchased in front of him.

Once she had pulled Ronald's jacket from him, she set him gently on the floor, turning then to give George a hand with his.

"Hi, Daddy," Theresa Ruth chirped, as she tried shedding her coat on her own, twisting and turning until it wound up on the top of her head.

"Hi, kid," Floyd answered, smiling at the little girl. "Need some help?"

"No," she answered, "I can do it." Mary Barbara reached over and took the coat from her and shooed the kids into the living room to play, leaving Floyd to his paper. As usual, he was seemingly undisturbed by whatever arguing had taken place.

Mary Barbara slowly passed her sister's bedroom, hesitating. After mulling over the idea for a moment she tapped softly on the door asking, "You okay?"

"I'm not any different than I've ever been, living with that man!" Orpha said loudly, to be sure Floyd could hear. She opened the door angrily and went into the kitchen, grabbing Ronnie from the floor where Mary Barbara had placed him just moments ago. With the baby sitting astride her hip she noisily pulled the high chair

90

across the floor to the other end of the table from where Floyd was sitting. Once she had placed Ronnie in the chair she laid a couple saltine crackers on the tray in front of him to keep him occupied as she went about putting things in order. She banged drawers and slammed cupboard doors letting Floyd know she hadn't gotten over his selfish antics nor was she the least bit convinced by more of his hollow promises. "Hey—can it," Floyd snapped, obviously irritated. He was scanning the help wanted section, something he always did, never with any particular purpose, it appeared to Orpha.

She shot him a look of distaste.

"Here," he said, laying the paper down, shoving it across the table in her direction. "Who knows, it might be just the ticket we're looking for."

Orpha picked it up and began reading where Floyd had circled with his pencil.

WANTED, COUPLE TO LIVE IN, RUN LARGE FARM, CALL 534-1000. New hope sprung forth numbing her anger. "This might not be such a bad idea," she mused. She knew with Mary Barbara leaving, paying the rent was going to become even more of an uphill battle. "Good God, if we could get this we won't have to worry about food or rent," she declared, her voice bordering on excitement.

"Yeah, I figure," Floyd interjected, "I could stay on at the hospital through the winter with no crops needing tending to and then on the weekends do what has to be done that you can't handle by yourself."

Orpha looked at Floyd, impressed that he had taken the time to give this some thought, and decided to make the best of this day and call a truce. "I'm going to use the phone down the street. Be back as quick as I can." Throwing on a coat, Orpha snatched the section of paper with the ad and headed out the door for the confectionery.

"Tell them we can be there Saturday or Sunday morning as early as—" Floyd's voice was abruptly cut off after she let the outside door slam behind her. Making short order of the block and a half Orpha rushed into the small store, laying her nickel on the counter and dialed with hope.

"Hello," a deep male voice answered.

"Hello," Orpha said pleasantly. "I'm calling about the ad in the paper. Is the job still available?"

"Yes ma'm," the man countered. "But I would prefer making arrangements to discuss it in person. Business on the telephone is not my way of doing things."

"Oh, uh, sure," Orpha replied, taken aback slightly by his directness. "May I ask with whom I'm speaking?" she asked.

"Bill O'Dell is my name. And what is yours?" he asked in turn.

"Orpha Wilkerson. My husband, Floyd, and I would be very interested in talking to you about this job. We could really use it," she pleaded, scolding herself silently for she knew she sounded desperate and hadn't intended to. "Sir, would you mind giving me directions on how to get there?"

"Sure thing. Be happy to," he answered. "But when was it you were planning on coming? And where are you coming from? Let's not get the horse before the cart," he chuckled.

"Oh gosh, I'm really sorry," she said, embarrassed by her childlike enthusiasm. "We are coming from St. Louis. Saturday or Sunday would be fine, that is, whatever you say is just fine," she stammered.

"If you could make it before noon Saturday that would work out better for us here," he told her. "Now let me give you directions on how to find us." As he patiently gave his instructions, she quickly scratched them about the margins of the newspaper. "That's all there is to it. You shouldn't have a problem, Mrs. Wilkerson."

"No, I'm sure we won't. We'll be there first thing Saturday morning. Thank you very much. Goodbye." After putting the phone back in its cradle, she called out,

92

thanking the old man who owned the place and hurried out the door running the full distance back to the apartment. Bounding up the stairs, taking two at a time, left her all but winded as she entered the kitchen where her husband and sister waited.

Confident and exhilarated, Orpha smiled brightly as she sputtered the account of what took place. "We have it. I just know it. I don't know why, but I have a very good feeling about this whole thing." Draping her coat over the back of a chair, Orpha pulled it from the table and sat down. "The job is still open," she continued, enthusiastically. "This move could change everything for us. The guy's name is Bill O'Dell. I think he's the boss. We got to be there early Saturday morning." Excitement for the future now completely engulfed them all.

Chapter Eight

Saturday morning, Orpha, Floyd, and the children were up early as planned, and with the help of Mary Barbara—who prepared coffee, breakfast, and a few sandwiches to take along—they headed out for Murphysboro, Illinois, and the O'Dell farm.

The children, still groggy from having been awakened before they were ready, settled quietly back in the seat of Lemvel's old Model A Chevy that Floyd had borrowed and quickly returned to sleep.

"Light me a cigarette, would ya?" Floyd asked. Orpha took two from her pack, sticking both in her mouth. Once she had lit them she handed one to Floyd. Dragging deeply on hers, she stared out the car window trying to make out the passing homes and buildings. Though it was still dark, daylight was edging its way in. They traveled in silence for a very long time, with the car finally making its way out of the city and into the open country. The lightning in the distance caught Orpha's eyes. While she intently watched the storm, she noted that the sky seemed to be wearing a veil of opaque gray with the lightning flashing repeatedly behind it. It put her in mind of a child who had gotten hold of a light switch and was enjoying turning it off and on.

She continued watching it, fascinated, trying to guess before it got there where it would flash next.

"Hey!" Floyd said, as he nudged her, "I've been talking and you haven't heard a word."

"Uh, what?"

"Looks like a storm a brewing," he repeated himself to her. "Let's hope we'll make it there before it breaks. Looks like we're heading right into it."

Orpha grew edgy as the wind blew hard enough now that the car was being pushed, and she could feel it moving a bit to the left on the road. She could see whole stands of trees bending and giving in to the wind's ever-increasing strength. She looked over at Floyd, hoping he would give her some reassurance, but he had his jaw set tight and seemed to be concentrating on keeping the old car on the road. Huge drops of water started banging against the windshield and were followed by what appeared to be buckets of water being tossed. Floyd reached for the knob, and turned on the wipers, although Orpha could not see that they were of much help. Floyd insisted he could see just fine. "Relax!" he snapped. "Don't keep at me woman!"

Ordinarily these words would have set them off into an argument but she let it slide for she was more concerned about getting where they were going than correcting him on how he was speaking to her.

They drove on without conversation, other than Orpha's occasional "maybe we should pull over and wait," and Floyd's "nah, we can make it."

It was nine o'clock according to the large, round clock hanging in the filling station window at the edge of town just after passing the sign for Murphysboro.

The storm had now subsided yet it remained overcast and a chilly wind was blowing. The kids were up now, hungry and asking for the bathroom. Orpha opened the bag of sandwiches and gave them each a half, at the same time telling them that where they were going had a bathroom, and to hold on for they were almost there. Floyd turned the car left off the main highway and headed down a narrow, gravel road with tall, thick weeds growing on either side that at present were being beaten about by the strong wind. Beyond the weeds were empty fields that had been plowed under, stretching as far as the eye could see. The road twisted and turned, going farther and farther back, with only an occasional house sitting way off by itself in a mowed area of a field. Although one very large house, Orpha noticed, strangely hugged the road's edge.

The area suddenly became heavily wooded, with the road dipping and moving deeper in through tall, heavy underbrush until the car was forced to stop in front of a large metal gate suspended across a shallow creek that had all but dried up.

Floyd jumped from the car. Running to the gate, he lifted the heavy chain that held it in place, then gave it a good shove, causing it to swing wide open. Once he had taken the car through he again went to the gate, closed it, and quickly replaced the chain.

"Must help keep in stray cattle," he said while getting in and slamming the door shut.

"Mommy, I have to go bad," George whispered in his mother's ear as he stood on tiptoe in the back seat.

"Floyd, wait a minute. The kids can get out here. There isn't a soul around." After disembarking, she opened the back door. Taking George's hand, she pointed him in the direction of a small bush. "Over there and be quick about it. Theresa Ruth how about you?"

"No, Mommy, I don't have to go," the little girl said, shaking her head firmly.

"Good," Orpha said, smiling at her petite, young daughter who was pressing herself firmly against the back seat, reflecting her preference to remain. Nestled in the corner, Ronnie began to stir, uttering small noises. Orpha bent down and scooped him up into her arms, holding him close to her body so the wind could not find him. She cooed gentle assurance.

George made a hasty return and once everyone was back inside they drove on. It was just a short distance to where the road took a left bend, then made its way abruptly into a huge clearing. Off to the right and at the top of a sloping hill sat an imposing white house with green awnings and shuttered windows. The road that had now become a driveway made a second small turn, this time to the right, heading for what Orpha presumed to be the main house. As they came closer she could see an expansive apple orchard rising from the embankment to the left of the driveway and then more buildings all apparently freshly painted and as well kept as the first.

Floyd brought the car up alongside the huge house that Orpha found impressive, and as he stopped, a tall, imposing figure emerged from the doorway. His head lowered slightly as he walked toward them, his sandy-colored hair blowing forward from the top of his head by the persistent wind. He reached for the door handle on Orpha's side with one hand and, with his free hand, took a quick swipe at his hair, trying to put it back in place. Still clutching the baby, Orpha stepped from the car, and, as she rose, facing him, noted his eyes were an appealing green.

"You must be Orpha," he smiled. "I'm glad you folks could make it." But before Orpha could respond, Floyd had made it around the car, extending his hand cheerfully, saying, "Yeah, that was one hell of a storm. I wasn't sure we'd make it." The men started walking to the house as Orpha helped the children out from the back seat and hurried along behind them.

Once Bill had ushered them into the large vestibule, he called out, "Laverne!" Within moments, a short, pleasant-looking woman clad in a crisp, white apron that was worn over an equally fresh printed housedress hurried down the staircase toward them. Her hair was firmly knotted in a generous gray bun on the back of her head with a few wisps of escaping hair that floated above the white skin of her forehead as she descended the stairs. "Yes sir?" she replied, as she reached the place where they stood.

"Can you give us a hand here?" he asked, nodding in the direction of the children. "Be happy to," she said, sounding delighted, as her soft blue eyes came alive with a twinkle and her round face wore a broad smile.

"Would you two little ones like a cup of hot cocoa and some cookies?" she inquired, as she bent over helping them shed their coats. "If so, let's hang these in the closet, and then come with me, okay?" Theresa Ruth and George looked to their mother for a sign of approval, and once she nodded her okay, they left, each holding on to one of Laverne's hands.

"Let's talk," Bill stated, as he motioned with his head for them to follow. Stopping, he slid open two large, highly polished wooden doors that disappeared into the walls on either side of the vast doorway.

He led them into what could be deemed a man's world. The shelving along the walls was heavy with books, which impressed Orpha immediately. She loved books and got lost in them any chance she could. Although in the last few years it was something she could ill afford.

The room had a soft leather sofa and chairs, and the distinctive smell of a rich pipe tobacco hung pleasantly in the air. The crackling of the fire in the stone fireplace warmly welcomed them.

"Have a seat," Bill said, gesturing toward the chairs and sofa that sat on either side of the hearth. "Let's see if we can work this out to suit everyone." The three discussed at length what each could contribute. Floyd would be expected to help with the crops and take care of the livestock on the three-hundred-acre farm. Orpha would, of course, take over Laverne's position in running the house and all that was connected to it.

"Big job, think you can handle it?"

"No doubt in my mind," she replied, smiling at him.

"Well that's that then," Bill O'Dell declared as he slapped hands on his knees and rose from the chair. "I'll be here some of the week, but on the weekends I'll have to be in the city tending to business there.

"This is the backbone of my business," he continued, as the three of them walked to the door. "I run and supply my restaurant with what I get from this place. If

98

this goes well, then it goes without saying, the rest of it will follow."

Orpha found herself intrigued by this tall mountain of a man, who had a forceful air about him, and yet you could almost touch the sensitivity that lay just beneath the surface. She guessed his age to be somewhere in his early forties. His face could be described as handsome in a rugged sort of way—definitely a man's man. Although she wondered about the woman in his life or if there was one.

"Orpha would you want to see the rest of the house?" the deep, now-familiar voice asked, shattering her thoughts.

"Oh . . . yes, I would," she quickly answered.

"I want you to have some idea of what you're getting into," Bill went on. "I'll have Laverne show you around. After shaking Floyd's hand and saying welcome aboard to the both of them he left the room to retrieve Laverne and the children.

Orpha was somewhat disappointed when Bill did not return with them, and was surprised at her curious reaction, quickly brushing it aside.

The house was every bit as lovely and spacious as she had guessed it might be and she could see without doubt a woman's hand in every room. "Is there a Mrs. O'Dell?" Orpha asked Laverne, as they left the master bedroom.

"Yes, there is, as a matter of fact, but she's sadly not with us."

"Oh?" Orpha probed but did not push.

"She's been in the hospital for sometime now and from what I can gather she won't be coming home anytime soon, poor soul."

"What's wrong?"

"Well," Laverne went on, "I suppose you could call it a mental sickness of some sort. Mr. O'Dell is out there any chance he gets. Between seeing her, the farm, his

99

restaurant, and the two apartment houses he owns, I'm surprised he's still up and walking around."

"Doesn't he have help here other than you?"

"Oh sure he has, but not nearly enough as far as I can see."

"How many other hands are there?" Floyd broke in.

"Two," she answered. "You'll be meeting them at lunchtime if you care to stay. If not, Monday will be soon enough. When do you folks plan on moving in?

"The sooner the better. If we can swing it— tomorrow," Floyd stated.

"Oh, that soon?" she smiled. "Well than I guess I had better show you where you'll be living."

Orpha looked at Floyd with a quizzical expression on her face. He answered with a shrug, and, with all three children in tow, they followed the woman down the staircase, through the kitchen, and out the back door.

Stepping out onto a large concrete pad just outside the door, they took a walkway that passed through a long, arched arbor thickly covered with barren grapevines. Once past what Orpha guessed to be a brooder house they entered a small screened-in porch that was attached to a much smaller home than what they had just left. Laverne bent over, rattled the key in the lock a bit, and threw open the door. She stepped back, allowing Orpha, Floyd, and the children to enter. Once inside, Orpha looked about and was pleased even with the rooms being undersized. There were five rooms in all, modestly furnished, and as neat as a pin. A sewing room with the latest machine and a kitchen with a large pantry to store her canned goods was the most impressive.

"Now if you have your own furnishings you would rather use, Mr. O'Dell says we can store any or all of what's here."

"No, this will be just fine," Orpha answered. "What little we have we can store," she said, knowing full well that their possessions, for the most part, weren't worth storing.

"Well, I guess that's it folks. I'll be leaving you now, but will be staying on for a few days yet to help you along and show you how things run," she said with a smile, and then was gone.

"I can't believe this," Orpha said out loud, almost bubbling. "It's a godsend, Floyd. This is the chance I've been waiting for. Let's try and make the best of it, okay?"

"Yeah, you have everything you need here, don't you?" A short silence ensued as they looked about commenting on different things.

"Well, I think it's time we head back. It's a long ride ahead of us and you know I'm the only one that does any driving, so let's get going," Floyd complained.

They stopped back at the big house long enough to retrieve the children from the kitchen where they still sat at the table with paper and pencil drawing pictures and munching cookies.

"It's time to go," Orpha told them. After a brief resistance, they all made their way back to the car.

"Yoo-hoo! Yoo-hoo!" Orpha turned to see Laverne running toward them with a large paper sack in her hand while waving her other hand frantically.

"I thought these sandwiches might come in handy," she said with a big smile on her amiable face. "I put a few cookies in as well. The children seem to like them."

"Thanks! You didn't have to do that," Orpha said, smiling back at the woman. "But I'm tickled pink that you did." Taking the sack, Orpha once again thanked Laverne, then went about helping the children into the back seat of the car and shutting and locking the doors. They said a final goodbye to Laverne, then drove ahead a short distance until there was enough room to turn around, finding just such a place on the other side of one of the barns. The ride back was filled with positive thoughts expressed in almost giddy conversation, and once back at the apartment the packing and discarding began with a rush. Orpha and Mary Barbara filled pillowcases with clothing and small items that wouldn't break, while Floyd went to the confectionery for empty boxes or crates.

"I talked to Arline this morning," Mary Barbara said while reaching for more things to stuff into the pillowslip she was filling. "She says it's okay for me to stay with her if you get lucky with this job and have to move right away. And besides, we figured if that's what happens I won't be there long, cause Lemvel and me want to get hitched real quick and move to his mama's house down south. But in the meantime I can watch the boys for her until she can find someone."

"Oh good! I was worried about both of those things. Did she sound upset about having to find a babysitter?"

"No, not at all. She told me that a woman two doors down from her place had offered once before and that she would ask her. She was pretty sure there was no problem."

"By the way, I was meaning to ask you, whatever happened to Frank Wierzynski?" Orpha asked somewhat puzzled. "We never saw him again once we moved here. He certainly was nuts about you. That was easy to see."

"Yeah he was sweet, but there was just something missing. Maybe because he was so much older," Mary Barbara answered with a tone of regret in her voice. "It reached a point that he had the last say on everything. I don't think he saw it that way but I sure did. And I really think he got tired of the long hall from St. Louis and that's okay.

"But, you know, Orpha, he could have told me that instead of just dropping out of sight and not even sending word through his friend Doc. He could have done at least that, don't you think?"

"Well, yes," Orpha replied. "And I'm pretty sure Doc would have mentioned it if something had happened to him or he was very sick. But you have to remember, Mary Barbara, given how seldom we see Doc, that probably would not be the best way for him to get word to you."

Now with a tone of regret in her voice Mary Barbara continued, "I don't know, we started out so good. It was probably me. I'm not too quick at figuring people out. And most likely he got tired of hanging out with a kid, right? Even so I can't say anything bad about him. We got along great in the beginning and he is still a nice guy. I still would like to know what I did to make him head off as he did."

"Well, someday you may get that chance seeing that he and Doc are close friends, but until then we have a lot going on here," Orpha said. "We better get moving."

"But he'll find somebody for sure, he's a nice man."

"Hey!" Floyd yelled from the kitchen, letting the crates and boxes he was carrying fall from his grip. "There's a man out here that wants to know what time we'll be ready to roll in the morning." The women looked at each other, and, as if on cue, stopped what they were doing and went to see who the man might be.

"Hi," Orpha said as she entered the room. "Hi," Mary Barbara echoed.

"How do," the man returned pleasantly, quickly taking his cap from his head. A shock of thick, red hair exploded from beneath, giving the appearance of having more hair than face. His beard, too, was thicker, shaggier, and longer than most men wore it. And this giant of a man, with quick, darting blue eyes and an easy grin carried an air of relaxed sociability.

"What did you say your name was?" Floyd asked.

"I didn't," he retorted. "It's Radar, Radar Lie. I work for Mr. O'Dell. What time would you folks want me here tomorrow?"

"Six is fine," Orpha broke in. "That is . . . if it's okay with you."

"Okay, dat's good for me," the man said, placing his cap back on his head as he turned to leave. "See you in the morning." He was gone as quickly as he had appeared, leaving the door slightly ajar as he went out.

"A man of few words," Orpha announced, as she closed the door tightly behind him.

Chapter Nine

Once settled in their new home, cold weather followed close behind. With no harvest to occupy them, Orpha had more time to adjust to her new way of life. With Laverne's help, she learned what was expected of her. Floyd had made arrangements with the hospital to work part-time during the week, then the full weekend. It all seemed to run smoothly for awhile. At first Orpha was willing to agree that the weather was bad and therefore driving the distance from the city might not be such a good idea for Floyd. But as the winter months waned he spent more time away than he did at what she had thought could be a new beginning for them.

Bill hadn't mentioned Floyd's absence yet, but Orpha knew that if he didn't make more of a showing come planting time it might not go so well for them, and she hated the thought of going backward.

"For God's sake, Floyd! We can't botch this! We need it too badly! What the hell's wrong with you?" she asked, feeling helpless and irritated at the same time. She had been waiting for him that weekend, and within moments of his coming through the door, she jumped him with all the anxiety and frustration that had overtaken her thinking of what might happen.

"Aw, stop your goddamn bellyaching," he snarled, as he brushed past her. Removing his cap and jacket, he hung them forcibly on the large screw-in hooks that ran along the wall behind the kitchen door.

"No, damn it," she shouted. "We both know you're doing more than working. You're not pulling the wool over my eyes. Not for a minute, you jackass!" With that she stormed out of the room.

Floyd, in hot pursuit, followed her—yelling back that maybe he might just stay there permanently, for he sure got a lot better treatment from his fellow workers than he received from her.

"I'll bet you do! And if they're fellows, I'll eat my hat. I'm aware of the floozies you work with. I get all the news. Don't think I don't." She hadn't really heard anything, but she knew this man, and a quick jump in bed with someone other than his wife was not, in his mind, a mortal sin. She had no proof, but the telltale signs were there.

She remembered the weekend he came home drunker than a skunk. He dropped his pants to the floor, fell in bed, and slept until noon. She picked the trousers up that morning, and as she emptied the pockets to prepare them for the laundry, she noticed a thin white coating that was smeared about the fly. She didn't have to think long to know what it was, and murmured to herself at the time, "That son of a bitch. That's it. He better not think of coming near me."

Orpha kept it to herself in hopes of holding on to her job, but she was determined that she would have a talk with Bill and maybe he would let her stay on by herself.

This argument, like most of the arguments they had, solved nothing between them. It started with a bang, then after the threats and hot accusations were thrown about for a period of time it would fizzle into a strained truce.

"Good morning! Sure smells great in here. Any pancakes on the menu?" Bill asked with a broad grin upon entering the kitchen of the big house the following morning.

The breakfast table had been set an hour earlier, giving Orpha time to fix a selection of Bill's favorite breakfast foods. She took special pains with the setting of the table, choosing the cheeriest print tablecloth with matching napkins. A huge platter of scrambled eggs encircled by fresh ground sausages. Hot, homemade biscuits with sausage, milk gravy, and pancakes still on the griddle waiting to be transferred to their own platter with lots of butter and a steaming pitcher of maple syrup to back it up.

"My God, woman!" Bill exclaimed, obviously pleased as he watched her put the food on the table. "Is this a special day that I don't know about? Did I forget my own birthday?" he teased with a smile as he pulled a chair back and beckoned for her to sit with him.

Once seated, she was uncertain of the best way to start.

"Bill, I've got to talk to you."

"Now, Orpha, you're not going to tell me you're leaving me?" he interrupted with an imploring smile.

"Oh no. To the contrary. I'm hoping you'll let me stay."

"Why on God's good earth would I want you to leave?"

"We, that is, Floyd and I, have, err, uh, decided to go our separate ways," she said, sounding silly to herself as she groped for the right words. "I wasn't, err, um, really sure that—"

"Orpha, I have never met anyone that works harder than you do. Tell me why I would allow you to go anywhere?" he asked, looking straight into her eyes. "We'll do just fine you and me," he said reassuringly as he took her hand in his and patted it gently.

She thought she detected a flickering in those green eyes that she had not been aware of before, a strong fondness maybe? She really wasn't sure how to put it into words, but she allowed her hand to stay in his warm grip, not wanting to take it away. Their hands separated at the sound of voices.

"I had better pour the coffee. The men are here," Orpha said with some reluctance.

Turning his head, Bill greeted his farm hands. "Good morning! Grab a chair and dig in! There's a spread here fit for a king."

"Hey, what did we do to deserve this?" one of them asked. "Who cares! Let's eat," another chortled. Once seated the men enthusiastically served themselves continuous large portions of Orpha's special breakfast.

With breakfast over and the back door banging behind the last hand as he left, Orpha determined that it might be a good time to face Floyd. She would return shortly to tidy up the kitchen.

Throwing a jacket over her shoulders and carrying a container of breakfast leftovers, she hastened out the door into the bitterly cold morning, stepping carefully over the icy spots on the walk that had been revealed by a quick shoveling earlier.

The air was still, and as cold as dry ice she thought, as her nostrils seemed to stick together when she took a deep breath.

Orpha hurried toward the house in the back to a situation that had finally been forced to happen. She would make Floyd aware of her decision. Although she couldn't guess what his reaction might be, she felt less concern about that as she knew it would be hard for the kids to understand. "One day at a time, one day at a time," she repeated to herself as she took hold of the doorknob and let herself into the warmth of the small kitchen.

She felt a surge of panic as she thought of the encounter she might be facing with this man she could no longer live with. Taking in a deep breath and the few steps that were necessary to enter the living room she plunged ahead. George and Theresa Ruth were on the floor still in their night clothes busily working with their coloring book and crayons, looking up long enough to let her know they were hungry.

"Let's take care of that right now. To the table with you both," she said, once she had them seated and eating. Orpha went to the back bedroom where Ronnie was sitting quietly in his crib, looking about, not making a sound. However, there was a loud noise in the room nonetheless. Looking over at the bed she had not shared with Floyd for some time, she could see him in his normal sleeping position—on his side with his pillow shoved lovingly (or so she interpreted) between his legs, snoring with each breath.

Once she had picked up the baby, she purposely bumped into the foot of the metal bed frame. "Floyd, come on! Get up out of there! I have to talk to you before you leave." She started walking away but noticed he had not moved.

"Floyd!"

"What, damn it?!" he shot back at her, angered with her for being awakened so abruptly.

"I want a divorce," she blurted out. "And I want you out of here that's what."

With that said, she left the bedroom not knowing what might happen next. She hadn't meant to handle it quite that way but there it was out in the open and she would deal with whatever he might throw back at her. He thinks I'm mad and it's just another empty threat. There have been so many. I'll let him know that I have already talked with Bill and everything is settled. As she placed the baby in the high chair, Floyd came up behind her, encircling her waist, and began nuzzling her neck. "Come on, sweetheart, don't be mad."

"Will you get the hell away from me?" Orpha said angrily, pushing and twisting from his arms. "I mean it, Floyd! It's done! It's over!"

"Just like that?" he asked. "You tell me it's over and I take a walk? Forget it, lady."

"I worked it out with Bill this morning," Orpha went on, quickly trying her best to impress upon him that she was dead serious. "He said the kids and I could stay."

"I'll bet you worked it out with him," Floyd spat at her sarcastically. "What else did you work out? Or is it in?"

"Don't be a pig," she snapped. "I'm not going to fight with you." She looked him straight in the face, trying to let him know she was following through this time. "You knew very well this was going to happen sooner or later. So do us both a favor and don't make it any tougher than it is."

"Hey, babe, if this is what you want it's fine with me." He started to leave the room turning back long enough to get his last shot in. "But I can tell you one thing. I won't be doing without my sex!"

"Come on, Floyd, did you ever? I'm not entirely stupid," she called after him.

"Mommy, why don't you like Daddy?"

Orpha looked down to see her small son standing beside her holding onto her dress. "Is Daddy bad?"

"No, George, it's not that Daddy is bad, he's just not very bright."

"What's 'not bright,' Mommy?" the small boy inquired.

"Honey, go play. We will talk about it later, okay?"

With a gentle nudge she sent him back into the living room with Theresa Ruth close behind.

Once Floyd had left, Orpha sat at the table with her head resting in her right hand trying to sort through what she was now feeling. Definitely relief for her own sake but also panic—not knowing what was ahead—and some guilt for her failure at this marriage that produced three adorable kids—and how unfair it was to them to send their father away.

But it was done and there was no going back. "I'll have to make the best of it," she told herself out loud as she rose from her chair and started getting the children ready to return to the big house to finish her morning's work.

Chapter Ten

The weeks passed, with Christmas just around the corner. Orpha would have to see if she could find a way to town to pick up necessities for the children, but they would have to be wrapped as gifts. All needed shoes, boots, coats, and mittens and maybe if lucky she might squeeze out candy canes. She had been saving every dime possible from what Bill paid her since Floyd had left. Not sure he would bother to think of the kids for Christmas, Orpha was prepared to do the best she could. A Christmas tree had already been delivered. It had been left outside the back door. Orpha noticed it that morning as she and the kids made their morning walk from one house to the other.

"Mommy, is that our Christmas tree?" George asked.

"Yes, yes," Theresa Ruth excitedly answered. "It's ours, it looks like ours," she said, jumping up and down.

"It might be," Orpha answered, smiling. "But let's wait until we find out for sure before we get too carried away," she said, coaxing them to walk ahead.

All three were busily eating at one end of the table when the men arrived for their afternoon meal.

"Bill, would that be some of your handiwork outside our back door?"

"What handiwork would that be, Orpha?" he asked with a sheepish smile.

"Oh, just that beautiful pine tree sitting up against the back of the house."

"Nah," he said with a big grin on his face. "I think you'll have to blame Radar for that."

Orpha, surprised at her benefactor exclaimed, "Well, for Pete's sake! Thanks, Radar! That was really sweet of you!"

The big Norwegian's face flushed a few shades darker than his hair and he responded with, "Oh . . . sure."

"It's a beautiful tree! The kids got so excited when they saw it," Orpha went on. "Thanks again."

"Sure, sure," he said, smiling, while reaching for the hot cakes.

Radar had taken it upon himself to cut the tree short, but exceptionally full, and bring it down from the woods behind the acreage that was farmed.

He was a quiet man, Orpha had been told, dedicated to his family, and the best worker Bill had—not to mention probably the biggest and strongest. He was said to be fond of children, and the number of his own offspring seemed to verify that—seven at last count.

Orpha made a mental note that apple pie would be on the next night's dinner menu, with fresh hand-churned vanilla ice cream, the big redhead's favorite desert. Her small thank you.

Having finished eating, the men left the table and the big house to take care of whatever had to be done around the farm. The kitchen was now left for Orpha to put back in order once again as the children played in the next room.

Lost in her thoughts while reaching to replace a large platter on an upper shelf, she hadn't heard the footsteps behind her.

"Orpha?" a voice spoke her name.

Startled, she spun about dropping the platter to the floor." "Oh shit," she cursed. Then seeing the intruder, she mumbled, "I'm really sorry, Bill. I'll replace it." Flustered, she bent over and began picking up the large white chunks of dish that lay scattered across the floor.

"Hold on," Bill said, taking the fragments from her hands and putting them on the table. "Let me help you." Enclosing her hands in his, he gently pulled her to a standing position directly in front of him. Orpha stood looking up at him.

"Forget the dish! I should have let you know I was there," he exclaimed. "I got to thinking, maybe you needed to go into town sometime before Christmas for the kids. I'm planning on going myself. I'd be happy to have you come along if you're interested."

A little nervous now, Orpha slowly pulled her hands from his, dropping them to her sides while stepping back. The closeness they were sharing was becoming strangely uncomfortable and she was detecting a certain amount of excitement.

"Gee, I, uh, I don't know," she weakly answered.

"Well, let me say it this way. I would like very much to take you Christmas shopping and then out to dinner. I think it could do us both a great deal of good, and, to be honest, your company is what I'm really after," he said now, looking her straight in the eyes.

Completely caught off guard, Orpha stammered, "Well, yes, um, of course, but I have to find someone for the kids."

"Maybe I can take care of that," Bill went on. "I'll give Laverne a jingle and see if she'd be willing. How about this Saturday? What's a good time?" he asked, smiling.

"Well, probably noon or a little after," Orpha answered. "Once the children go down for their naps will be fine."

"Great," he said, with a clap of his hands. "It's a date, then!" With that, he turned and left.

Orpha stood there recalling somewhere near a month or so back when she thought she had detected an interest on Bill's part but pushed it aside. "Well now, don't jump the gun," she scolded herself. "The man simply wants some dinner company, and besides he's twenty years older than you and he is married—very married—more so than most." Taking hold of the broom Orpha began sweeping the scattered shards into the dust pan.

Charged with nervous energy now, she diligently threw herself into her work, her mind occasionally darting to the outing ahead. With Christmas just a few days away the stores were brimming with activity that next Saturday, and the special excitement that goes with last-minute gift buying permeated the air about her.

The glistening of the fresh snow and the many strings of colored lights and decorations everywhere made Orpha suck in her breath with exhilaration.

The Salvation Army had Santas out in force ringing the small gold bells that drew people's attention to the red kettles waiting to be fed by good will. As they passed the Santa stationed near the door of Famous-Barr department store, Bill, obligingly, made his contribution.

"Merry Christmas!" the man dressed in red called out as Bill ushered Orpha into yet another bustling store. "Merry Christmas!"

Orpha could still hear his voice mingling with the ringing of his bell as she went through the revolving doors, stopping on the other side to wait for Bill. She spotted him following behind two elderly ladies, who seemed to be the only ones not in a hurry. Once he reached her, Bill took Orpha's arm, guiding her into a corner out of the way of the hubbub that surrounded them.

"How about stopping for a cup of coffee and giving these old feet a break," he suggested, smiling, then forcing a look of great pain.

He stood in front of her resting his hand on the wall above her head shielding her from being jostled by anyone rushing past. His Stetson was positioned just above his now-intense green eyes that, to Orpha, once again, spoke of his silent feelings. He gazed down into her face and the closeness of him she found almost intoxicating.

"Sure, why not?" she responded, looking away, trying to get better control of herself.

Bill put his arm about her waist and began threading them through the sea of shoppers, and in the direction of the restaurant located conveniently on the main floor. Once they had been seated and their orders taken, Orpha inquired, "Is Christmas shopping something you enjoy?"

"No, not particularly, but I couldn't think of any other way I could spend time with you and I guessed you might not be interested in going out with anyone. Cad that I am, I figured if I took you shopping we'd spend time alone."

"I would hardly call this alone," Orpha said, teasingly.

"True enough!" Bill answered, smiling. "But I want to make sure you know I expect only that, your company. I hold you in the highest regard."

"Thanks," she said, relieved, as the room emptied itself of all but the two of them.

Once their food arrived they took their time eating while making small talk. Orpha's problems faded momentarily and time seemed of no importance as they sat enjoying each other's company. Bill slowly pulled his pocket watch from its hiding spot, glancing at the time. The soft click of the gold lid closing signaled to Orpha that the day that had been full of holiday spirit was soon to end. Reluctantly, he announced that they should be moving on. Pushing their chairs back they gathered up their parcels and shopping bags, which were becoming increasingly difficult to manage.

"We're going to need a couple of pack mules if we don't quit soon," Orpha cheerfully pointed out.

"We'll manage. Only one more stop to make if you wouldn't mind," he smiled. "Then I promise we'll leave."

Bill was insisting upon picking up something for each one of the children. After moments of protest from Orpha, followed by gentle coaxing from him, he won, when he said," It would make my Christmas brighter, and, after all, Christmas really is for kids."

The elevator was packed tight as it rose to the next floor, stopping with a gentle lurch, bringing Orpha's stomach back to its rightful place. The little man clad in the store's snappy red uniform with gold trim and brass buttons reached over, opening the gate and then the large glass door, exposing a small child's wildest dream. Toys everywhere, a huge tree brightly lit and heavily decorated with candy canes and large glass ornaments of assorted shapes and colors.

"Watch your step please, ladies and gentlemen, watch your step," the operator cautioned. "People now spilled out of the elevator into the enormous toy department. Many were parents, who led their children off to the side where good old Saint Nick sat on his immense red velvet throne doing his ho ho ho for the seemingly never-ending line of young believers, as they waited for their turn on his knee.

"What would they really like?" Bill asked. "No hedging now," he teased, smiling his most beguiling smile. Keeping in mind Orpha's obvious discomfort but wanting to make it a good Christmas for them, he gently urged, "Come on, now! Out with it!"

"I don't really know offhand," she answered.

"Let's take a walk through and see what happens," he suggested.

Just then, the elevator doors once again opened and a large nun dressed in the familiar habit of the Sisters of Charities began ushering a carload of noisy, excited youngsters out with orders of "Let's stay together now! Quiet please!" Then a final check—"Are we all here?" And, indeed, they seemed to be as the group started moving. However, one round cherub had stopped, looking up as high as her chubby little neck would allow. She beamed a wide smile showing two empty spaces. "Hi!" she said to the police officer on duty.

"Hi, yourself," he grinned back. Leaning down to meet the small child at her own height while putting his hands on his knees to steady himself, he said, "Don't you think you had better catch up with your friends?"

"Yes," she said in an obedient tone. "What's your name?"

"Fred. What's yours?"

"Becky," she answered with a happy smile still covering her smitten face.

Bill and Orpha had been caught up in the ongoing scene, which was about to end abruptly. One of the sisters happened to take a backward glance and spotted the young straggler. She put Orpha in mind of a large black and white mother hen as she came scurrying back to claim her missing chick. "Bye," the little girl waved as she was being hurried off. Orpha could hear the nun saying, "Scoot, scoot." As the long line of excited, noisy children made their way slowly between the red velvet roping, Orpha could hear the faint voices of carolers coming their way, closer, and closer. Then upon entering the toy department they broke into a bouncy, high-spirited rendition of "Santa Claus is Comin' to Town." The air in the store seemed literally charged with the excitement of the holidays.

A kewpie doll, a large red fire truck, and a tall bag of brightly painted, lettered blocks were selected for the children. Again Orpha and Bill entered the elevator but not without a struggle. The three additional gifts put them over the top, making it tough getting in and out the doors. Dinner would have to wait for another time, perhaps. Besides, it was getting late, and, as they stepped out onto the main floor, they could see—through the large store windows—very large flakes of snow floating through the air, and the light of day was beginning to dim. The streetlights had already come on and with the long ride ahead they agreed it would be wise to head home.

They trudged back to the car, which now wore a thin white cover of snow. Once the packages were placed in the trunk the two set about brushing some of it away. The snow covering the windows fell easily with a dusting by hands and forearms. Bill tried forming a snowball, only to have it fly apart and back in his face as he playfully tossed it at Orpha.

"See," she laughed, "you're not supposed to throw things at a lady!" She opened the car door and quickly darted inside.

"Is that right?" he called out, and before she knew it he was sitting beside her with a handful of snow threatening to wash her face by moving his hand in a circular motion directly in front of her nose. They were both laughing as Bill discarded his melting weapon out the door. Turning to her with great urgency, he collected Orpha in his arms and kissed her hard and deeply on the lips. He released her, apologizing, "I'm sorry. I hadn't planned on that. It got away from me. I've been wanting to do it for such a long time."

"I know," she responded. "I could sense it coming." He looked somewhat surprised at her confession.

"Bill, in all honesty," she went on, "you haven't been alone with what you have been feeling. I've been working hard trying to keep myself in check. I didn't want to start something we'll never be able to finish."

He knew what she meant instantly and it brought him back to earth with a thud.

It was a quiet ride home as they both sat with their thoughts. Orpha could almost feel Bill's sadness and she was wishing she had handled the situation differently than she had. What had been a wonderful mix of exuberant and lighthearted feelings now faded into pensive silence.

The car made its way slowly around the final curve in the driveway leading to the darkened main house and then to the brightly lit back house.

Bill pulled up, parking a short distance from Orpha's back door, the car's motor still running and the headlights still shining. He turned to her with the expression of a man resigned to his fate.

"I want you to know it's been a good time and I've enjoyed being with you. I hope my indiscretion won't keep you at a distance."

"Please don't feel bad," Orpha pleaded, as she placed her hand over the top of his. It's been a long time since I've enjoyed myself so much. Thanks for everything. I know the kids will be thrilled with your gifts, even though you really shouldn't have done it. And, Bill, maybe if we move gradually we could work things out between us."

Bill brightened at the thought that he might have a chance and his gratefulness was mirrored by his smile.

Christmas Day came and went, and as Orpha busied herself with her chores she remembered how excited the kids had been while opening their gifts and especially those given to them by Bill.

Theresa Ruth never turned loose of her doll during the entire day and it had remained her constant companion ever since. Orpha reflected on one other moment of that day. George had drawn a picture for his father and carefully wrapped it in a page from an old newspaper that she had brought from the main house. Tying it with a piece of string he handed it to her, solemnly saying, "Mommy, would you give this to my daddy when he comes?" She brushed the thought aside quickly, for tears of hurt started to form and they would serve no purpose. Here it was going into the last part of February and Floyd hadn't so much as called since he left, and maybe it was for the best. It was hard to say.

The kids asked about him less as the days wore on and if they did Orpha gave them an assortment of reasons for his absence, which, at the moment, seemed to satisfy them.

Bill had been scarce around the farm as well. The winter months left little to be done and what chores there were the farm hands easily took care of. So, Bill's time was spent in the city.

Orpha found herself missing him and looking out the windows whenever she happened to be near one, in hopes of seeing his car coming up the drive. She now wished that she hadn't been so reluctant with his advances, and thought he might have interpreted her reaction as not being interested.

The ringing of the phone interjected itself and scattered her thoughts. But deciding to let it wait, Orpha finished smearing a coat of wax on the kitchen floor while backing out on her hands and knees into the hallway, lightly bumping the table that held the telephone, whose persistent ring, demanded to be answered.

Pulling herself up by the doorframe, Orpha grabbed the phone from its cradle. "O'Dell's," she answered. A short silence and then the voice on the other end was unmistakably that of her husband.

"Hi, doll."

" Floyd," she said with distaste. "What do you want?"

"Just called to see if you miss me. How's things going?" he asked in a lighthearted manner.

"If this isn't just like you. It's hard for me to believe you care how things are with not even so much as a Christmas card to the kids."

"Come on, I didn't call to fight with you," he pleaded. "Hey, I miss you. I was thinking maybe we should have another go at it. What d'ya say?"

"Floyd, seven years is more than enough for me. What you don't understand is I don't want your kind of life. You're nothing but an irresponsible kid and I'm sick of hoping things will get better. They never do. It's always the same old crap."

"You're right, sweetheart. I'll do better. Give me one more shot at it, for the kids' sake."

Her hair instantly stood on end. "You've got your damn nerve! For the kids' sake? When did you ever do the right thing for the kids' sake?" With that she slammed the phone down hard. "God, I can't believe him! The only person he has ever thought of is himself." She was furious now, and if he were in reach she might be tempted to throw something at him. "God, I can't believe he really thought I would even consider," she muttered as she went to check on the children. The sound of the back door as it was opening and closing caught her attention just as she had reached the playroom doorway.

"Who's there?"

"Just me," Bill's voice called back.

"Oh damn," she muttered to herself as she ran her hand over her hair, then her clothing. "I look like hell." She quickly untied and brushed the knot from the front of her skirt that had been put there to keep it from getting in the way while doing the floor. A fleeting glance into the large hall mirror as she passed, told her it was hopeless.

"Hello, how are you? Other than busy," he asked with a smile.

She knew he could see her embarrassment and tried to make light of it.

"Oh fine. As long as I keep moving," she smiled. "Did you need something, Bill? Coffee? Something to eat maybe?" He followed her into the kitchen.

"Well," he answered slowly. "I'm wondering if I told you, what your reaction might be."

Turning toward him, she wasn't sure she heard correctly. Bill stretched his opened hand to her, motioning for her to take it. "What I really need and want more than anything is to be with you." Orpha now placed her hand in his and he drew her close. Bending his head down he laid a tender kiss upon her mouth. Then, pulling back just far enough, Bill could see into her eyes, and what he saw made him smile as he gathered her to him once again. "Oh God, woman, I want you so bad, and I know as it stands a future for us may not be possible."

Orpha stood engulfed not only by his strong, hard arms but by her own feelings of longing. And at this moment whatever he wanted she was willing to share. For the strong, urging sensation of desire would allow anything. She lifted her head from beneath his chin, then standing on her tip toes wrapped her arms around his broad neck, kissing him with a hunger she had never before experienced. They were straining desperately into each other's bodies as they continued to kiss with deep passion, unaware of their audience.

"Mommy," a small voice calmly spoke out. Orpha broke away from Bill abruptly. The interruption brought her back to reality instantly and somewhat unnerved her.

"Hi honey," she said sweetly to her young son smothering her true reaction of embarrassment.

"Mommy, I'm hungry," he announced, all the while scowling in Bill's direction.

"Here, son," Bill smiled, as he offered him an apple from the bowl on the sideboard. "Will this do?" Bobby took it, but with what appeared to be some reservation, then walked slowly from the room looking back once at his mother.

They stood quietly for a moment. Bill then gestured to her with his open arms, and Orpha once again returned, laying her head on his chest.

"Do you think we might find time next weekend for dinner and a late night?" he whispered softly against her ear.

"Yes, I would like that. I'll look better than I do now, I promise," she said teasingly.

124

"Hard work could never hurt your looks in any way. I have yet to see you looking anything but beautiful."

Orpha tossed her head back, laughing mockingly. "That's one of the things I love about the Irish. They know just the right thing to say and when to say it."

"I would never lie to you," he said with conviction as he gave her one last squeeze. Then with his arm about her waist they walked to the back door, where he kissed her lightly on the cheek and was gone. She smiled to herself, thinking of his flattery and how it tickled her.

Her evening with Bill that following Saturday, was turning out to be every bit as wonderful as she had anticipated throughout the days before.

She had never been to such a plush restaurant before and found herself a bit uncomfortable in the surrounding elegance.

The women coming in on the arms of well-dressed men made her take a quick notice of her own appearance, and as she looked up from herself she found Bill smiling broadly. "They can't hold a candle to you," he said, softly leaning across the table. Orpha felt a warm flush come to her face. She was embarrassed at being caught feeling insecure. The waiter sat a silver bucket on legs next to the table. She knew that Bill had ordered champagne and she was silently hoping she would like it better than the vinegary champagne she had once before tasted. But pleasantly, the wine was very much to her liking, and she drank glass for glass right along with Bill all through dinner. In fact, she seemed to be doing more sipping than eating, which she laughingly made mention of in their conversation.

Soft, beautiful music filled the dining room now and Orpha found herself swaying hypnotically within herself. She watched as couples began moving slowly to the dance floor.

Orpha and Bill rose from their seats at the same moment and with her hand in his she led the way. Cupping the side of her waist with his free hand Bill pulled her in just close enough that she found herself wanting to be even closer. She was aware that the wine was making her lightheaded, and a fleeting glimmer of common sense warned her to check her behavior or she could be sorry. But Orpha had never been wined and dined as it's called, quite like this, and caution was not a concern for this night she foolishly decided.

Months later as she thought back on that night, she was never sure who initiated what happened next. All she knew was that it was a wonderful night—maybe the most romantic she had ever known. Bill aroused in her such intense feelings, feelings she had never before experienced. Even now she felt small butterflies in her stomach as she remembered how they left the restaurant hand in hand without really saying anything to each other, taking the elevator of the hotel where the restaurant was located up to the seventh floor.

In her mind's eye she watched as Bill opened the door to the beautifully decorated suite, with a key he had not in her presence asked for. At the time she never gave it a thought that he had to have made the arrangements long before they arrived for dinner. But in all honesty at the time she would not have cared even if she had thought about it. Although later she mentioned it to him and he assured her that it was where he stayed while in town tending to business.

Chapter Eleven

Warm weather had finally arrived. Orpha was enjoying the bright, sunny morning, sitting out on the concrete side porch with a cup of coffee, watching the hummingbirds dipping into the honeysuckle vines that had twisted their way about the supporting posts on either side. The kids were chasing each other in the now-soft green grass directly in front of her, letting out occasional squeals and laughter. Her thoughts lingered on Bill and how much she enjoyed his company. What a tender man he was and just maybe somehow, something miraculous would take place. Her thoughts faded off as she mentally immersed herself in the beautiful weather, conscious of the warm rays of the sun laying softly on her face she had tilted upward and on the length of her bare arms.

"Good morning," a voice called to her. "Good weather, yes?"

"Oh, hello, Radar, yes, it's gorgeous."

"You have more men for lunch, Orpha," he matter of factly reported to her. "The mail and supplies I put in kitchen. I leave now." And that was that. Still a man of few words, Radar said what he came to say, then left. In all the months she had lived at the farm, Orpha had never been able to engage him in long conversation.

Leaving the children to play, she went back to the kitchen, and began putting the few things away that Radar had brought from town. The envelope on the table caught her attention. She knew immediately from the postmark and handwriting that it was from Mary Barbara. She hadn't heard from her in a very long time. Quickly, she tore it open, unfolding the lone sheet of paper, and began reading.

Dear Orpha,
Got here and found things much different than I had thought.

The big white family home on the river that Lemvel had talked about? Turns out to be a big one-room shack. With us included, at least four other families are living in it, with no running water or electricity. I was really surprised and a lot disappointed, but I'm crazy about Lemvel, and he promised me in a couple of months we'll have a place of our own. I sure hope so. I like his family. They are good people but they don't seem to be willing to work for their keep. Everyone here is on welfare and instead of applying for WPA and working for what they get by fishing for mussels from the river, and selling them to a nearby button factory, they pretty much just lay around, including Lemvel.

All the women other than the grandmother are pregnant and maybe even myself, not sure yet. Will let you know as soon as I know. How are the kids? Tell them hi for me.

And say hi to Floyd too. I even miss him believe it or not.

It's sure beautiful back here in these hills. Everything is so untouched and wild. The underground springs are icy cold and clear as crystal. At night the air carries through the open windows (that, by the way, don't have glass in them) a hot muggy breeze saturated with green smells, and more than a few insects. The loud frog and bug music takes a bit of getting used to but I've been sleeping better the last couple of weeks.

I'm hoping we get settled in our own place before too long so we can have everyone come see us and stay awhile.

By the way, they are very religious here. Nothing but church music can be played on their radio and nothing but gospel records on this very old Victrola. I went to church with all of Lemvel's kin Sunday. Just a small place, but boy did they ever pack them in and they really get in the spirit of things. People were rolling on the floor, shouting

128

*and praise being the Lord. They also were talking some
kind of strange language, which I could not make head or
tail of. It's really different from what we were brought up
on. Well, not much else to write about, so here's hoping we
hear from you soon.*

    Love your sister,
    Mary Barbara Murphy

"Another hot, clammy day on the way," Mary Barbara
thought, as she wiped at the sweat building on her face with
the palm of her hand.

    She had just finished her follow-up letters to Orpha,
Arline, and Mama, letting them know she was definitely
pregnant and that the baby was due, to the best of her
figuring, around the last of October, possibly the first of
November.

    After laying the stub of pencil down that she had
sharpened with a knife, she quickly picked it up again
thinking out loud, "I better keep this in a safe place. I might
not see another."

    "Mary Barber! Mary Barber!" Her name with a
slight bend to it was being called from outside the house.
Lemvel says for youn to come on down to the river now
and take a dunking with 'em.

    " Okay, I'll be there directly," she shouted to Isaac
in the same manner that these people spoke. She could not
see him but picturing him in her mind, she was amused
with his image. Lots of blond hair, being somewhere
between eight and nine years old, as round as he was tall,
always barefooted. His shirts short enough for a child half
his size. His round little cheeks were forever peeking over
the top of his pants, until one of the adults would scold him,
whereupon he would hoist them quickly, only to have them
return to their original resting place soon thereafter.

    "Granny, anything I can get you?" Mary Barbara
asked as she stepped out onto the makeshift back porch.

The frail old matriarch moved rhythmically back and forth in her rocking chair that creaked out a tune of its own. "Nope!" the woman snapped, not bothering to look up.

Mary Barbara stopped, intrigued by what she saw. For as Granny rocked, she would periodically reach out with the toe of her shoe for the edge of a small trap door affixed to the porch, and without missing a beat, she'd lift it and spit her chaw into the black opening. Staying long enough to see the synchronized rocking and spitting once or twice more, Mary Barbara then pulled herself away and headed down the well-traveled dirt path that cut through the high weeds and led to the river.

"Come on in!" Lemvel called to her. "Me and a big fish is waiting for you."

"What big fish?" Mary Barbara laughingly asked as she started wading in toward him, with her clothing still on. "It feels strange," she thought, "but if it makes them all happy . . ."

"You shouldn't be showing your flesh. It's not Christian-like," Granny had grumbled when she had seen her swimsuit. "I never heard of such a thing," she thought, while looking about for Lemvel. "Even the men go swimming fully clothed."

"Where did he go?" Mary Barbara said out loud as she quickly spun around in the water that had now reached her waist. "Lemvel," she called, closely scanning the surface, expecting him to pop up and grab her. "Lemvel, come on, where—"

"Gotcha!" he said as he seemed to come from nowhere, taking her under with him and then with a hand on either side of her hips he projected her up and out into the water. Sputtering as she came up and brushing her wet hair back from her eyes, she began paddling after him laughing and telling him that she was going to hook herself that big fish he had been talking about.

With that, Lemvel came to a quick stop, extending his hands, palms up and the fingers motioning, come ahead. "I dare you," he challenged. "Come and get this big fish!" A sly grin now covered his face and Mary Barbara knew what was being offered. She swam to where he stood, pulling herself up on him and wrapping her arms about his neck. She began blowing softly in his ear and then nipping it very gently. He yanked her in close as his open mouth covered hers and his one hand feverishly explored the private parts of her body.

As they pressed into each other with growing passion, Lemvel started slow walking her backward to the river's edge. Once on the bank they lowered themselves to the ground, with just a thin screen of young saplings and some underbrush nearby to hide them from view. They tore at each other's wet clothing making hungry noises as they found the hot, damp flesh beneath. He entered her with one hard thrust and continued driving in deeply. And she rose to meet him with each move until the greatness of their act drove them to an ecstasy that was so intense it contained a delicious pain for her, and she told him this as they lay beside each other limp and spent.

"You know," Mary Barbara said, as she slowly began to redress herself in a bent-over fashion so as to take advantage of the scant natural screening, "if we had a place of our own we could do this as much as we wanted and whenever we felt like it. It's so hard to find time alone with everybody around."

"You're right!" Lemvel answered thoughtfully as he stood up while buttoning the last button on his trousers. He then leaned down, pulled her up from the ground by her wrist, and with long strides began hauling her along behind him.

"Wait a minute, wait just a darn minute!" she yelled out, stumbling as she was trying hard to keep up with him.

They stopped at the river's edge a distance from where they had made love. "Where are we going?"

"To find a place of our own. Isn't that what you want?"

"Yes, but—"

"Get on in," he instructed, pulling the small, old rowboat in closer on the bank.

"Okay, okay, but where are we going?" she repeated.

"You'll see," he smiled. Picking up the ores he began paddling down the river. They had gone just a short distance when he proudly proclaimed, "Well, there it is." He was looking out past her and pointing. Turning her head as she shifted her position on the wooden seat she could see a small, weathered old cow barn. Her heart sank. Lemvel, for Pete's sake, it's a barn. Is that what you want us to live in?"

"Well, I can't think of anyplace better presently."

"Can't we at least try to find something in town or even move back to St. Louis? A barn? That's all there is?"

"Now wait just a dang minute. You haven't even seen inside yet," he snapped, becoming irritated and somewhat bewildered by her disappointment. "You was just moaning cause we had no place to be alone and I thought we could do some fixing and sweeping." The boat bumped gently as it ran aground. Lemvel stepped out into the shallow water, then onto the bank, as Mary Barbara remained seated.

"You coming?" he asked as he turned from her—not waiting for an answer—and started up toward the building that sat just a few hundred yards from the river.

She stood up looking first at Lemvel in disbelief and then at the old cow barn, swiftly raising her arms from her sides then letting them fall back to her in a hopeless gesture. She stepped from the boat and ran to catch up with him. The rusty hinges barely affixed to the side door screeched loudly as Lemvel pulled hard and the heavy wood gave way. Stepping down and into the old barn that still smelled of livestock and stale hay they moved first to the center then turning in a small circle side by side, they slowly took in what could possibly be their new home. The hayloft's shuttered window had been left open, and from it the streams of sunlight escaping through the wide cracks of the floor overhead were peppered with the dust from their walking about. Mary Barbara spotted the ladder reaching upward to the loft.

"Let's see what it's like," she said over her shoulder, resigning herself as she started carefully climbing what appeared to be a sturdy ladder.

Once she reached the floor of the loft, still holding tightly to the sides of the ladder, she swung her leg aside and stepped out onto the loft's heavy boards, and began walking noisily about.

"Maybe we could fix it up just enough for now. It will be better to be by ourselves, I suppose, even if it's here."

"Who owns this?" Mary Barbara thought to ask.

"My pa's uncle," he shouted up at her. "He stopped farming years back. Too much work, not enough money, I hear tell."

"Where's his house?" she inquired.

"Ain't none. If so, it would be on the other side of that hill yonder. But from what I heard, reckon it burned down one night, cause uncle had too much moonshine and not enough sense left to stomp the fire out." He laughed at his own attempt at humor, then went on. "We haven't seen hide nor hair of him for nigh on to three years, but as the old saying goes, a bad penny always comes back."

Mary Barbara gently corrected him, "No, you mean, a bad penny always turns up."

"Yep, that's right," he agreed, smiling at her.

Mary Barbara came back to the edge of the loft and looked down into his smiling face. "You know, I'm thinking, either I'm so crazy about you or I am just plain crazy!"

"Now why would you be thinking a thing like that?" he asked, as his grin grew even wider.

"Just that I'll probably live here or anywhere you ask me to and what's more you know it, don't you?"

"Yup," he replied with a short sucking sound to the side of his mouth and a quick accentuating nod of his head. "Yup, I guess I do at that."

"You big booger," she said, as she descended the ladder and stepped down onto the dirt floor.

She took a playful swipe at him, as she walked to the broad strip of cement in the center of the barn that at one time held hay for livestock to feed on.

Slowly she was resigning herself to the fact that this was all Lemvel had to offer. And as she surveyed her surroundings she knew she would have to make the best of the situation, although her voice reflected the disappointment and sadness that lay deep within. She tried desperately to appear interested. It's going to take a lot of elbow grease, sweeping, scrubbing, and gallons of hot, soapy bleach water, and I can't believe I'm letting you put me in a barn," she said just above a whisper.

"Hey, put me down!" she yelped. "What are you doing? You're gonna drop me."

He had crept up behind her, sweeping her off her feet and into his arms, kissing her playfully about her face while taking long striding steps toward what would be their front door. "This is our house and I'm gonna carry my bride across the—what d'ya call it, darling?"

"Threshold," she answered with a smile as she gave up her struggle with despair surrendering to his childlike charm as she clung to his neck.

"Well, that's what I'm adoin', I'm taking you across it."

The days spent cleaning the barn and making it as livable as possible had at the beginning been a challenge to both of them. But Lemvel grew tired of it quickly, and for a short time it became an interest only to Mary Barbara.

The months wore on, and as her pregnancy grew more obvious so did Lemvel's laziness and indifference to doing what should be done. Other than an occasional fish he might catch or some small game he would bag he did little else than rest, as he called it, and for the life of her she couldn't figure what he thought he was resting from.

As Mary Barbara's delivery date drew closer, her own energy level, along with her driving desire to keep things clean and neat were noticeably ebbing. She seemed to be fitting in with Lemvel's way of living and more resigned to her bleak surroundings. She could feel herself slipping into passivity and would occasionally promise herself, "Once I have the baby, I'll do better."

"Hey, woman, looky here," Lemvel yelled out as he kicked open the old door entering the barn. Two grotesque-looking opossum dangled limply by their tails from Lemvel's fist, dripping a scattered trail of blood onto the dirt floor as he walked in her direction. "I got these here critters just for you," he chuckled. Beaming proudly, he held his trophies high as he came alongside the bed where she had stretched out earlier.

"What d'ya say? Want to git goin' on these here beauties for supper?"

"No, I don't, but I will."

Slowly she rose from their old metal bed, and as she did, the rusty springs announced her departure. Adjusting her large, feed-sack shift so that it would cover her now-rotund body, she followed him, shuffling slowly across to the end of the cement pad, numb and indifferent to the small spattering hitting the floor just ahead of her.

135

Mary Barbara hated cleaning and preparing opossum let alone eating it. She found it much too greasy for her taste, and had told Lemvel this time after time. But she suspected it was easy kill for him and her pleadings weren't considered.

She watched as he slapped the carcasses on the surface of the oilcloth-covered kitchen table and walked off the slab to the old kerosene stove. Lifting the lid from the iron skillet he exposed the leftover cornbread from yesterday's meal. "Want a piece of cornbread?" he asked, as he tore a handful out and stuffed it in his mouth. Mary Barbara didn't bother to answer. She was now face to face with the two ugly beasts she had to skin and prepare for that night's meal. "Ugh," she said out loud. With a sharp knife she took the heads from their bodies, then cut off the legs and tails, dropping them in a bucket sitting near the table. Mary Barbara then went about skinning. With two swift slices down the center of the stomachs she opened them, removed the entrails, which joined the parts already in the bucket.

Mary Barbara washed the carcasses inside and out, rubbed them with salt and pepper, and sprinkled them with flour. The two small bodies were laid on their backs in the old enamel roasting pan with six large, peeled rutabagas. Once she had added just the right amount of water, Mary Barbara opened the oven door and slid the roasting pan in.

"Lemvel, come get this bucket and take it out and down by the river so the critters can feast! Lemvel? I will probably wind up doing it myself, damn it," she said out loud.

She busied herself next with the drop biscuits, which were easy enough. Mix a batch of biscuit dough and then drop them from a large spoon on a baking sheet one by one.

Preparation for this meal always took considerable time, leaving Lemvel ample opportunity to complain that he was starving to death.

Now seated, he dug into the cooked marsupials with unrestrained gluttony and plenty of lip smacking to go with it.

"Lemvel, do you have to make so much noise?" Mary Barbara snapped. Lemvel looked up from his meal long enough to mutter something that sounded like "uh huh," and returned to his food with the same audible enthusiasm.

Mary Barbara was and had been for some time a little on edge. She told herself it was because of the baby, who was due any day. But now she realized it was more than that. She sat watching Lemvel with opossum gravy on his chin, as he ate with his usual passion.

Reaching over, she took a biscuit, nibbled at the edge for just a moment, then placed it alongside her plate. She helped herself to a spoonful of rutabagas, which she poked at a couple of times before deciding they weren't what she wanted either. Laying her fork down, Mary Barbara pushed her chair back and left the table.

"Hey, where ya going?" Lemvel asked with his mouth still full.

"Not hungry," she answered over her shoulder as she went back to her rumpled bed, at the other end of the slab, the springs screeching as she lowered herself onto the secondhand mattress, that was well broken in and more than a bit lumpy.

"Get a hold of yourself," she scolded. "He's a good man. It's not his fault you feel bad." Slowly she drifted off to sleep.

Waking with a start, Mary Barbara checked the Big Ben alarm clock that sat on the chair by the side of the bed. "Ten o'clock, gosh," she said out loud, surprised at how long she had been sleeping. It was pitch black in the barn except for the soft glow of the kerosene lamp on the dinner table, which silhouetted the dishes and leftovers still there. Sitting up on the edge of the bed she squinted as she looked about, thinking Lemvel must have gone to town again, which he had been doing more often lately.

She didn't mind all that much except she worried he might not be there when she needed him.

A sudden loud noise made her heart jump and she shot up from the bed quicker than she would have thought possible. Looking upward to the loft where the sound had originated, she guessed at what it might be. "That damn door," she muttered to herself, as it now banged loudly against the wall behind it. The wind had picked up, whipping it open. She could feel the draft as the heat rose and found its way to the large opening.

Knowing she had no choice but to take care of it she reached for the lamp next to the bed. Once lit, she held it out allowing its soft glow to light her way to the ladder.

"Holy Mother of God, I hope we make this," she said out loud, and began slowly and deliberately taking one rung at a time, her bare feet curling as best they could for a better grip about the thick wooden rods. Pulling and pushing her swollen, pregnant body up was no easy task she soon discovered.

Reaching the edge of the loft she held the lamp out to get a better look. But as she went to swing her right leg out and step on to the loft her left foot slipped. "Oh my God," she blurted as she tried balancing the lamp while reasserting her footing, her free hand hanging on as tightly as she could. The heavy ladder moved, but only slightly, then stabilized. Taking a deep breath, she once again reached out for the floor of the loft and made it. Hurrying to the black gaping hole in the wall she peered hard into the pitch of the night hoping to see some sign of Lemvel. Seeing nothing she banged the door closed, and quickly propped a board firmly against it. "There, that should hold

138

it," she said out loud, her voice swallowed by the emptiness of the loft.

Making her way down the ladder was not as difficult once she made it past the first few splintering rungs.

In the dim light she cleared the supper table, taking a portion of the hot water that perpetually sat in waiting on the surface of the stove and began washing the food-caked dishes, vigorously scouring them with her fingernails. As she took the last cleaning swipe at the table, Lemvel pushed his way through the door, singing happily his favorite song when drinking, "South of the border down Mexico way." Staggering over to where she stood he put his face near hers as if he wasn't quite sure of her identity. Abruptly stopping his music, he declared, "Hey thar's my sweetheart. Waiting up for me, are ya?" He was wearing a grin as wide as his face would allow.

"You're drunker than a skunk," she scolded. "Go to bed!" she ordered in a voice of disgust.

"What d'ya mean," he slurred as he put his arms about her trying to get as close as her pregnancy permitted. "I'm just nuts about ya. Come on, let's make another baby." And with that he started snickering and fondling her.

"Lemvel, go to bed!" Her irritation with him heightened as she worked at pushing and guiding him to the bed, whereupon she gave him a firm shove in the right direction and he fell into the mattress hard enough that both sides of it reached up in a welcoming fashion then flattened out as did its drunken occupant who lay spread eagle and as still as death itself.

"Whew!" she said, fanning her hand in front of her face. "You stink!"

She finished unlacing his boots that were only partly laced to begin with. Taking them from his bare feet she let them drop to the floor. Going to the other side of the bed she lay down beside him, and as she did her mind scanned briefly over her new life. How very different it was from what Lemvel had told her, and she found herself resenting that fact. Looking over at him she could barely make out his features because of the darkness. But she knew his handsome face well and smiled in spite of her annoyance with him.

Turning to her side to avoid her husband's liquor-soaked breath she made herself a promise. "Tomorrow I'll clean this place and myself, then sit down and write Orpha and Mama a letter."

It seemed as though she had just blinked and it was daylight once again. Throwing the covers back she drew her heavy body into a sitting position. And once she had her legs dangling from the side of the bed she slowly stood up, taking a long look at Lemvel. He was stretched out on his back, and in need of a good scrubbing, his hair going every which way, while his mouth wide open, sent out strange noises.

"My hero," she thought, sarcastically, as she walked away to prepare coffee. Her morning was spent scouring and sweeping and doing anything she could to make the place a little more livable. When she decided she could do no more she sat down. Looking about she thought how much nicer it looked and how much better she felt about her surroundings, only there was a big lump in the bed. She smiled looking over at the form of her husband still rolled up in the covers.

"Hey you, over there in the bed," she called out. "Are you going to stay there all day?" No answer. "Lemvel," she tried again, "it's almost noon. Are you going to get out of there?"

"Leave me be woman," he called back, and burrowed deeper into the bed.

"I'll tell you what," she went on as she rose from her chair and walked to his side of the bed, "if you get up so I can fumigate that bed I'll make you biscuits and gravy and even throw in an egg or two, how does that sound?"

"It sounds like you're going to keep pecking at me until you get your way is what it sounds like," he said, his words muffled by the covers that still hid his head.

"Then stay there all day if you want," she snapped, her patience in short supply this morning. "I don't give a crap," she shot back at him as she walked away. "Rot in the damn bed, see if I care." She padded across the cold slab in her bare feet to where the dishpan full of hot water sat in waiting. Bending over with some effort she held her head low to the center of the large vessel and with a cup began pouring water over her head after which she began firmly rubbing a bar of ivory soap into her hair trying hard to work up a suds. Having rinsed it with cups of the same water she wrapped her head in a dingy towel, and went on with her sponge bath.

While combing out her wet hair, a trickle of warm water ran freely down the inside of her leg and gushed onto the pavement floor. She knew instantly what was about to happen. Dressing quickly, she hollered, pleaded, and demanded, "Lemvel! Get up! I mean get up now!"

He stirred, but did not make a definite move. Again, she walked to the bed. "Lemvel, come on now, get yourself up! I think I'm about to have the baby." There was a slight stirring from the breathing mound of quilts and then as if a light had been turned on, he came from beneath his hiding place in a rush with wide-eyed expectation. "Now? You're having it now?" he asked excitedly.

"What should I do?" he asked.

"Nothing you can do, just get me to the hospital in plenty of time." Packing wasn't a problem—she had nothing to take. The few things she had managed to buy for the baby were still in their original wrappings, lying in the bottom drawer of the secondhand dresser.

Her pain started slowly but rapidly increased. "Let's go," she forced herself to say in the middle of a strong contraction, while holding her hand to her rock-like stomach. "Get the truck. I'll meet you out front."

"Please, God, let me make it in time," she prayed to herself, as Lemvel tore out of the barn.

The old Ford pickup rattled on down what she referred to as Washboard Ave., and it felt to her as though it wasn't missing a hole. "Shit," she swore in pain. "This ride has got to be worse than having any baby," she said as they violently bounced down the road, her head making contact with the roof once or twice. "Son of a bitch," she lashed out, partly at Lemvel, because in her pain-racked mind he was responsible for every bump and pothole in the road. Also the contractions were very close now, and she had little time between them to steel herself.

They finally hit the main road and Lemvel tore down it like a bat out of hell. "Hang on darlin', I'll get you there. Don't you worry none," Lemvel said with conviction.

He went on talking but Mary Barbara couldn't hear and didn't care to hear what it was he was saying for she was in her own world of pain and trying desperately to handle it bravely as she knew Mama would want her to. Trying to draw strength, she told herself what she had remembered hearing Mama say, "Women have been having babies for centuries, and in fact Chinese women would drop their babies in the rice fields, pick them up, and go on with their work." Hard to believe, but Mama had said so, and she would not lie. "God, I'm such a namby-pamby," Mary Barbara scolded herself.

The truck came to a sudden halt. Lemvel jumped out, raced to Mary Barbara's side, flung the door open, and helped her down. Now bent over in deep pain, she forced herself to walk as she smothered her moans. Once inside the hospital staff took over and instructed Lemvel to wait in the father's waiting room until the baby arrived.

Chapter Twelve

It was late afternoon and Orpha was in the middle of pinching off dough from a large mound, making clover leaf rolls for supper. She heard the side door open and then close, but no one came into the kitchen. While dusting her hands on the sides of her dish towel apron, she walked to the door, noticing a stack of mail that had not been on the hallway table earlier. One of the men must have just dropped it off and gone back to work, she figured.

She wiped her hands carefully, then picked up the mail to see if there might be something for her. What first caught her eye was a long business-size envelope with the return address of St. Regis Sanatorium.

Orpha held it for a moment just looking at it, knowing that the person it concerned had great influence on her life, and there wasn't a whole heck of a lot she could do about it. She slowly and thoughtfully laid the letter back on the table, then continued inspecting what was left.

"Oh good," she said out loud when Mary Barbara's handwriting became apparent on the very last envelope. She tore it open and began reading.

Dear Orpha,

I had the baby last week. It was a boy. We named him Bobby. He is really a pretty boy with lots of dark curly hair and big chocolate-brown eyes. You forget just how tiny newborns are, with the exception of Ronnie of course.

I'll bet he has really grown since I've seen him last, as I'm sure they all have. How is everyone? I don't mind telling you I'm really homesick and would love to see all of you. Did you and Floyd work things out or is he living life free and easy? Something I'm learning down here—some men can be very selfish and some of them can also be very, very LAZY. Other than that we're okay. Lemvel promised me he would go in town to the button factory and get a steady job so as we can get out of this damn barn he found us to live in. We'll see. Not that he's not a good man—he is. It's just he has no get up and go.

Well, enough of my bellyaching as he calls it. Have you heard from Mama? I wrote her to let her know about Bobby, but haven't heard a word from her yet. Is she okay? Next time you talk to Arline ask her to drop me a line when she gets a chance.

In your letter you mentioned more than a few times this Bill person. Is there by any chance something going on there I might be interested in? Ha, ha! Just kidding. He sounds really nice to work for. Well, got to go. Bobby's screaming bloody murder. He must be hungry again. Just like these guys, never get enough of the tit. Write when you can. Give the kids a hug for me.

Love your sister Mary Barbara

Orpha spoke out loud, "Short letter. They live in a barn?"

Returning to the kitchen she went back to pinching rolls. With the last pan filled she covered them and set them to rise. It would be suppertime soon and the men would be coming in from their chores to wash up for the evening meal. She moved quickly, putting finishing touches on the large pot of beef stew.

"Mommy, Mommy," she could hear the kids calling excitedly as they banged their way through the door. "Daddy's here! Daddy's here!"

"What?" she asked, not wanting to believe what she was hearing. She felt intense resentment at Floyd's unannounced appearance even before she laid eyes on him. But there he was—coming through the doorway with Ronnie in his arms and the other two hanging on his pant legs laughing as he tried to walk. "Look at this big fella I found outside," Floyd said, jumping the boy up and down in his arms.

"What do you want, Floyd?" Orpha asked caustically.

"Just what's mine," he said. "Just what's mine."

"You know, you have a lot of nerve, waltzing in here for the first time in how long? Saying something as stupid as that. I suppose you expect me to fall all over you. Well, it's not going to happen. So, leave! Get out now before I toss something at your thick head."

"Come on, sugar, you're scaring the kids," he said, smiling.

"Like you really give a damn," she shot back.

"Would I drive all the way out here if I didn't?"

"You damn right you would, if you thought there was something in it for you."

"True enough," he replied with a sly grin. "So I'll tell you what, the four of us will go back to the house and wait for you to finish here, and then we'll talk about our lives together."

Not waiting for her response, he urged the kids—who appeared nervous and apprehensive as to what might be taking place—to come along with him. The door banged behind them, and Orpha stood there, furious with this man who thought he could just walk in and out of their lives whenever he felt like it. "How dare him! That son of a bitch! Damn!" She finished her cursing as she picked up the pan of rolls and opened the oven door, feeling the need to bang something, but knowing if she slammed the door hard she could flatten the bread.

Her mind was racing. "Damn him to hell! Just who does he think he is?" she muttered in anger. She soon heard the men coming in from the fields for supper and dreaded when they would leave. She was never one to enjoy confrontation. But never one to shirk it when it was necessary.

The farm hands gathered about the sink, passing the soap around as they washed up. Once seated, they ate with enthusiasm while their clinking of silverware and voices in conversation became a backdrop to her thoughts. Moving about the supper table, Orpha automatically stacked more rolls on the platter and made trips back to the kettle on the stove to refill the large tureens with steaming stew. She was silently pleading with God to give her some kind of answer to her problems—one that might be good for all concerned. Lost in deep thought she however felt a presence. "My compliments to the chef," Bill said, smiling at her warmly.

"Bill, Floyd's at the house," she told him in a low voice, as she turned with a bowl in each hand and walked back toward the table.

Returning to his seat, Bill lingered behind with a cup of coffee until the rest of the men had left. He pushed his chair back standing quietly behind it, as Orpha went about scraping and stacking dishes.

"You'll let me know if you need me, won't you?"

"Yes, thanks, I will."

He smiled, then left.

Orpha hesitated with her hand on the door knob before entering the small kitchen of the back house. As she opened the door Floyd was coming out of the bathroom that was located at the other end zipping his trousers. "Hey, perfect timing, sweetheart," he teased. "That's the last thing I want from you, Floyd. Why are you here?" She had primed herself for what she decided would be their final run-in.

"I want my girl back," he said. "I know I've been a horse's ass, but I can tell you that part of my life is over."

"What part? Your skirt chasing, your acting like a kid, or just being irresponsible? What part, Floyd?"

"Come on, honey," he pleaded, sounding as sincere as he possibly could. "I'll prove it to you. You'll see I can do right by you and the kids. I swear."

"Floyd, we've been through this too many times in the last seven years. You are what you are."

She felt just a little sorry for him now because she could see the water rimming his eyes as he realized she wasn't having any more of his hollow promises.

His self-pity now turned to indignation and anger as he tried another ploy to weaken her resolve.

"Let me tell you something, lady, if you cared so damn much for these kids you'd want them to have their daddy. You think you can do it on your own miss high and mighty, and not have them hate you for kicking my butt out?"

"Floyd, get out! GET OUT! I know you better than you know yourself."

"Yeah, bet you know mister big shot O'Dell even better don't ya? Ya little tramp." His hand shot out, grabbing her by the arm, twisting it painfully behind her back.

"Let go of me you bastard," she cursed, wrenching her arm free, as she stumbled into a chair, knocking it over.

"I'll let you go when I'm damn good and ready," he yelled back, making another lunge at her.

"Mommy, Daddy, don't," the kids cried from the doorway, hysterically begging for the fight to end.

"Get the hell out of here or—"

"Or what? Go on, call the son of a bitch. I'll kick the shit out of him. He can find his piece of ass somewheres else— not with my wife."

"You are pathetic," she yelled back. "You poke every woman that's available and you still think you have a right to tell me what to do."

A loud knock on the back door brought a quick silence.

Radar's large form filled the open doorway, his hand still gripping the doorknob. "I heard da kids, wondered if all is okay?" He stood there looking at Orpha and then at Floyd and then at the children still huddled together.

His eyes now fixed on Floyd with a steady gaze, as he continued talking.

"I'll be right outside here if you want, okay?"

"Thanks, Radar. I think Floyd was just leaving."

"Hey toots, I'm gone," Floyd quickly responded with a shrug of his shoulders. "But don't call me when you get in a pickle. I'm done. This guy knows when he's whipped."

Floyd found the space in the doorway a little tight in his hasty retreat, but once through, he muttered, "See you later, big fella," and quickly walked away.

"You'll be okay?" Radar asked as he turned to go.

"I'll be fine," Orpha said smiling faintly. "Thanks."

She felt sure it had been Bill who sent Radar to her rescue, not wanting to intrude himself. She slowly closed the door and went to her children, hugging them as she tried to reassure them that everything would be fine, and at the same time hoping that they would be. George, now going on six, had become quite the big brother, taking charge whenever he could. As Orpha walked in she could see he had his arm around Ronnie with Theresa Ruth standing as close as she could to him. They had gone from crying out of fear to soft sniffling as he was reassuring them. "See, it's okay. We'll be all right. Mommy's here." George did not have a problem being sensitive or strong for his younger sister and now his baby brother, Ronnie.

"Mommy, is Daddy mad at you?" George asked.

"Is he gone away?" Theresa Ruth wanted to know, her eyes still red from crying. "What did we do to make Daddy mad?"

Scooping Ronnie from the floor, Orpha motioned for the other two to join her on the bed so she could talk with them. "You did nothing wrong. You're all wonderful, and you are the very best children that any mommy or daddy could have, do you hear me?" she said, looking at them one at a time and smiling, trying hard to make them believe her.

"Sometimes even Mommy and Daddy forget to be nice to each other just as kids do and that is not good, so we have to try harder to not yell or be mean. I promise there will not be any more yelling, is that okay?"

"Okay," George agreed. Theresa Ruth echoed him. Ronnie started getting restless and bouncing about the bed.

"I know what we can do after dinner," Orpha said, changing the topic. "We can take a nice long walk down the road. It's a pretty evening and the fresh air will be good for us. How does that sound? Would you like that?"

"Yay! Let's take a walk! Yay," George cheered.

Theresa Ruth smiled a weak smile in agreement.

In the days following, things ran smoothly for Orpha. She hadn't heard from Floyd for some time and the kids appeared to be adjusting nicely.

Bill was spending more and more time with them and they had grown close. Even George, who would occasionally ask about his daddy, appeared to be forming a bond with this man who couldn't do enough for them.

"Please allow me to have some pleasure in life," he would say with an affectionate smile. "I am not being entirely unselfish you understand."

Bill enjoyed squiring her to elegant restaurants and showering her with small expensive gifts. Toys for the kids were abundant. In fact, it had reached a point where she had to request that it stop. The children were expecting something each time he came over, she had told him.

"They have grown greedy, and as much as I appreciate what you do for them, toys all the time and every time they see you is not good for them."

Bill reluctantly understood but started taking them into town. And while there, he would beseech her to let him buy them shoes and clothing. He appeared to get such a kick out of it that Orpha did not have the heart to stop him.

Besides, he had numerous times let her know that he loved her and if he could have his way and be free of his predicament he would ask her to marry him in a flash.

On returning from one such day in town, they had just slammed shut the last car door, when Radar hurried to Bill's side announcing that there had been an urgent call from St. Regis, and that he must call them as soon as possible.

With his brow deeply furrowed, and without another word, Bill rushed off to make his call.

"Come on, kids. Let's get these things into the house and put away," Orpha said, looking in the direction of the big house and wondering what had happened at the sanatorium of such importance.

It was not until the following day, late in the afternoon, that she caught a glimpse of Bill as he pulled into the driveway, going the distance to turn around and come back, so that his passenger could alight from the car on the proper side.

Orpha watched from the playroom window, barely hearing the children at play, as she watched a lady emerging from the front seat.

Offering his hand, Bill assisted the tall, regal-looking woman's exit. Orpha knew instantly who the woman was. Her long, blond hair caught up neatly in a snare, her features finely chiseled and inexpressive. She wore a stylish gray suit, and a smart spring coat thrown across her shoulders. All in all she appeared well kept. Not at all what Orpha expected for a woman just released from a mental hospital, and after so long. Her heart sank, as the lady hung on Bill's arm while he guided her up the sidewalk and into the house.

She could hear the front door opening and closing, along with their indistinct talking, until it disappeared up the stairway and behind the muffled sound of the bedroom door softly closing behind them.

Leaving the children to play, she walked slowly but purposely to the foot of the staircase. Looking up and not knowing what she expected to see or hear, she just stood there. Voices first in speaking tones and then steadily rising could be heard. There was silence. And then with a burst the woman's voice, "I want them out of here! Do you hear me?" A door opened, and the same shrill screaming continued. "I may have been ill but my ears work just fine." The voice was softened once again as the door shut it off.

Orpha turned to leave hoping to escape before Bill reached the top of the landing.

"Orpha, wait!" Bill hurried down to where she stood. "I take it you heard what was said?"

Embarrassed at being caught eavesdropping, Orpha replied, "Yes, I'm sorry. I did hear. We'll go, Bill. You have enough to worry about."

"Orpha, I know you understand that I care a great deal for you and the kids and I don't want you to leave. But this situation would not be good for any of you. And knowing I'm to blame that it went as far as it did makes me feel like a heel. Hold on here for a few days or for as long as you want until you can make other living arrangements. In the meantime, I'll see if I can unravel this mess I've made."

"Bill, please, you are not entirely to blame. I'm a grown woman with three children and didn't do anything to stop you—but could have. We'll be just fine, but I may need those couple of days you offer."

"Take all the time you need, but perhaps it might be a good idea not to come to the main house. Ina is very excitable, and it appears that someone has been carrying tales to her."

He took her by the shoulders, looking down into her eyes, and softly said, "I do love you, and we will—be—together!" With that, he turned and went back up the stairway.

Orpha stood frozen until she once again heard the sound of a bedroom door closing.

Tears rimmed and spilled over, making cool, wet paths down the warm flesh of Orpha's face. Quickly wiping them off with the back of her hand, she tried hard to get a grip on her emotions. "I don't have time for this foolishness," she scolded herself. "He has a wife and you knew it. Now where are you?" She continued to flog herself, adding to her unhappiness as she approached the playroom. "Come on, kids. Let's go," she called to the children." "Time to go home." An empty, hollow feeling settled in the pit of her stomach.

With supper over and the kids tucked away for the night, Orpha sat at the narrow, white-enameled kitchen table, staring blankly ahead, oblivious to the heavy smog that hung in the small room as she smoked one cigarette after another. Forcing Bill from her mind, she tried to think of somewhere to go or something she might do. She sat for hours with no firm solution forthcoming. It was very late when she finally forced herself to bed.

Morning came too soon, and, as she awoke, Orpha was looking straight into the face of a red-haired, blue-eyed cherub, who carried a spattering of freckles across her tiny nose.

"Hi, Mommy," the little girl whispered as she knelt next to the bed, her face almost touching her mother's. "I'm hungry. Can we have pancakes before we go to the big house?"

"Sure, honey," Orpha answered, sitting up. Pausing for a few moments, she threw her cover back, stood up, and ran her hands through her hair as the terrible feeling of being lost and very much alone came creeping back to her. "This is worse than any hangover I've ever had," she thought. "Now I know why I never looked to fall in love— it hurts too damn much."

155

Once she had dressed herself and encouraged the three little ones to do the same she went about preparing breakfast for them. Amid their chatter and noises, along with her deep concentration of solving her problem, she did not hear the back door opening.

"Hi, Mr. Bill," she heard George say.

She looked up from watching the pancakes in the skillet to see Bill, wearing a face of remorse, taking time to answer the boy.

"Hello, son," he said, ruffling the small boy's hair. "I'll only stay a minute. I want you to have something to help you get resettled," he sadly smiled. "Hope you won't take offense at this. It's not conscience money or a payoff." He now held a long, white envelope he had taken from the inside of his shirt. "I want to know you're safe until I can be with you." He extended his offering for a moment and then gently forced it into Orpha's hand that hung at her side.

"Bill, I—"

"Orpha, if you need help of any kind, you know how to reach me, promise me?" Taking her chin between his thumb and forefinger, he held her head still while he placed a brief kiss on her mouth. Turning, he forced a smile for the children and left.

Orpha listened to the door as it found its place, then the releasing of the knob. She stood there with a spatula in her one hand and envelope in the other just staring. She smothered a strong urge to call out, run after him, and once catching him, she would reach up on her tip toes, wrap her arms about his broad neck, press herself firmly against him and kiss him deeply. "Oh God," she moaned, "I'm already missing him!" She stood in the center of the tiny kitchen feeling desolate as though she had been abandoned to a cold, empty wilderness that at any moment would swallow her whole.

Forcing herself to put aside her pain she began clearing away the breakfast dishes, then guided the children to the backyard, with instructions, not to disturb Mrs. O'Dell who is sick and needs sleep not a bunch of little Indians running around her house. She reentered the kitchen and, picking up the telephone, dialed her sister's number.

"Hi, Arline."

"Hi," Arline responded. "How's things?"

"Well, to be honest, not so good. I need a place to live."

"You need a place to live? Why? What the heck happened?"

"Oh, it's a long story. Can you put us up for a while? I have a little money, so we won't be a financial burden."

"Sure sis," Arline said without hesitation. But once again she asked, "What's happened?"

"Tell you all about it when I see you. It may be a couple of days by the time I get everything together. I'm hoping Radar won't mind bringing us in."

"Gosh, kid, I'm really sorry but I've got to go to work. I'm running late, which, as you know, is not something new for me," Arline chuckled, trying to lighten things. "But I'll see you when you get here, okay?"

"Okay, bye," Orpha answered, slowly hanging the earphone back on its hook. She sat there thinking of all that had to be done, when it occurred to her that she had not even opened the envelope Bill had insisted she take. Rising from her chair she picked it up from the space in the middle of the range where she had left it. Inside, she found bills of different denominations encased in bands of paper. Orpha removed the bands and counted. "This is way too much. I'll never be able to repay it," she murmured. "My God, there is a thousand dollars here!" she exclaimed, laying it on the table in a fanlike fashion and looking at it. She had never

157

seen so much money at one time in her life. Gathering it together, she returned it to the envelope while making a mental note to herself. "I'll just keep half and return the rest. It will take long enough to repay five hundred let alone a thousand."

Orpha didn't like borrowing money under any circumstances, but in this instance she realized she had little choice and was grateful for the help.

She never returned to the big house before leaving, nor did she see Bill, and she felt deep in her heart the chances of them getting together again were slim to none.

Radar drove his truck in front of Arline's apartment house stopping with a lurch. The long ride into the city had been a quiet one aside from the discomfort of being cramped and the kids fidgeting on occasion.

They had all shared the front seat with Radar— Theresa sitting on George's lap and Ronnie curled up napping on his mother's.

"Looks like we made it," Radar declared.

"Yes it does," Orpha answered, with sadness in her voice, as the feeling of emptiness and uncertainty washed over her once again.

"Come on, kids, let's go," she said as she pulled on the door handle of the old pickup and bumped the door open with her shoulder.

Once inside, they all trudged up the stairs to Arline's second-floor apartment. Orpha rapped softly, hesitated, then knocked again a bit harder. "Coming," her sister's voice called from the other side of the door while the padding of her footsteps could be heard moving closer. "Hi, come on in," Arline smiled, stepping back from the open door, allowing room for them to enter.

"Hi, thanks a lot," Orpha smiled weakly. "I know it's not fair to you, barging in like this, but we have no choice."

"Don't worry about it, kid. We'll do just fine."

"Where are the boys?"

"In the back playing. Thank God for good weather."

"Come on, you two, let's go find Donny and Raymond," Arline offered, inviting George and Theresa Ruth to follow.

With a nodded approval from their mother they ran to catch up with their aunt. Orpha stood looking about, seeing that this was really going to be tight, all of them in this tiny apartment. At the same time Ronnie began stirring in her arms, reminding her that he was becoming too heavy to hold for any period of time without her arms aching.

Walking across the narrow front room she slowly laid him down on the couch. After a quick fluttering of his sleepy eyes he went back to his nap.

"Orpha, I hope it's okay with you," Arline said upon re-entering the apartment. "I told Radar to put your things other than clothes in the basement. We're allowed a corner for storage, and it's a pretty large area.

"That's fine, thanks," Orpha replied. "I'm really sorry to put you out like this, and I'll find something as soon as I can, but with having to leave so quickly from Bill's—"

"Orpha, you know we have always been there for each other. Why would I refuse now? Anyway, what's family for if they can't help each other out. Come on let's have a cup of java and you can tell me what the hell happened out there. I swear, never a dull moment in this family."

The kitchen was smaller than the one Orpha had left behind, and it appeared that everything in it had been cut to fit. The tiny, white, apartment-size range sat off-center on one side of the room, with a long, one-basin sink to the left, and wooden icebox to the right. Overhead, the length of the wall held long white wooden cupboards with glass doors and matching round wooden knobs. Orpha noted the pretty scalloped shelving paper that Arline had taken time to place

159

inside. A drop-leaf table on the opposite side of the room, sat beneath the small, fancy-curtained window. On the narrow end walls stood matching radiators tightly encased and obviously painted a few times, for nicks in the paint revealed different colors.

"You really have this place fixed up cute," Orpha commented.

"Thanks, it's small but it's home," Arline smiled back. "Come on. Let's sit while we can."

The large, white doily was removed from the center of the table, and the coffee pot took its place on a potholder. Arline took two cups from the cupboard, and filled them almost to the brim leaving just enough room for a bit of Wilson's canned milk.

Amid the children running in and out, Orpha tried hard to appear in control of her feelings, while telling her sister what had occurred at Bill's.

"I'll be leaving now," Radar called in from the hall.

"Oh wait," Orpha said, as she pushed her chair back and hurried to him. "Radar, thanks for all your help, not only for today but since we've met. You've been so good to us."

The large man stuck out his hand to shake hers, but Orpha ignored it and gave him a big hug instead. "Take care of yourself and tell your wife and kids goodbye for me."

"If you and the little ones need help, we help," he stated firmly. "Don't you forget, okay?"

She smiled, and said, "I know. I'll remember."

"Oh, Radar, would you do me one last favor? Give this envelope to Mr. O'Dell. He will know what it's about."

"Sure, I give it to him as soon as I see him. Sometime maybe we see you, huh?"

"I sure hope so," she replied, touching his arm.

Then turning from her with obvious regret he disappeared down the stairs.

160

Orpha listened to the sound of Radar's steps and the heavy glassed wooden door closing behind him. "Well, that's that," she said soulfully turning and walking slowly back into her sister's apartment.

Chapter Thirteen

It had been a little over two months since she had moved to Arline's with not much luck finding work. Famous-Barr had said they would give her a call when they had an opening, but so far she hadn't heard from them. The money that Bill had given her was a big help but she knew that she could not stretch it forever. To make matters worse, her period had not shown up. She decided to keep that fact to herself if need be for as long as possible. Abortion was not something to be considered.

Orpha sat at the open kitchen window. A light, warm breeze came through the small window, disturbing the curtains just slightly.

It was a hot and muggy day in St. Louis. Down below the children played in a large galvanized washtub that she had filled with water, and their laughter and squeals seemed in the distance as she watched them.

She considered giving Mama a call. Perhaps she could talk with Sister Mary Barbara, the mother superior of Saint Mary's Home for Girls. She and Mama become fast friends years ago when Mama had lived next door to the convent. Mama even named Mary Barbara after her. In later years, when their father left, Sister Mary Barbara saw to it that all three girls had a home at Saint Mary's for as long as it was necessary.

For a few moments, Orpha's mind drifted over the very short story she and her sisters had been given by Mama of their father's abandonment when they were very young. Which to this day made her feel resentful and lonely when he came to mind. She never could figure out why the lonely part for she never had a chance to get to know him.

According to Ruth their father and his brother spoke of the theater often and made it clear they dreamed of returning. Which, of course, is what they did without warning or any serious provision for their children's care.

Ivan's wife and her two children moved in with her parents, and Ruth found a small apartment next to the Sisters of Charity convent where she met and became close friends with the mother superior.

Needless to say, Ruth was very bitter about her past and the topic rarely came up in front of her. The last thing Orpha heard her mother say about it was, "I hope they both burn in hell—the sons o' bitches."

Shortly after the move to the apartment next to the convent the three girls were accepted at Saint Mary's Orphan Asylum and remained there until they reached high school age. Orpha would often think while still in the home that maybe their father got lost or maybe he lost his memory and some day he would find himself as well as his memory and come looking for them, but it never happened.

At a very early age, she had a deep feeling of being very much on her own without anyone to protect her or care much about her. Ruth would visit with them for a short period every Sunday after Mass with not much of anything to say other than behave and do what you are told. Affection did not come easy for Ruth.

Maybe the sister would be willing to help her, as she once helped her mother. Orpha felt she could no longer impose on her sister, though Arline protested to the contrary. George and Ronnie, if accepted, could be boarded at Saint Joseph's—a boarding school for boys. Orpha worried that if she did not seek help in this manner in time everyone would suffer, including Arline and her children. The idea of losing them even for a short while was painful, and she felt tears rising at the thought of the children's reaction of being put there.

If only she could have enough time to get on her feet. Arline was just making ends meet for herself and her two boys and was considering calling the boys' father for some assistance. Orpha knew she could expect nothing from Floyd.

The thought of calling Bill kept coming back to her, but she decided that would appear rather silly, seeing that her pride had forced her to return half of the money he had given her. She also feared she might in a weak moment reveal her condition. The prospect of having him with her was ideal, but the idea of railroading him into divorce and marrying her would not be the right way to go. Hog-tying any man to have him would only be asking for more problems down the road.

"Where was all this brilliant deducting months ago?" she chided herself as she poked her head forward to the screen door and called the children in.

"Orpha?" a voice softly called out from the living room.

"Yes?" she responded, getting up and going to see who called.

"My God! Mary Barbara, what the . . . How did you get here?" Orpha stood looking at her in dismay. "Are you all right? You look awful—the both of you."

Bobby was asleep in his mother's arms, with his head on her shoulder and his frail, little body limply sprawled across her. They both appeared exhausted and badly in need of a bath.

Looking down, Orpha could see not only a crust of dirt on her sister's bare feet but blood caked between her toes. "Where are your shoes?"

"They hurt more than they helped. I got rid of them."

"When was the last time you two ate?" Orpha asked as she took Bobby from his mother, laying him gently on the couch.

"Oh, it's been a while."

"I was just about to feed the kids lunch. You better have something."

Mary Barbara followed her into the kitchen, and after dropping herself into a chair like a beaten rag doll, she uttered, "Dear God, I didn't think we were going to make it. Orpha, you don't know how good it is to be here."

"Well, I can take a pretty good guess just by looking at you. How did you get here?"

"Hitchhiked."

"Hitchhiked! With that baby, you walked from Arkansas? Oh, Mary Barbara, why didn't you call? Things are tight, I'll grant you, but we could have figured out something. Look at your feet! They are all bloody! I wish you had written, letting us know. What was the big rush?"

"Orpha, I had to get out of there. It had reached a point that we were living like damn animals. Lemvel loves me, I know. And I'm still nuts about him, but to just lie around day after day and become one of the pigs—I couldn't do it anymore! And that's only part of it," she continued. "He—my gosh it sounds like a herd of buffalo coming!" A tired smile crossed her face.

"He is too!"

"He is not!"

Two of the kids were yelling back and forth as they came bounding into the room.

"Quiet, you two! Orpha instructed.

"Mommy, who's the baby on the couch? asked Theresa Ruth, who was at her mother's side tugging at her skirt.

"He's your cousin Bobby. Now all of you sit down."

Giving up her chair, Mary Barbara now leaned against the icebox, wolfing down a thick sandwich she had helped herself to, washing it down with a cup of coffee she had not taken time to heat. "A bath would really feel good, Orpha," she exclaimed. "Could I, while Bobby is still sleeping?"

"My God, of course! After what you just came through, soak as long as you want. We can finish talking once the kids go down for a nap."

165

After tugging at her badly soiled button-down dress and her tattered underwear, they fell to the floor. Kicking them aside, Mary Barbara leaned over, put the plug in the drain, and as she reached to turn on the hot water, every muscle in her body was aching.

She filled the tub as full as she could, allowing enough room for the water to rise once she lowered herself into it. Her bruised, bloody feet hurt, and she grimaced as she stepped into the steamy bath. Once seated, Mary Barbara sank beneath the warmth of the water and let it wash over her head—staying as long as her lungs would allow. Coming back up, she grabbed the bar of soap and began vigorously scrubbing.

"Bobby must still be sleeping, poor little tyke," she thought to herself. "Sleep is the best thing for him now, later food and bath."

"Mary Barbara!" Orpha called from the other side of the bathroom door. "I'm going to open the door and put these clean clothes on the chair for you, okay?"

Not waiting for an answer, Orpha opened the door making enough room for her arm. Reaching just inside, she placed fresh underwear and one of her own house dresses on the wooden chair that stood by the doorway.

"Thanks!" Mary Barbara called out as she lay back in the warm water, closing her eyes. She could feel the perspiration trickling down from her forehead. The combination of the hot water and the intensity of the muggy day hurried the sweat across her eyes. As she sat low in the water with it covering her chin, she caught herself starting to doze. "Better get up before I drown myself," she thought with a start. Once out, she dried her hair as best she could, wrapped the towel about it, pulled on the underpants, and was just barely able to fit into Orpha's dress. Even with losing a fair amount of weight she was still much larger than her sister.

Mary Barbara took time to scour the tub, then picked up her dirty clothes from the floor and walked barefooted out to the living room past her sleeping son, then into the kitchen where Orpha sat alone blowing her cigarette smoke out the screened window.

"Where should I put these?" Mary Barbara asked as she offered up what now appeared to be rags rather than clothes.

"Are they worth saving?"

"Guess not," Mary Barbara said, walking to the wastebasket and dropping them in.

"There's coffee left if you want some. What's going on with you and Lemvel anyway? Want another sandwich?"

"No thanks. Just coffee." Pulling the chair from the table, Mary Barbara sat down, taking a long sip from her cup. "Well," she began, "to be honest, it scared the hell out of me when I began to fit in, Orpha. I was becoming one of them—dirty, lazy, and no get up and go. I could see where I was headed, and besides that, Lemvel was taking to staying out a lot at night with his moon-shiner friends and then sleeping all day. He never did go to the button factory for a job. I don't mind toughing it but not wanting to help yourself at all?"

"What did he say when you told him you were leaving?"

"Nothing. He wasn't around. I knew if he were to ask me to stay I might not go, and I had to get out of there. I don't think he will ever change, and I could not live that way forever. I tried telling him, but he refused to listen, so—Do you think Arline is gonna be mad about us staying here?"

"I hate to tell you right off the bat, things aren't much better here. But I know Arline would rather have you in here with us than out on the streets, so don't worry about that."

167

"Actually, I've been thinking about giving Mama a call, and seeing if she could get the kids into the homes for a time. I know she has some pull with the mother superior at Saint Mary's. I'm hoping it will give me a chance to get to my feet. It's tough all the way around. You're not alone, Mary Barbara. Arline's struggling on her last leg, and that SOB she's married to promises but never delivers, and to make matters worse, I'm pregnant."

It was out of Orpha's mouth before she could catch it. "Oh, damn, I wasn't going to say anything until I had to."

"Orpha, my God! You've got to get a hold of Floyd and let him know. Don't you think he would help if he knew you were pregnant? Is it Floyd's?"

Orpha did not answer. "Oh shit, it's Bill O'Dell's," Mary Barbara exclaimed, answering her own question. You're gonna tell him?"

"Slow down!" Orpha exclaimed. "What good would it do to tell him? He's in no position to do anything about it. He is still married and his wife is back home with him. However unhappy he might be, the fact remains he is with her—not me."

"Do you love him?"

"Yes, for all the good it's going to do me, I just don't want him to feel he owes me anything because I'm pregnant with his baby. I'll work it out somehow. I'm not kidding myself. It's not going to be easy, but maybe there's some truth to the old saying, 'God takes care of fools and drunks.' It's not hard to guess which one I am. By the way, I would like you to promise not to tell anyone about this. It's important to me that it stays under your hat until I'm ready, okay?"

"Sure, whatever you say, but I think—"

"Mary Barbara, please don't," her sister implored.

"Okay, whatever you want. Just kind of worried."

"Well, it looks like there is plenty of that to spread around."

Orpha nodded her head at the open doorway where Bobby stood quietly looking like a little street urchin. He was in need of a bath badly. His small, dirty face had been mapped by occasional tears inflicted on him by his long ordeal on the road. His dark, curly hair was matted to his head. She couldn't remember ever seeing such sad brown eyes on a baby. "Why don't you stay put and rest while I feed him and give him a good bath?"

Orpha went to Bobby, scooping him up in her arms. "It's going to be all right sweetheart. Let's have something to eat." Sitting him down in a chair, she fed him until he finally shook his head no. She left him sitting with his mother long enough to run water in the tub. Once putting him into the warm water, she tenderly but effectively scrubbed every inch of him. "You poor little thing. You have no fight left in you, do you?"

Bobby had just turned himself over without any resistance. Not a sound came from him.

"Okay, we're done, Bobby." Wrapping the towel about his small form, Orpha lifted him from the tub and placed him on the couch. She sorted through the dresser in the living room, finding some of Ronnie's clothing she figured might fit.

"Here he is, like new," she announced, walking into the kitchen, holding him high in her arms for approval.

Still seated, only now with her head on the table sleeping soundly, Mary Barbara did not stir.

"Hey, go lie down, and get some sleep. I'll take care of Bobby," Orpha coaxed with a nudge of her hip.

Pulling her head up, Mary Barbara wiped the side of her mouth, where the saliva had escaped her lips. "Thanks," she uttered, rising from her seat, slowly leaving the room.

"Well, little man," Orpha exclaimed as she looked at the new member of her ever-growing nursery, "looks like we're all in this together. As the old saying goes, 'It's a poor hen that can't scratch for another chicken.' But even with three hens here, I don't have much hope for us, Bobby," Orpha confessed. "It's not at all like being on a farm where you raise your own food and can it for the months ahead or for any tight spots you might run into."

The weeks slipped by, and the month of July was "as hot as any firecracker," Mary Barbara had commented that morning. "That's very clever," Orpha chided her with a forced laugh. "I hate this heat. I wish we would get some rain. Maybe it would cool things off a bit."

She found herself somewhat irritable lately, with very good reason, she allowed herself. She had gotten no response from her mother on temporary boarding of the children at the homes, and their day-to-day living experience wasn't getting any better.

The money was really tight. Aside from the little Mary Barbara brought in from ironing and an occasional house cleaning job, the only money coming in was Arline's small paycheck. They were a month behind in the rent, and although the landlady was a patient sort, this would more than likely come to an end when she was denied the next payment that soon would be due.

The sound of the phone—shared by all tenants— ringing in the downstairs hallway, caught her attention. She could hear it clearly, for she had purposely left their door wide open in hopes of catching any draft that it might create.

Mrs. Rapply could be heard talking, and then silence.

"Orpha! Are you up there?"

Hurrying to the top of the stairway, she leaned over the banister answering, "Yes, I'm here."

"Telephone, dear," the landlady said as she looked up at her past the two flights of stairs.

170

"Thank you," Orpha called back. "I'll be right there."

"Come on, Bobby, you'll have to come with me. Everyone is napping." Snatching the little boy up, she quickly ran down the stairs, catching a smile crossing his face as he bounced in her arms. "Oh, you like that, huh?" she asked, smiling back at him and bouncing him even more. Once reaching the telephone where the earpiece now dangled slowly to and fro from its long cord, Orpha stooped to pick it up and placed it to her ear.

"Hello?"

"Orpha, I just received word from the archdiocese that if you will bring the children with you, they would like to interview you for the openings they have both at Saint Mary's and Saint Joseph's. But one draw back," her mother continued, "both parents must be there and in full agreement. So it's up to you to find Floyd and have him agree."

"Thanks, Mama. I'll do my best. It's certainly in the best interest of the children."

"I'm not convinced of that, but they are yours and it's your decision. They will see you two weeks from today at two o'clock. You will need all papers pertaining to them and yourselves. Don't be late and, for God's sake, don't miss it. I went through a lot of trouble to set this up. The address is, do you have a pencil?"

"No, but I'll remember."

"It's 4140 Lindell Boulevard. Got it?"

"Yes, Mama. Thanks a lot." Orpha hung up the phone with mixed emotions. "Is this the only way?" she asked herself. "Am I doing this right? Oh God, I don't know of any other. Please let this be the best for my kids?" Already her chest had tightened and fast-building anxiety caused her to suck in a deep breath before she began mounting the stairs to return to the apartment.

171

The hot, muggy weather was making everything sticky to the touch she thought as she grabbed hold of the banister. The still, heavy air seemed to make it more difficult to breathe, and then—as if her thoughts were heard—Orpha was startled by a loud clap of thunder followed by the sound of a fearsome, driving rain.

She hurried up the stairs, with Bobby still riding on her hip, to close the windows. Without a doubt, rain would be driven in by the strong wind. The storm woke all of the kids. Theresa Ruth came tearing into the room, crying, "It's going to get me! It's going to get me!" And the boys were close behind asking if they could go out and play in the rain. Orpha assured her little girl that nothing was going to harm her, and took time to impress her with what the nuns used to tell them about the thunder—that it was the sound of the angels moving their furniture around. Once Theresa Ruth appeared satisfied, the boys pressed for an answer.

"When it lets up a little, okay? Orpha said. They raced to the living room window to watch for any letup and with the passing of just a few minutes were back again informing her it was time.

"No, not yet," she told them. "I'll let you know."

The kids stood at the two long windows watching diligently. Orpha sat with Bobby on the couch until the storm had lessened to a soft rain and just an occasional clap of thunder. "Okay, you can go now," she called out.

"Yay!" George yelled.

"Let's go! Yay!" the rest repeated after him, and off they went out the door and down the stairs as fast and as noisy as they were able.

"Should we go watch the kids?" Orpha asked her small companion, his large brown eyes looking at her, uncertain of what she wanted. "Sure, let's go!" she said, swooping him up and once again placing him on her hip for the ride down the stairs.

They stood in the doorway and Orpha was amused at the children's antics in the rain. Running madly in a large circle on the slippery, wet grass of the front lawn, they were screaming, yelling, and more often than not losing their footing, only to get up and once again join in with those left standing.

Orpha found herself laughing out loud as a loud clap of thunder would make them jump straight up in the air and tear off for the coverage and safety of the front porch, screaming all the way. "What fun they're having," she thought, feeling a pang of guilt for what their future might hold.

"Just for a short while," she said to herself. "Just for a very short while."

Chapter Fourteen

Once she had made contact with Floyd and he assured her that he would go along with putting the children in homes, things moved very quickly. The day of the appointment they were told that they would be expected to pay half the room and board. And although the home would supply everyday clothing, any special outfits for holidays, holy communion, or confirmation, would have to be purchased by them, or the fabric could be brought to the home's seamstress and a reasonable fee would be charged to make the garment. The children would also have to be baptized in the Catholic faith, and a thorough physical examination along with vaccinations would be given.

Orpha and Floyd signed the documents necessary to enroll and turned over full legal guardianship to the Catholic Charities of St. Louis.

Orpha was numb. She thought she might be in a state of shock. It all seemed like a hazy dream and a heartbreaking one at that. She only spoke to Floyd when she had to, and it appeared not to bother him at all as he smiled broadly and used his best manners to charm the administrators.

"You just don't give a damn at all do you?" Orpha spat at him as they left the building.

"I wouldn't be here if I didn't want to be. What the hell's wrong with you? I come to do you a favor and all you can do is be sore about it?"

"Is that what you had the gall to say? I should have my head examined for staying with you as long as I did."

"Look, honey, to be honest, this saves me a lot of money. It's a good business deal for the both of us and you're just not honest enough to admit it."

"You—" Orpha swung at him with a flat hand but missed her mark as he grabbed her wrist, holding it long enough to reach over and lay a quick peck on her cheek.

"See you around, sweetheart," he snapped, giving her a short, jaunty salute before leaving.

"Oh God, I hate that man! That selfish bastard!" she said out loud stomping her foot on the sidewalk, watching as he disappeared around the corner.

The two blocks to the bus stop were walked in a brisk, angry fashion, her heels clicking loudly and her arms vigorously swinging in time with her feet.

She could see the bus coming down the street and fast approaching. Braking into a run as best she could with the heels she was wearing, she waved at the driver to let him know she wanted to board and to wait.

"Easy does it, young lady, watch your step," the man behind the wheel said pleasantly. "We weren't going to leave you behind."

"Thanks," Orpha smiled weakly, dropping her fare into the box, then heading down the aisle in search of a seat. She chose a seat next to a window near the center of the bus, sitting down abruptly with the assistance of the bus surging forward once again. The windows were cracked open for the most part, and while in motion it was bearable. Although once it had stopped for passengers she would become acutely aware of not only the heat, but heavy doses of what she guessed to be Lily of the Valley cologne and perhaps a dime-store fragrance by the name of Blue Waltz. "Never cared for either," she thought. "Too sweet." Now fused with all else in this intense heat she found herself breathing through her mouth in order to escape the overpowering smell. The bus rolled along stopping and starting.

She now fought hard to hold her tears in check. The welling up of them almost choked her, while the awful hollow feeling came back in full force. She felt so lost and heartbroken. Deeply sucking in her breath, Orpha murmured, "Oh dear God, please help us." And with that a tear escaped and she left it there to dry.

"My babies," she went on silently. "I promise you will be home very soon. I'm so, so sorry." Dwelling on what she had just been forced to do was so painful and she knew the sick hollow would be with her until she was able to be with them again.

People watching seemed to make the ride go faster, and it kept her mind from her troubles for a short time. Across from her sat a thin, dissipated-looking elderly man, badly in need of a shave and a bath. In his lap he held a small brown paper sack with the top having been rolled backward from the center forming a small bowl—from which she guessed he took quick swigs. His eyes were closed and his head rested and bounced on the back of the seat. With each bump in the street, low, rasping sounds fell from his open mouth.

Orpha turned her attention to two middle-aged women whose corpulence overflowed the seat they shared across the aisle from her. Their lightweight summer frocks strained at the buttons that ran down the front of more than ample bosoms. Whispering in each other's ears, they were quite caught up in their topic, which, Orpha figured out after a moment or two, was a very well-dressed, very dark-skinned black man, who had boarded the bus at the last stop, taking a seat directly in front of them.

They discontinued their whispering, and began speaking in either Polish or Italian—she wasn't sure which. But she decided that one was guilty of Blue Waltz and the other just as guilty of Lily of the Valley. They continued with their discussion quite openly now until the next stop.

Orpha noticed the object of their whispers rising as the bus slowed. He hesitated momentarily as he grabbed hold of the hand rest on the back of his seat, in front of where the women sat. Very quietly but proudly he announced to them, "Madam, from the blackest soil comes the richest crop!" He tipped his hat politely and left. The women sat with their mouths gaping in shock. For in their ignorance a black man speaking their language was unheard of.

"Can you believe it?"

"Well, I never!"

Their faces were flush with embarrassment.

"Good for you," Orpha thought to herself. "Maybe that will teach you to hold your wagging tongues."

Looking out the window as the bus pulled away, she could see the man adjusting his straw hat, shading his eyes from the bright sun. And as it happened he looked up as her window came in front of him, and they shared a fleeting smile.

Taking note of the passing street signs as the bus bumped along, Orpha knew once she left the bus she had a couple of blocks to walk in order to catch the streetcar to Washington Avenue. The neighborhoods were now becoming familiar to her. She pulled herself up from the seat and stepped out into the aisle in preparation to leave.

The street car ride was short and uninteresting compared to the bus ride, and she quickly walked the distance to her sister's apartment. Her mind went to her children, and that awful feeling returned to the pit of her stomach.

"God, please help me," she prayed to herself as she walked. "I know I've done many things wrong, but please let the punishment be only mine." Her next thoughts came hard and fast in the form of self-condemnation. "Who are you kidding? Grow up! Your penance will be done by all involved, aside from maybe Floyd, that cad!" Once again, her anger stirred, along with fear of the unknown.

Turning off the sidewalk and starting up the short, paved path to the apartment house, she observed a still figure of a man standing at the far end of the long front porch. Not recognizing him, Orpha nodded her head in a mannerly hello, but as she reached for the doorknob she

177

took a second look. "Lemvel? What are you doing here?" she asked, surprised at seeing him. Does Mary Barbara know you're here?"

"Nope, don't think she does. Not likely she'll ever care. Been working up the guts to go up but ain't got there yet."

"Do you want me to send her down?"

"Yeah—okay." Nodding, he shoved his hands deeply into his trouser pockets as he moved backward, returning to the far end of the porch.

"Hi, I'm back," Orpha called out, loud enough to be sure she would be heard over the children at play.

"I'm in here," Mary Barbara called back.

Orpha found her sister having a cigarette, while sitting on the foot of the bed taking deep, fast drags.

"Oh, I see you already know you have company?"

"Yeah, he's been there most of the afternoon. Mrs. Rapply told me there was a tall, skinny, good-looking young man asking about me. I knew right away, but I wanted to wait until you got home. I didn't want to leave the kids up here by themselves, and for some reason he decided not to come up."

"He's not coming up because," Orpha chortled, "he's afraid you're going to throw him out on his hillbilly ear, that's why. Are you going to see him?"

"Sure I'll go talk to him," she said, stubbing her cigarette out in the ashtray that was cradled in her lap. She rose from the bed, taking the ashtray with her.

Orpha followed her to the open doorway, giving her a pat on the shoulder for encouragement, then watched as she trudged down the stairway.

"Well, what time is it anyway?" she asked herself as she stepped over the kids playing in the middle of the living room floor. "And how come all of you are indoors on such a nice day? If it were raining outside you would want to go out! Isn't that right, George?"

178

The little boy did not answer. His mind was completely absorbed in the game of cars he and the other three boys were playing. Their pretend noises of motors revving and cars crashing filled the apartment. Orpha decided it might be best if she were to go back and shut the door, in order to keep most of the racket inside.

She realized it was getting late, and it wouldn't be long before one or all of the kids would be complaining that they were hungry. "Might as well get started," she said out loud, checking the cupboards to see what there was to prepare.

Taking four cans of pork and beans down, Orpha began methodically opening them and dumping them into a large pot. While reaching for a lone bean stubbornly sticking to the bottom of one of the cans, Mary Barbara returned.

"Orpha, would you mind if Lemvel and I took a walk?"

"Well, of course not. Why would I mind?"

"Well, I don't want to take advantage."

"You mean, Bobby? Go, please. What's one more kid? I was just getting ready to feed them. Take your time, but, Mary Barbara, make sure you don't make any hasty decisions, okay? You've told me what a charmer he can be, remember?" Orpha smiled to let her sister know she cared and that she didn't mean to intrude.

"Don't worry. He's going to really have to do some tall talking to convince me," she affirmed as she turned and left the room in a flurry.

"Oh boy, I can see the handwriting on the wall," Orpha exclaimed to herself as she pulled a package of hot dogs from the back of the icebox.

It was close to dusk by the time the children had eaten, but Orpha shooed them out into the backyard for a couple of hours of play before bedtime.

179

The summer air coming in through the open window was still muggy but a bit cooler. And as she cleared the supper dishes from the table she could hear a singsong call rising from the back alley. "Rag sheen'y, rag sheen'y" and the clopping sound of the old horses hooves as they hit the ground. She remembered being told that the rags collected by the rag man were sold to factories who made paper from them. Her mind skipped briefly over this bit of knowledge, then back to the chore at hand.

With everything tidy and in place she sat at the open window looking down on five noisy little kids running in different directions in hot pursuit of lightning bugs. She observed George as he found a small canning jar on the ground close to the large cement trash burner. Picking it up he passed it around telling the others to put them in here, put them in here. After a number of the captives were snatched and jailed in his glass prison, George, with his little hand still covering the mouth of the jar, held it up so they could all watch the entrapped insects flashing. "Ooh," she overheard Theresa Ruth exclaim. Orpha left her position at the window, long enough to start the water running in the tub for the evening ritual of bathing. Theresa Ruth first, the four boys, two at a time, next. Bobby was given the full treatment by his mother in the kitchen sink, but it appeared that Mary Barbara might not make it back in time.

"Give them a few more minutes," she thought as she once again sat at the window, conscious of the water still running in the bathtub.

"Okay, everybody come in now! George," she called out through the screen, "bring them in! Time for everyone's bath. Come on now," she coaxed, "make it snappy! And don't bring those bugs in with you either. And all of you be quiet coming up the stairs, do you hear me?"

"Shush, hey shush," Orpha instructed with her finger over her lips as she stood in the doorway of the apartment, making sure the kids did not get too rowdy on their way up the stairs.

The following half hour carried its own unique sounds that accompanied every night's bedtime ritual— small protests of no consequence, light squabbles among the children, water pouring into the tub for bathing or into the toilet as it was being flushed time and again. Prayers and good nights softly followed, then all was quiet.

It was dark out now and getting late. Arline had gotten home just a short time ago from work. After a quick snack of warmed-over hot dogs and beans, she announced she was bushed, but before going to bed she shared one last thought. "I really hope she knows what she's doing. I've got this feeling she'll be heading back to Arkansas. What do you think?"

"Well, whatever it is she decides to do, I pray she does not put herself in my position."

Arline didn't respond to her sister's comment, instead gave a wave of her hand, saying good night, leaving Orpha sitting by herself.

Her thoughts turned to Bill. Leisurely, she went over some of the time they had spent together, and she found herself missing him beyond belief. She quickly pushed him from her mind, deciding her only concern at the moment should be her children.

Pushing her chair back she started getting up but sat down once again, as Mary Barbara with a smiling Lemvel came into the room. "Guess what? Lemvel and I are going to give it another try. What do you think?"

"I think first, I'm not the least bit surprised, and for all of your sakes I hope it works out."

"It will. Don't worry. We have made each other promises that we have to keep, right Lemvel?"

"You're right darlin'," the tall, handsome man flashed a smile, while putting his arm about her waist and squeezing her to him.

"Orpha, do you think it will be all right if Lemvel stays the night?"

"Well, of course. He's still your husband, isn't he?"

"Yes, but do you think Arline will get mad with all that's happened?"

"No, I doubt it. Why don't you just make a pallet on the living room floor? And we'll see you in the morning. I better get to bed. What time will you be leaving?"

"What time do you want to head back?" a visibly happy Mary Barbara asked. "No hurry," Lemvel answered.

"Well, then, I'll see you in the morning. Goodnight." She left them and went to the bed that she and Arline were forced to share. Orpha heard an occasional giggle and soft thump on the living room floor before dropping off to sleep.

The morning came too early for Orpha. She swore to herself that someday she would stay in bed all day just for the hell of it. She threw her side of the covers back, leaving Arline sleeping. It was her day off from the defense plant where she had been working for almost a year.

For a few moments Orpha thought back to the day she had learned of the outbreak of World War II. She had just put the finishing touches on the evening meal while the radio was sending out holiday music, one song after the other, and in fact she had been singing along on a few. Suddenly, and most unexpectedly, the program was interrupted. The message was loud and startling. She remembered she was frozen in place. The United States of America was now at war. "Oh my God," she remembered saying out loud as the very fired-up announcer continued with his frightening news. The United States of America was, on this day, December 7, 1941, a date that that will live in infamy, attacked suddenly and deliberately by the Japanese navy and air force.

The war effort was now at a fever pitch. Work was there for any woman that needed or wanted a job. The

182

hours were long and the pay decent, but not enough to support a family. And without any help forthcoming from her husband, Arline's situation was almost as desperate as Orpha's. Arline was to make contact with Harry today and see what could be worked out between them. Their divorce was close to its finality. Harry had been living with a woman he said he was planning to marry as soon as the divorce was granted.

Orpha was surprised to find the pallet in the living room taken up, with Mary Barbara, Lemvel, and Bobby gone.

"For Pete's sake," she said out loud, as she headed for the kitchen where she found a note beneath the ashtray in the center of the table.

Dear Orpha and Arline,
Left early to get a head start. Hope you don't mind but didn't want to wake anyone up. Thanks for everything. Will write as soon as I can, and you write me too, okay? Don't worry. Everything is going to be fine.
Love your sister Mary Barbara.

Chapter Fifteen

It had been sheer hell today. Orpha had taken the children to the homes and her heart was broken. She spent a lot of time hating herself, hating Floyd, condemning her very existence for what she was forced to put her kids through. She would never forget watching her small sons' that day at Saint Joseph's. Trying to comfort his younger brother, George put his arm about his little shoulders, saying, "It's going to be okay, Ronnie. Look at all the kids we get to play with." But Ronnie kept crying, wanting to go home.

"Go now! Quickly!" the nun in charge instructed her. "The longer you prolong it the worse it becomes, believe me." Orpha turned and left, hoping the boys would not see her.

Theresa Ruth had reacted with wide eyes. She appeared frightened and somewhat confused, but there were no tears at her mother's departure. Looking back as she left her little girl, Orpha could still see her holding Sister Mary Joseph's hand and sadly waving goodbye with the other.

Orpha managed to hold herself in check until she reached the apartment, but once inside and alone her pain escaped in long, tortured sobs and tears that came flooding from her heart, and pouring from her eyes. She cried until she couldn't cry any longer. She was numb now and somewhat dazed. She rose from the bed, went to the kitchen, and began making coffee. Her mind seemed to have frozen and didn't want to process any more mental suffering than it had to. The hurt was just as acutely felt in her body. For it ached with sadness. Orpha sat down and vacantly stared out the window. The sound and smell of fresh, percolating coffee began to fill the long, narrow kitchen. The emptiness was so painfully heavy she was praying she could bear it.

As she filled her cup with the steaming brown liquid she could hear the muffled ringing of the phone in the downstairs hallway. It stopped suddenly, telling her more than likely that Mrs. Rapply had answered it. A soft knock on the door came a few moments later with the landlady calling out, "Orpha, are you in there?"

"Yes, Mrs. Rapply, I'm here," she called from across the room, hoping the women would give her a message and then leave. For she would rather not be seen in such a state.

"There's a gentleman on the telephone for you, dear."

"Thanks, I'll be right there," Orpha pleasantly responded, aware of the woman's shadow in the space below between the hall floor and the door, where it paused for a brief second or two, then broke away.

Allowing Mrs. Rapply enough time to return to her own apartment, Orpha hurried down to answer the phone. Putting the ear piece to her ear she stretched upward on her tiptoes to reach the receiver.

"Hello?" she said. There was silence and then a familiar voice made her heart leap. "Bill? Oh my God, Bill, how are you?"

"I'm fine. How are you and the children?" Orpha fought her tears back at his question. "Well things are a little tough, but I'll work it out. Everything takes time I'm told."

"I want to see you," he continued. "Is there any chance of taking you out for dinner? There is something important I would like to discuss with you. Will you see me?"

She looked down at herself. Her condition was becoming noticeable, but she could still get by with a loose-fitting dress. Mucking up the waters any more than necessary was not at all in her plans, and hooking Bill for anything connected with this baby she would definitely not do. But the desire to see him was too strong, and she heard herself saying, "I would love to. When?"

"Could I pick you up at eight tomorrow evening? Is that too short notice?"

"No, that's fine. I'll be ready," she assured him.

"Until tomorrow then," he answered.

"Tomorrow," she repeated. Not ready to turn loose of his voice she hung on listening for the sound of Bill hanging up, then the breaking of their connection. Her mood was still dark, but a glimmer of light was flickering now. Just being in his company would ease the pain.

Orpha climbed the stairs and once again sat in the apartment by herself. It seemed so lonely and quiet, and she decided not to dwell on it. Getting up from the sofa she picked up the daily paper and busied herself with the want ads.

The jobs for the most part made her distinctly aware of her lack of education and skills for the business world. She circled a few to be checked out in the morning and hoped one would be fruitful. For the sooner she got to work, the sooner she would get her children back.

In the midst of scouring the ads, Orpha became aware of Arline's return. On the stairway, Arline could be heard scolding her two boys for running and being so noisy. "Where's the other kids?" Raymond asked upon bursting through the apartment door with his younger brother directly behind him—the two obviously ready for their cousins and play. Puzzled by the empty rooms as they looked about they received no answer.

"Out, you two," their mother instructed. "Go play outside for a while," Arline said, cutting their questions off by changing the topic. "Supper will be ready in a little bit. Stay in the backyard! Don't leave it, do you hear me?" She then shooed them out the door.

"Do you want to talk about what happened today?" Arline asked her sister as she settled into the chair across from her. "Maybe it would help." She could see Orpha's eyes were swollen from crying.

A firm shake of Orpha's head, still down and peering over the newspaper let her know that now was not the time.

"Although I do have something to tell you," Orpha said as she looked up squarely into Arline's face. "Bill called today. He wants me to have dinner with him tomorrow night."

"You're kidding, really? Are you going? What in God's name took him so long? Aside from his wife, of course," Arline commented as an afterthought.

"Yes I am. I need to see him. Just talking with him will help me."

"Orpha, are you going to tell him? He does have a moral right to know."

"Let's not talk about morals, Arline, or the lack thereof that brought me to where I am today."

"So, who do you know that's a saint?" her sister said, coming to her defense. "Orpha, your pride is going to hurt all of you. Can't you let it go just this once, if not for yourself, maybe for the kids' sake?"

"For the kids' sake? Is that what you said?" Orpha shot back. "Do you think I haven't twisted and turned my mind in every direction trying to come up with the right solution for my kids' sake?"

Orpha was furious. She stood with both hands spread on the table, bracing herself as she leaned toward her surprised sister, allowing her anger to erupt.

"Arline, I couldn't begin to tell you what I have considered doing for my kids' sake. So don't go preaching to me. I am at my wits' end, and if it weren't for my so-called pride as you say, I could take the easy way out and let someone else solve my problems. But they are just that, my problems, and I'll do my best to solve them. You and a

187

host of others might not approve of my methods, but that is definitely not one of my problems."

"Orpha, please. I'm sorry. I didn't mean to make you mad or imply you weren't trying. I'll mind my own business from here on." Arline rose to leave, and before she cleared the table Orpha reached out, touching her arm.

"Wait, don't—" she pleaded. "You're probably right," Orpha admitted, reclaiming her seat. "To a certain extent, my pride does get in the way sometimes, and this could be one of them. I promise if Bill insists on helping, I will let him, but I won't ask."

Arline smiled. "Can't ask for anymore than that, kid."

The evening went by quickly, yet the night seemed to never end. Vivid pictures of the children crying out for her tormented her soul as the wetness of her tears could be felt running off her face and on to the pillow beneath her head. Arline lay next to her sleeping soundly. Orpha could see the outline of her form and the slow rising and falling of her breathing. She forced her mind to stay on Bill, so as not to dwell on her pain, and finally she fell asleep.

Orpha bolted into an upright position, squinting at the small alarm clock sitting on the top of the chest of drawers across the room. "Oh damn! I've slept away the whole morning," she muttered, kicking back her covers. Bounding from the bed, she hurried into the kitchen where she found a note from Arline by the coffee pot explaining why she had let her sleep, and that she would be dropping the boys off at the neighbors two doors down who had agreed to watch them. She would see her later. Take it easy and good luck!

Orpha poured half a cup of coffee. Not wanting to take the time to reheat it, she gulped it down as she hurried back into the bedroom where she pulled her gray and white sharkskin suit from the closet. It had long served her well as a durable and multifunctional garment. Hoping it would still fit her she tossed it on the bed along with the newspaper she had snatched from the kitchen table. Rushing into the bathroom she quickly washed up. She took time to wind her long dark hair onto the round rat pad that she had secured about the crown of her head—a hairstyle she thought might make her look more serious, efficient, and competent.

With the help of a large rubber band looped through the buttonhole of her skirt and then around the button itself, she gained a couple inches. The jacket was snug, but fit passably. Slipping into a pair of open-toed heels, Orpha bolted from the apartment, with yesterday's help wanted section tucked under her arm, slamming the door harder than she meant to behind her. She stopped briefly on the front porch to decide what address and job to locate first. The large ad for the defense plant caught her eye. She had circled it yesterday with red pencil; this would be her first stop. According to Arline, she should have no problem getting work now, for there seemed to be new people coming on the line every day, and as far as she knew all the factories were in full swing.

After a short bus ride and a walk of no more than a block and a half, Orpha entered the one-story brick office building where the interviewing—and hopefully hiring— would take place. She took a number from the table stationed just inside the door along with an employment form. Filling in the blanks with the little she had, she waited to be called. There was an atmosphere of muffled efficiency, with people coming through the propped-open front door. They took a seat, filled out the forms, rose, moved to the front of the room where they sat to be interviewed for a slightly longer period, and then, after a quick encounter with a camera, they were gone.

Orpha was hired on the spot, assigned to the McQuay-Norris ammunition plant. She was to begin the very next evening on the early shift, inspecting the cores of bullets for nicks and imperfections.

Her spirit lifted as she stepped out into the early afternoon sun. Tilting her head up, she let the warm rays bathe her face momentarily, and at the same time she found it necessary to lay the flat of her hands on either sides of her skirt as the playful breeze seized the hem promising to lift it.

With the beginning of a new job, regardless of what might happen with Bill, she had begun a process that would help restore her children to her.

She looked forward to visiting day at the homes this weekend and yet she knew it would be very painful each time she would have to leave them behind. It would never get any better—she was certain of that.

The bumping bus jolted her forward in her seat when it came to the stop just ahead of her own. Standing, she made her way to the rear, where she grasped the pole next to the back-door exit and planted her feet firmly to brace herself against any sudden move. The door screeched open as the bus came to a full stop, and Orpha stepped down and back and waited for it to continue on its way. She took her time walking home and once inside the house she hesitated in the hallway, gazing at the telephone, contemplating another call to Saint Mary's. Concluding it might be best not to check on her kids again due to the unwelcome sound in the nun's voice after she had called two days in a row, she made her way up the stairs. The apartment greeted her with empty silence for Arline had not made it home from work and Donald and Raymond were still with the lady two doors down.

Although her appetite was not there, common sense insisted she should fix herself something. She made a peanut butter and jelly sandwich, after which she turned on the flame beneath the coffee pot. "It's this morning's leftovers, probably stronger then hell, but it won't kill me," she said out loud. She sat down at the table, biting into the bread, and the sweet pasty mixture clung to the roof of her mouth.

After the second mouthful she pushed her chair back, rising to pour the now-lukewarm coffee into a cup. With a large swallow, she cleared her mouth for the next bite.

Glancing at the clock, she could see she had plenty of time before her date with Bill and the thought created a twinge of excitement that danced about inside of her now anticipating the evening ahead. "Time always drags when you want it to hurry and flies when you want it to stand still," she thought. Her thoughts wandered about each one of her children, but once she felt the tears building she forced her thinking in a different direction.

"Floyd has been a real son of a bitch," she thought. "He doesn't seem to care at all." As far as she knew he hadn't even been out to see the kids. "Well, to hell with him. I'll do this myself somehow." Her anger with Floyd seemed to bring forth some form of energy. Pushing back her chair, she got up and began cleaning the kitchen, doing the breakfast dishes, then working her way through the rest of the apartment, until everything held its rightful place.

Turning the faucet on in the old claw-footed bathtub she sprinkled her usual few drops of cologne, as she went about preparing for her evening with Bill. It would be a good idea to use the bathroom before Arline and her boys came home she surmised. She could take her time while giving herself some much-needed special attention.

Once in the tub she tried to relax, but she found herself scrubbing unnecessarily hard and fast. Dropping the cloth and bar of soap into the bath water, she leaned back, letting the warm liquid reach her chin while closing her eyes. "Think good thoughts," she heard herself say. These words were what she would often whisper to her kids at night when tucking them in. "Just think good thoughts!"

The afternoon had slipped by. Orpha could hear Arline coming up the stairs with the two boys in tow, shushing them all the way. "You guys are so noisy!" she was saying. "For being such little twerps, you make enough noise for ten kids. Come on let's move. In you go."

"Hi, what happened?" Arline called out. "You guys can go outside or go play in your room."

"Outside!" they answered.

"Well then, go! Scoot!" she instructed with the wave of her hand toward the door that still stood open. "Stay in the yard. I want to be able to see you from the kitchen window, okay?"

"Okay," they shouted back as they ran down the stairs.

Joining her sister in the living room, Orpha plopped onto the couch, lit herself a cigarette, then after a long hard drag exhaled the smoke in a strong gust toward the ceiling.

"Well, I must tell you I have some good news. Guess what? I'm a working girl now. Things feel better just being able to say it!" She tossed her head back dragging in and letting another cloud rise.

"Hey, that's great, kid! When do you start?"

"Tomorrow, early evening shift."

"What plant? Not mine I'm sure. They don't let relatives work in the same buildings."

"No, sorry to say, but across town at the McQuay-Norris plant. But that's fine with me. Just so I'm working."

"Don't you have that big date with Bill this evening?"

"Yes, I'm ready," she smiled. "All I have to do is slip on my dress. Nothing anxious about me. It's only three hours from now."

"So tell me," Orpha inquired, "what's it like working in one of these places? You've already mentioned the women can be pretty tough and some of them talk like Mac truck drivers. What else should I know?"

192

"Well, let's see. Aside from what I'm sure they already told you about loose lips sink ships? You won't be able to forget that, because there are posters throughout the plant warning you day in and day out. I know I wouldn't want to speak out of turn or say anything that could be misinterpreted. Something on that order happened just today. There's this big woman, really loud and obnoxious, who needs to shave her upper lip."

Orpha giggled in disbelief.

"Yes, I'm not kidding, but anyway," Arline went on, "she may not have a job come tomorrow. She said something really stupid today on the line. I thought for sure she would get hurt, but all that took place was a shoving match with three other women and herself. They were furious with her."

"Well, for God's sake what the hell did she say?"

"She jokingly made the comment that she hoped the war lasted until she had her mink coat paid for. God those women almost jumped the table to get at her."

"Jeez, what an awful thing to say even if she was kidding," Orpha commented.

"Yeah, I know, she left early and I didn't blame her. That parking lot could have been her funeral. Umm . . . let's see, what else? I know you've heard me crab time and time again about it being hotter than blazes in there in the summer with very few fans going. They do have salt tablets in a box as you come in the door. Supposedly they help. I don't know for sure. I just take them hoping for any help I can get. Oh, and another thing. I only take two cigarettes with me. Otherwise you have moochers after you all day long. Smokes are just too hard to come by to be passing them around, and it's the same ones always with their hands out. You have to wear a hairnet or at least have your hair up and out of the way of the machinery, as I'm sure they told you. I can't think of anything else, other than for the most part there's a feeling of singlemindedness and unity among everyone that works there, and a lot of joking and teasing goes on. That's about it. What's your job?"

"Inspecting bullet cores for nicks is what I was told. Doesn't sound too hard to me," Orpha said, matter of fact.

"Don't be too sure, Arline smiled. "The foremen on those table lines are pretty tough. You never know whose box they are going to check next, and I hear it only takes one slip-up and you're gone. Just one small mistake someone makes could cause the life of a serviceman and that's the thinking on that."

"Well then I guess I'll have to do a perfect job as I always do," Orpha teased, feeling a little better about her predicament. She had made a decision earlier while soaking in the tub that she must keep the kids from haunting her mind constantly so she can function effectively on their behalf. For it was a crippling way to think, reviving their cries and little faces every moment of the day.

"Must be nice to be so all-fire perfect! What did you say your name was?" Arline shot back with a snort. Getting up from her seat she tossed her head and pointed her nose to the ceiling with a snooty look on her face. "Hello, dears! Nice to meet all of you! My name? Oh, my name is Perfect. Everything about me is perfect!"

Orpha was laughing now at her sister's antics. "You crackpot," she called out as she tossed a small pillow at her.

Arline disappeared into the kitchen. The noise of dishes and the clanking of pots announced she was preparing supper. "You're not eating, right?" Arline called out to her.

"That's right," she answered. Orpha did feel better, and she would try to enjoy her evening out with Bill. The anticipation of seeing him in just a short while gave her butterflies. She found herself smiling as she let her best dress slip down over her arms and then tugged at it to cover her now-thickening midsection. "Oh, this is not going to work," she thought, while pulling it back over her head and dropping it on the bed. She reached for Arline's pink and brown lightweight crepe dress. It was short-sleeved, with a soft-pink diagonal insert running from under the bust line up to the neckline and deep chocolate opposite that line down to the hem. She found it very flattering, for it was loose fitting and just skimmed her hips and flared about her legs. "Perfect!" she thought as she checked her reflection in the dresser mirror. It all but hid her condition. Makeup was not something she used much of. For one thing she couldn't afford it. Other than a hint of Vaseline on the lashes and even less on the brows to groom and darken them she would apply a very light touch of lip rouge, for it was all that was needed. She brushed her hair loose and free about her shoulders. As she gave herself one last going over she heard a firm rap on the living room door.

Although she had the urge to race to open it she forced herself to count to three before she started walking slowly in that direction. She had picked up the notion, she wasn't sure from where, that a lady shouldn't appear overly anxious when a man came calling for her. A second fleeting thought from her conscience followed: of course, her condition and situation was certainly not that of a lady.

"Do you want me to get that?" Arline called out from the kitchen.

"No, I've got it," she answered, at the same time turning the knob and pulling the door open to find Bill standing on the other side with both arms full of packages. With his Stetson cocked to one side and low on his brow, he was grinning broadly. "Hello, angel! It's great seeing you."

"You, too," Orpha answered, just a bit nervous as she stood there looking at him. "I mean, it's also good to see you."

"Do you have somewhere I can put these? Bill asked, moving his laden arms up slightly. "Just a little something for the kids. Didn't want them to think I forgot

195

them," he continued, still smiling broadly. "Where are they?" he asked, as he stepped in front of the couch, letting the gifts tumble onto the cushions. "But first things first," he continued as he straightened up and took two long strides back to where Orpha stood. He reached for her hand, giving it a gentle tug. "Come here, sweetheart," he said, smiling down at her as he brought her in close, wrapping his arms about her tightly. "You have no idea how much I've missed you," he whispered in her ear. Then just as softly, "You know I love you."

"Oops," Arline exclaimed as she walked in the room. "Don't let me stop you. I'll just stand here and quietly watch," she teased.

Bill, have you met my sister?" asked Orpha, turning from his embrace. "Yes, as a matter of fact, I think we met briefly at the farm a while back. Arline, isn't it?"

"Why yes, I'm flattered that you remember," she said, smiling coquettishly and extending her hand for him to shake.

"Oh brother," Orpha thought to herself. "She's just as bad as Mama. What a flirt! Say you're jealous!" a little voice in her head accused. She forced herself to back away a couple of steps from Arline's and Bill's exchange to prove to herself she would not allow such petty feelings to rule her, or at least she'd try not to—she had enough problems going.

"Okay, now where are those ragamuffins?" Bill asked.

"In bed by now, I'm sure," Arline quickly replied as if to head off any discussion in her presence.

"Hmm," he grunted, obviously disappointed as he reached inside his coat, pulling a silver-chained watch from his vest pocket. After quickly glancing at the timepiece, he asserted good-naturedly, "I'll just have to wait until next time, won't I? Ready to go?"

"Anytime," Orpha replied.

Taking her by the elbow, Bill led Orpha through the door and down the stairway.

"Have fun you two!" Arline called after them as they made their way out the front door. Orpha was silent and somewhat pensive during the ride and her mood had not changed even after being seated at their table. Neither the restaurant's posh ambience, nor Bill's ordering of their dinner seemed to reach her.

"How do I tell him what has happened with the children? Will he think I'm awful? What else could I have possibly done?" Her mind was reeling.

"Orpha!"

She jerked her head up, meeting his eyes with her own, smiling faintly. "Oh, I'm sorry, Bill. It's just that I have so much to tell you and don't know where to begin."

"I know, sweetheart. We have the same problem. Shall I start or . . . you?"

His news, she sensed, from all outward appearances was more positive than her own.

"You first," she nodded.

"Ina and I have worked out all details, and have agreed that a divorce would be best for both of us," he announced in a burst of cheerful resolution. "It's being processed now," he went on as he reached for her hands. "She has settled for a cash amount that we both feel is fair, leaving the business and farm with me. Now what I'm hoping is that—," Orpha watched as Bill lifted his right hand into his jacket pocket and then with his fingers concealing something within them, he laid his fist on the table in front of himself as he proceeded.

"Orpha, you know how I feel about you and the children. Would you want to marry me? Once I'm free? There it is, I've said it . . . What do you think?" He was leaning into the table at the same time searching her face and watching for an indication of what she might say next.

Overwhelmed by Bill's proposal, Orpha sat stunned. Only tears moved and spilled from her eyes as she sat motionless.

Completely perplexed by her reaction, Bill asked, "Are you saying yes? You're not telling me no, are you?"

"Yes," she said in almost a whisper. "I mean, yes, I'll marry you."

"That was a yes! I heard it!" he said jubilantly, his voice now loud enough that people were looking their way.

"Bill are you sure you want to do this? A readymade family and all?" she asked, hoping he would reassure her.

"Will this convince you?"

Turning his hand over, Bill exposed a small red velvet box. He opened it, never taking his eyes from hers. Technically, he stated, neither one of them was free, but he hoped to remedy that within a short period of time. Until then, he asked if she would accept and wear his ring as a promise to each other and to the future they would have together.

Brushing the wet from her cheek, she extended her left hand. He then slid the ring onto her finger. "Look at that, a perfect fit," he beamed at her.

"It's so beautiful, Bill. How did you know what size to get?"

"I didn't! It was a good guess, but the ruby was what I wanted for you. Its deep red glow in some way put me in mind of the spirit that owns you." Orpha cringed a bit inside at his words. Sweet talk was one thing, and she got plenty of that from Floyd and others, but having it border on poetry was different.

"Well now, what was it you wanted to tell me?"

"Bill, I still don't know where to start, but maybe I should tell you right out that I'm pregnant, and it's your baby."

It was his turn to be stunned as he sat stoically for a few moments making Orpha think he was displeased with her news.

"My God, woman, are you trying to give me a heart attack? When? Why didn't you tell me?"

"Around Christmastime. I didn't want you to feel that you had to marry me. I would never do that to you. Is it a let down, Bill?"

"Dear God, no," he smiled. "I'm pleased. It's just a little sooner than I expected." Taking her hand in his once again, he squeezed it gently. "We'll make it just fine. It will all work out. It's turning into quite a day, isn't it?"

"Yes, unfortunately, I have more to tell you. I took a job at one of the defense plants in order to save money to get the children back from the homes that I was forced to put them in."

" Homes?" he blurted. "What kind of homes? Foster homes?" His face showed deep concern.

"No, Catholic orphanages, but they're by no means up for adoption. The arrangement was to pay half of their support and the Sisters of Charities would pick up the rest until I could get situated and take care of them on my own."

"What about Floyd? Wouldn't he give a hand?"

"Bill, if I waited for Floyd to give me a hand we would all starve."

"Sweetheart, I'm not going to ask why you didn't give me a call or why you returned part of the money I gave you. I know you well enough to guess the answer to both questions. But I want those kids out of there as soon as we can work it. The big house will be empty and waiting." His brow now knitted in thought, as he hesitated. "We might be wise to ask Laverne for help at least for a time before and after the baby arrives. I'll give my attorney a jingle. He can handle any legal problem that has to be taken care of. But first thing in the morning we'll call that defense plant and let them know that the future Mrs. O'Dell won't be coming to work for the government."

Orpha was impressed by Bill's take-charge approach. He was solving all her problems in one fell swoop. Not something she had ever experienced. His straightforward manner instilled a feeling of strange calmness, and yet at the same time, stirring in her the need to be held closely in his arms as he kissed away any feeling of insecurity or fear she held deep inside.

Their food arrived, though Orpha was too distracted to eat. She would take an occasional sip of wine and fork something in her plate, never raising it to her mouth. "You aren't eating. Not hungry?" Bill asked.

"No, I guess I'm thinking too much. Everything seems to be moving so fast and yet it feels like years since I talked to you on the phone that day, asking for the job at the farm. I'm sorry, Bill, I guess I just don't have much of an appetite."

"Well then, what would you say to us leaving and going upstairs," he asked in all sincerity.

"I would love to be alone with you," she smiled, slowly placing her napkin on the table. As she did so a quick, constricting, warm surge took place deep in the warm private area of her lower body, signaling her growing desire and passion. She was eagerly looking forward to being completely consumed in the pleasure of their lovemaking.

Bill teased as he helped her from her chair. "Are you sure now? We could stay here and wish we were upstairs."

Orpha smiled affectionately up into his face. "Only if you want to, Bill."

Once alone and the door locked behind them Bill took her in his arms gently pressing her to him as though she might break. "I love you more than any man has ever loved any woman." He kissed her mouth softly, than brushed her neck with his lips while he slowly freed the buttons of her dress from their openings. Peeling the garment back from her body and down her arms he let it fall to the floor as he continued touching his lips to her shoulders. Orpha stood still as he took her clothing from her body lovingly, and kissing all parts as he exposed them, rising from his knees, he lifted, and cradled her in his arms kissing her on the mouth as he lowered her onto the bed. He stood at the side of the bed as he undressed himself, looking down at her. "You are one beautiful woman." His eyes were unmistakably filled with appreciation. Orpha felt just a bit uneasy about being so closely examined, perhaps because she did not feel at her best. Her figure was naturally fuller now. Bill lay down beside her, propped up on his elbow, his masculinity now enlarged and distended. He ran his hand slowly over her breasts, squeezing each one lightly, then down across her stomach, bending over to kiss it. As he moved further down with his hand, he slid it between the soft, warm, moist mounds of her opening. She caught her breath, reaching out, encircling her fingers about him, moving her hand very slowly back and forth. Pulling himself up and over her, he gifted her with warm, brief kisses followed by quick, hot, wet licks beginning at her eyelids finishing on the tops of her feet.

She was lost in their passion and wanting him to enter and complete their lovemaking, for she felt that if he didn't, she may leave without him. As if he knew, he was there, and the coming together, was of such intensity that Orpha heard herself moan with pleasure.

They lay encircled in each other's arms for a few moments, enjoying the deep peace and aloneness their lovemaking had created. Bill spoke softly, "I think I could eat something now. And, in fact, I'm so hungry I think I could eat you," he chuckled, pulling her into him, nibbling at her ear, then making a move for her neck. Pushing at his chest, Orpha laughingly freed herself from his grip, informing him that she, too, was hungry, but not hungry enough to become a cannibal.

Quickly sliding from the bed to her feet, she reached for her clothing from the small heap that had been made earlier. Bill lay watching her dress with a broad smile across his face. "You know, you really are a gorgeous gal."

"Sure I am! Just look at my tiny waist, slim hips, and undersized basooms," she responded with candor and self-mockery, amused by what appeared to be blindness on his part.

"Well, I suppose if you want to look at your body through eyes of pure vanity and measurement, you may not be seeing the real beauty." He was standing beside her now, wrapping his arms about her while kissing her lightly on the forehead. She looked up into his eyes impressed by the sensitivity coming from a man of such a stern and rugged appearance. After one last peck on Orpha's cheek, Bill vigorously rubbed, then clapped his hands together. "Let's get going my love and find us some food." He began dressing himself while she sat on the edge of the bed, waiting patiently, feeling hunger pangs that she had not felt or been aware of for a very long time.

The weeks ahead were busy and exciting. They had filed the necessary documents to take the children from the homes, as well as the divorce papers to be served on Floyd. The day of their release was one of pure joy for Orpha. The sisters had them ready and waiting. She would never forget the picture of the boys tearing down the hallway to meet them with grins as wide as their little faces, and Theresa Ruth standing just inside the large entrance of Saint Mary's, holding on to Sister Mary Joseph's hand, smiling as she turned to wave goodbye to the nun who had obviously taken a special liking to her.

Once at the courthouse, they waited for Floyd to show but—no surprise to Orpha—he was nowhere to be found. The judge finally went ahead with the proceedings, giving full custody to her as well as finalizing her divorce.

The kids' chatter and excited questions filled the car as they headed from the city in the direction of Murphysboro.

"Mommy," George said, leaning over and speaking into her ear as his little fingers held on to the back of her car seat. "Are we going to be with you forever, now?"

Orpha turned, looking into her small son's worried face, his eyes searching, looking for the one right answer.

"Forever," she smiled at him.

"Forever!" George grinned back at her satisfied and then joined the others.

By the time they pulled up in front of the big house, stillness had overtaken the children who now leaned up against each other, sleeping.

"Bill, wait, before we move another inch, I've got to say something." Covering his hand with her own as it still gripped the steering wheel, she continued, "I don't know how I could ever thank you enough for what you've done for us," she spoke softly and earnestly.

Moving his face close to hers he smiled and replied, "Just love me, sweetheart, just love me." He quickly kissed her on the mouth, opened the car door, and let himself out.

"Yoo hoo," a voice called.

"There's no mistaking that voice," Orpha laughed out loud.

Laverne was coming down the walk as fast as she could manage. "Oh, I thought you would never get here," she said, giving Bill a pat on the back as she bent over to peer into the window at Orpha. With a big grin covering her round, happy face she went on excitedly, "I have everything ready for the kids. What can I carry in?"

Chapter Sixteen

They settled in as a family without a hitch, Bill would later comment to Laverne, who decided to stay on permanently. The small house became her quarters. She cared for the children and did most of the housework, although Orpha would constantly insist, "I'm pregnant, not sick."

"I know, I know," Laverne would answer. Still, she bustled about, humming to herself, leaving very little for Orpha to do. Having never married or had children, Laverne made it clear that she felt she now had a family she could care for, and did so with great relish. The fact that she had been chosen along with Radar to witness Orpha and Bill's wedding cemented her dedication.

The heat and mugginess of the day to come could already be felt on this early morning of late August, as the sun laid long shadows running from east to west, while it slowly climbed higher and forced its light through the trees and the vineyard below. Orpha sat on the side concrete patio, sipping her coffee, listening to the birds calling back and forth as the insects continued with their tireless song.

She laid her head back looking into the blue of the sky wondering frivolously if anyone had captured the heavenly color in a fabric. "What a gorgeous dress it would make," she smiled to herself.

"Good morning," Laverne's pleasant voice offered as she appeared beside Orpha's chair.

"Oh . . . good morning," Orpha echoed.

"Anything in particular you see up there?" Laverne asked, smiling broadly as she looked up to see what she might be missing.

"No, not really, just looking. Kids still sleeping?"

"Yep."

"What time is it getting to be, anyway?" Orpha asked, glancing at her visitor.

"Six or thereabouts," Laverne answered.

A quiet interlude ensued as Orpha observed the morning sun's brightness reflecting off the dew that still lay on the lush green surroundings.

Stretching her arms out she sucked in a deep breath as she reveled in the fragrance of the newly cut hay wafting gently through the air.

"Sure looks like another scorcher, doesn't it?"

"I wouldn't be a bit surprised," Laverne answered, giving the top of Orpha's chair a couple of light taps. "And here I stand like I have nothing else to do! Best be getting at that bread, before the real heat sets in."

Orpha was amused at her new friend's seemingly tireless ways. I don't think I have ever seen her walking, she thought, watching Laverne skitter off into the house.

The month of September followed and unfolded quietly and uneventfully, but the summer weather dragged on. It had been unusually hot, and the fans in the big house were going constantly, moving back and forth, blowing and humming, as they brought some relief—however slight it might be.

Although Bill was home for the weekends, he spent most of the week in the city, tending to restaurant business. Even with the war raging in Europe, it was prosperous.

The running of the farm was left to Radar's very capable hands, while Laverne took charge of the house, with very little resistance from Orpha. She would occasionally feel a twinge of guilt but was grateful that not much was expected from her right now. Being in her sixth month and with the heat contributing to her discomfort, she lived as "a lady of leisure" (as she referred to herself), a luxury she had never been afforded before now. She spent a great deal of her time in books. She devoured them as a hungry person would food. Bill's extensive collection pleased and satisfied her appetite. The world was open and spread before her. The knowledge she obtained from constant reading, along with Bill's love, made her deeply grateful and more self-confident than she had ever been in her life.

It was the last Sunday of the month. Mama and Arline were invited to dinner. Arline's boys would not be coming, for they were now living with their father and his new wife.

That bothered Orpha. Knowing Arline's former husband was a heavy drinker, and since she had not met the woman who was now his wife, she was not sure what might be in store for Donald and Raymond. She worried about them, but she knew Arline had no choice. There were no openings at Saint Joseph's and she could not afford to raise them by herself—something Orpha was acutely familiar with. But things were really tough for a lot of people these days in the city. With rationing and shortages of all kinds, only the affluent fared well. As did the farmers, for most of what was needed they raised themselves.

"They're here, they're here!" George called out from his post at the front window.

"They're here, they're here!" Theresa Ruth yelled, parroting her brother.

Orpha hurried to the door, which George had already flung open. Bolting down the front walk with his younger brother in hot pursuit they went to meet their grandmother and aunt. Following behind as fast as she could run, Theresa Ruth plowed headlong into her aunt's legs, wrapping her arms about them.

"I can't walk, sweetie," Arline laughed, taking the little girl's hand. "Hi, Georgy," Arline said, leaning toward him as she spoke. "Gee, I swear you've grown a foot since the last time I saw you."

Looking up at his aunt, Ronnie waited for her to notice him next. "You're becoming a big boy, too, aren't you?" Arline smiled and patted Ronnie on top of his head. Grinning at her, he ran back in front of them past Orpha who now was waiting in the doorway.

"Hi, glad you two could make it," she said, stepping back so they could enter the house. "I hope you're hungry. Laverne has cooked enough food for an army."

"It smells great," Arline remarked.

"Oh, I'm sure I'll find something to my liking," Ruth agreed with a smile, "and that's exactly what I'm afraid of."

The meal was enjoyed, the conversation light. Ruth loved having center stage as she told stories about her past and one or two embarrassing anecdotes about her two daughters.

They laughed, and the children laughed with them, even if at times it was apparent, they had no idea what they were laughing about. Bill sat at the head of the table, getting a big kick out of the jubilant interaction between his wife and her relatives. He loved seeing Orpha happy. The atmosphere was open and relaxed.

Laverne outdid herself with dinner, and everyone raved about her peach cobbler. Ruth made a point of telling everyone how lucky Orpha was to have found Bill, and if she could, she would have given Orpha a run for her money. Bill smiled at her, appearing just a bit embarrassed, but obviously flattered as he excused himself to retrieve his pipe from the den.

Ruth leaned in toward the center of the table and in a hushed toned continued, "Now that he's left the room, I can say this—that's what I call a man! I'm right, aren't I?" Ruth asked with a mischievous grin.

"Mama," Arline lightly scolded, "you're bad, and that's none of your business, is it, Orpha?"

"No it's not. But she's right!"

With that, the three of them shared a girlish giggle.

"Has anyone heard from Mary Barbara lately?" Orpha asked as she stubbed out her cigarette.

"No, I haven't," Ruth said, expressing her deep concern, and quickly changing her demeanor. I don't mind telling you girls I'm worried. I feel strongly that something is very wrong."

"Now that's odd, why would you say that?" Arline questioned.

"Aside from not hearing from her, I just know."

"Good God, Mama!" Arline cringed.

Morbid talk, as she would refer to it, always unnerved Arline.

"As surely as I sit here," Ruth went on, "she is not well, and I know I'll hear of it soon. I have felt this so strongly in the last few days. What makes it even harder is that there is no way of reaching them. They don't have a phone."

"Mama, you're scaring the hell out of me," Orpha commented, obviously disturbed by the conversation.

"I wouldn't mind being wrong on this one," Ruth went on, "but . . ." Her voice trailed off.

The day ended on a high note aside from the discomfort and fear that Mama instilled in Orpha's mind about Mary Barbara.

The kids had long since gone to bed, and the evening air held a cool, comfortable breeze as Bill and Orpha walked Ruth and Arline to Radar's car. He was seated at the wheel, ready to play chauffeur again. They stood watching Bill's black Lincoln fade into the night, as it headed back for the city. Arline in the back and Mama sitting in front with Radar "to keep him company," she had jokingly said as she sat herself right in the middle of the seat.

"What a vamp! She'll never grow old," Orpha laughed. "I can't believe her sometimes."

"She's just young at heart," Bill allowed.

"Only when it comes to flirting is she young at heart. You know, she sees and feels things that most people don't."

"Are you telling me your mother has a crystal ball?"

Smiling down at her, he wrapped his arm about her shoulders as they turned to walk back into the house.

"Now just what has your mother seen and felt to convince you of her powers," he teased, giving her a playful squeeze.

"Go ahead and laugh! Next time she comes out, maybe she will make a table talk."

"What?" Bill threw his head back in a laugh of disbelief. "Come on, now, you can't really buy that."

"No, I never thought these things were possible either until one day she proved me wrong."

Once inside she followed him into the den, where they sat as she went on with her story. Bill lit his pipe, while Orpha did her best to hold his interest.

"I had at one time a small, three-legged end table much like the one in the back entrance hall here. At Mama's instruction we all sat about it with our fingertips touching."

"Who is 'we'?" Bill inquired.

"Oh, Arline, Mama, and I. We were to concentrate with our eyes closed and then she would ask the table questions. It was to reply with either one, two, or three cracks, depending on how she would tell it to answer. You can believe it or not," she went on, "but I looked under the table, saw nothing. Mama's legs and feet were nowhere near the legs, and our hands were just above the surface of the table when the table would crack. That was spooky enough, but then she told the table to rise on one leg. That was when I quit. I'll never forget the look on Arline's face. She was bowled over, same as I. Oh, I could tell you many stories I have heard about her and her mother. Mama has always said that Gramma was a witch, and the kids in their neighborhood were convinced of it. They were scared to death of her."

The aroma of Bill's pipe filled the room, as he would take small, soft puffs, then let the smoke escape his mouth. He sat intrigued by his wife's story, but Orpha knew he was only being entertained and was not the least bit persuaded.

"Well, I've heard of strange things but tables talking and rising on their legs is a new one to me," Bill said. "Maybe your mother could tell me what is in the future for us?"

"Go ahead, make fun. I don't think you would call me easily convinced. But I was there, and, no, we weren't drinking, before you ask."

"Well, sweetheart," Bill said, leaning forward and smiling, "I guess you would have had to have been there, but I can tell you this, if those kind of things can be done by anyone, your mother has my vote." Rising from his chair he tapped out his pipe in the tray. "Well, what do you think? Morning comes around mighty early in these parts?" He reached for Orpha's hand and pulled her up from her seat and to his side. Then putting his arm about her waist, which had all but disappeared, he led her slowly up the staircase and into the large master bedroom that at one time had served as a guestroom. But with Laverne's help, and with one of the hired hands doing the painting, Orpha had changed and decorated it along with every room in the house—carefully erasing signs of Ina as best she could.

The bedroom was soft and cool for she had done it in her favorite colors of blue and white. The long white lace curtains billowed away from the open windows like the clouds she had so often watched moving across the sky. The blue of the walls was as close to the shade of the heavens as possible. She worked for days mixing cans of white paint and different blues until she was satisfied that she had captured the hue of the sky on a warm, sunny day. On either side of the old canopy bed, which stood between the windows, were round tables, covered with beautifully hand-crocheted cloths that her mother and grandmother had made years ago. She had never used them for fear of something happening to them, but now they were displayed, and she enjoyed being able to appreciate them along with the entire house that she had grown to love and feel completely at home in.

Once in bed she curled up to Bill's back, kissing him on the right shoulder blade. "Good night," she said, pulling her pillow in closer under her head. "Good night," he answered, reaching back and patting her on the thigh.

It was late in the evening of the following day that the phone rang and, as if by decree, Mama announced she had indeed received a telegram stating that Mary Barbara was very sick and that she should come down.

"I knew it. I should have just gone on down before now," Ruth said, sounding impatient with herself. "What are the chances that you can go?"

"I'm sure I can, but Wednesday would be the soonest. I'll talk to Bill and ask Laverne if she would watch the kids for a couple of days. Mama, why don't I go down first, see how things are, do what I can do for her, then give you a call if it really is serious. That way you won't miss that much work if there's no need."

"No, that's all right. I'll be down as soon as I can get away. In the meantime, I'll give Arline a call. Although I really don't know what she can do with what she's got going on. That son of a bitch she was married to has loaned the boys out to some farmer to help him around his farm. They're nothing but babies. What the hell does he think the guy's going to get out of them? She asked him that and he told her it was good training for them. No, I know exactly what Harry's getting. He's getting rid of the kids and booze money."

"She's not going to let him get away with that is she?"

"Well, she said she would be picking them up as soon as she could find a ride to the farm where they are. When it rains it pours," Ruth grumbled.

"Mama, let her know that we can help if she wants. She knows I'm here if she needs me. No, better yet, I'll give her a call as soon as we hang up here."

"Okay then, you'll leave Wednesday, and I'll see you there in a day or so."

"Okay, Mom, bye."

"Goodbye," Ruth solemnly answered.

Orpha held the phone to her ear, until she heard the disconnecting click from the other end. She then lowered the phone slowly into its cradle, her thoughts full of concern for Mary Barbara.

Without further hesitation she dialed Arline's number. As it rang she remembered that it was Monday evening. More than likely Arline would be at work as a part-time waitress at a small diner two blocks from the rooming house. She had mentioned taking the extra job a few weeks back, saying she wanted to save money in order to get the boys from Harry. She wasn't sure how she would handle full-time at the defense plant along with evenings at the diner but what else could she do.

"Hello," the voice at the other end said.

"Hello! Mrs. Rapply?"

"Hello?" the voice called out again.

"Mrs. Rapply, this is Orpha. Remember me?" Orpha shouted into the phone.

"Who?" the old woman asked.

"Orpha!" she said even louder.

"Yes, Orpha, I know who you are. You don't have to shout, my dear. I'm not deaf."

"Mrs. Rapply, would you leave a message for my sister?"

"What was that? Speak up, dear."

"Would you tell Arline to call me, please? And if she can't reach me, tell her to give her mother a call, okay? Did you hear me?"

"I will, don't worry. Goodbye, dear."

212

Click. The conversation ended abruptly.

"Poor old soul," Orpha said out loud as she placed the telephone once again back in its cradle. "I hope she understood, she's becoming as deaf as a post."

Orpha's mind jumped back to the immediate problem at hand. She would leave as soon as possible the very next day and was hoping upon hope that Laverne wouldn't mind taking total care of the kids and that Bill would be understanding. She barely remembered his leaving their bed this morning, but she knew it was still dark out and that the downtown restaurant had early deliveries coming in. He made it a practice to be there when a shipment was due. He would go over every food item with an eagle eye, for nothing but the best was to be served in his two restaurants. Extra food would have to be bought from other markets. The farm could no longer supply everything that was needed on the menus—although the new, more upscale, establishment would not be formally opening until around the holidays, about the time the baby was due.

The thinking was, Christmas week would find everything in its place, right down to a stately, brightly lit, beautifully decorated Christmas tree, that would stand magnificently in the center of the main dining room. Orpha now hurried up the stairs, stopping just long enough in the hallway to peer in at Laverne, who was finishing her nightly rounds through the children's rooms, picking up their dirty clothing for the next morning's laundry.

"Laverne," Orpha called softly, then leaving the doorway, quickly continued on down the hall to the master bedroom. She yanked a large Pullman case from the back of the closet, slapped it on the surface of the bed, and, once open, began placing her things inside.

Laverne appeared in the doorway. "What's happened?" she asked.

Orpha explained the worrisome situation, then asked, "Could you possibly stay with the children until I return?"

"Don't you worry none. The kids and me will do just fine," Laverne assured her. "You just remember not to overdo it down there, after all—"

"Oh, thanks a lot. I really do appreciate this."

Orpha interrupted her packing long enough to give Laverne a hug of gratitude. "Are you sure you really don't mind?" she asked, taking a step back to look into the round, sweet face of this woman who was always so willing to help.

"Not at all. You just go and take care of your sister, but take it easy."

"I'll do my best," Orpha assured her with a grateful smile. "I'll do my very best."

The matter of whether Bill would approve of her leaving for any length of time and being that far away from him and the children was a question she was not sure she knew the answer to. However, she did know she wanted to be at her sister's side in the worst way. For that sinking, lost feeling in the pit of her stomach seemed to be warning her not to dally.

Orpha had just put her last article of clothing in the suitcase when she heard a car pulling past the bedroom window. "He's home—finally!" she spoke out loud, hurrying down the staircase to meet him at the door.

"Hi there," he grinned, greeting her as she walked toward him.

"Hi," she answered with a guarded smile.

"What's wrong?" he inquired.

"It's Mary Barbara. Mama got a wire today saying she's in a bad way and I have to go be with her. I know you can't get away, but Laverne said she would take care of every—"

214

"Whoa, just a minute. You're moving too fast. How about we go together? This is not something I want you to do alone. We'll leave in the morning. I'll make a few calls tonight. Where is it we have to go? I know it's some town in Arkansas. Which one?"

"Bald Knob," Orpha offered.

Amused by the name, he smiled. "I wonder who thought that one up?" After making the necessary calls, they walked together up the stairs and into the bedroom where a second bag was packed for Bill before going to bed. They intended to get an early start.

Chapter Seventeen

Mary Barbara lay in her bed—in acute intermittent pain. She tried to talk herself into dealing with it as a temporary thing and to rise above it, for "nothing lasts forever," she told herself. She could remember Mama saying those same words years ago. "I wonder," she thought, "did they call Mama like I asked them to? She might not be able to come . . . " her thought faded away. She kept her eyes closed as she let her fingers trail along the connecting threads of the old quilt that she lay beneath. It felt so heavy but she did not have the strength or desire to push it back. The music from the old windup Victrola made its way to her ears from the next room. It sounded so far away but she could make out the song "By the Sweet By and By." It reminded her of Floyd. She remembered him singing it while playing it on his guitar. A smile lightly touched the corners of her mouth as she thought back on Floyd and their battles. They could really get into some good ones. People were known to ask, "Who's the wife?" But the two of them never balked at fighting with each other either. "Oh—God," she could hear herself moan. Or, she thought it was her moaning. Even her voice seemed strange and off in the distance. But the pain was unmistakably hers.

She had no concept of time. The entrance to the room had an old army blanket nailed to the top and down the one side. It was of such thickness that not a glimmer of light could steal through from the other side. The room was shrouded in complete blackness. Even the tiny window had been covered, although the rhythmic sound of rain hitting the glass made her vaguely aware of its location.

Her pain seemed to completely engulf her now, and she became stubborn at its request to be announced, choking off the scream that was welling upward in her throat. At the same moment, she felt her head being lifted from the pillow and the hard rim of a cup being pressed to her lips as a biting liquid rushed downward making her gag. But she was too weak to spit it out. Mary Barbara could feel the bony arm her head now rested on, and she knew Granny was the pourer of some bitter home remedy.

Opening her eyes, she focused on the soft light emitting from the lone kerosene lamp, and the stern, frail, old face that wore wire-rimmed glasses, one lens of which had been fogged over so the dead eye behind it could not be seen.

The old lady now brought her arm up higher, elevating Mary Barbara's head even more, once again forcing the awful stuff down.

"Come on. Drink it up," she insisted. "It will kill the pain." With that promise, Mary Barbara gulped at the vile-tasting stuff.

Granny slowly took her arm from beneath her patient's head, letting it come to rest once again on the pillow. Then picking up her light, she passed through the cloth door into another world on the other side. A hazy glimpse of moving silhouettes was all Mary Barbara could see before the blanket dropped back in place, leaving her in the same dense blackness as before.

A loud clap of thunder shook the small frame house. A man's voice from the other side could be heard saying "Oooeee, the Lord ain't happy with youns tonight. What did you do?"

Mary Barbara heard laughter, then a scolding from Granny acidly followed. "I'll have none of that blaspheming in this here house!" she angrily informed them. "If you're gonna be talkin' like that you can go outside."

For a brief time it was quiet. "And besides," she went on, "we got a deadly sick woman in the next room, so you all hush up," Granny finished. The muffled tones of talk and activity resumed in the next room shortly thereafter.

217

The words *deadly sick* stuck in Mary Barbara's mind. "Am I dying?" she asked herself. "I wish Mama would come."

She could hear the rain now being driven against the house with great force, thunder and lightning booming and cracking with great exuberance, the air filled with God's power, which, according to Granny, might be taking her soon.

"What about Bobby? Who would take care of him?" Tears rolled across the lower temples of Mary Barbara's face, wetting her ears and hair. As much as she loved Lemvel she wasn't convinced that he would see to her son's needs when it came to cleanliness and education. For Lemvel was still largely illiterate aside from what she had taught him.

"I'm not the kisser or the kisser's son but I'll do the kissing till the kisser comes"—the rhyme danced across her mind. Lemvel would tease her with it while grappling with her for a kiss.

"We had a lot of good times," she reflected.

"Ooooo," she heard her own voice moan softly. The agony had let up some, and the time between the hurt was longer. Granny's concoction seemed to be helping. She let go of her thoughts and escaped into a deep sleep.

It could have been hours or just minutes that she had been sleeping, but the awareness of her hand being held made her force her eyes open and focus on the blurry figure sitting at the side of the bed. The grip was tight as she tried to spread her fingers to loosen it a bit.

"Lemvel?" she whispered.

"I'm here and I ain't goin' nowhere, darlin'," he said. She could see his chin was quivering with emotion.

He dropped his head into the sheets, his voice now muffled. "You got to get well," he pleaded, "for Bobby and me. You just got to get yourself better." She could feel the bed move with his sobs and felt helpless to console him.

218

"Lemvel! What are you doing?"

She could hear the words being spat out in a harsh whisper. Her hand was quickly released and Lemvel left without even answering his grandmother's angry question.

"Here now, girl. Let's try and get some food in you."

Mary Barbara could feel the spoon being worked into her mouth. And as much as she wanted to eat, she found it too much of an effort, so she turned her head to one side, only to have the brusque old woman force it back and insist on her eating another bite.

"You won't be dying in this bed. Not if I can help it. Once your family git here they can see you git to the hospital. I ain't had a good night's sleep since this whole thing started," she grumbled. "And I'm too old to be sleeping in chairs or on the floor."

Mary Barbara knew the old matriarch was disgruntled over losing the only bed in the house, which belonged to her, and from the beginning did not try to disguise her irritation with her grandson's wife for having taken it.

But what gave Mary Barbara hope was knowing that Mama had been called. She could be here anytime now.

Without warning the pain shot through her like a hot arrow. As it did she arched her back and groaned. She tried to deal with the return of her agony, at the same time turning her head to one side causing the spoon to drop from Granny's hand and spill its contents on her cheek.

"Now look what you gone and done. I can't be cleaning up after you all the time," Granny snapped. She was short on patience and did not care who knew it. She seemed satisfied to leave the gruel where it fell, then taking the only small hint of light with her she disappeared from the room.

It was quiet again as Mary Barbara lay alone, vaguely mindful of her dark prison as she slipped in and out of nothingness.

The storm had dissipated finally, leaving the room holding a dampness that penetrated her coverings. Her body began to shiver and within minutes uncontrollable shaking took over. She felt strong arms sliding beneath and then about her. She was being held in close. "I'm here, I'm here," Lemvel said softly in her ear. "Hang on, I'll get you thar." He had been sitting on the floor outside her door, peaking in on occasion. And could no longer restrain himself. He had to do something.

He had crawled into the bed with her, shoes and all, feeling that his body could warm her and make her stop shaking.

She leaned into his embrace and found his closeness comforting, and fell into a quiet repose. He was still there when she awoke, now sleeping himself with his arms having never let go of her. The unrelenting pain held a firm grip, but somehow she could now bend and go with it better than before. Maybe she was just becoming more tolerant in handling her tormenter.

They lay together for a long while, with neither of them stirring. Mary Barbara didn't want to lose him just yet. His presence seemed to calm her and to remind her that she wasn't completely alone. "Bobby?" she asked weakly. "Where's Bobby?"

Lemvel moved in closer to her, bent his head down as he spoke in a whisper, as if he did not want to be heard by anyone else. "He's just fine. Don't you go worrying yourself none about that boy. I'll see he gets looking after. You get well and that's all you need doing now."

Kissing her on the forehead he gently snuggled into her, stroking her hair back from her face. Once again, she fell asleep, but this time her mind was full of brilliant, colorful pictures from her life, the breathtaking beauty of

220

the places she had seen and enjoyed. Even the fragrances were there—the strong, invigorating smell of the rich, damp earth mixed with the scent of heavy, green growth along the country roads she had walked so many times. The sucking-in deeply of the fresh-scrubbed air after a spring rain, then watching as the sun, unable to wait for the shower to cease completely, began shining once again, and in its haste bringing a spectacular rainbow high in the sky. She could see and taste the icy clear water from the underground springs of the Ozarks that she had so often cupped in her hands and drank of. The season of fall and all its magnificence unfolded in her mind's eye, in panoramic view. Winter, wearing its majestic snow-white cloak, sprinkled with tiny diamonds, painted a portrait of a pristine fantasy so real she could feel the crisp cold air softly touch her cheeks.

The people she loved appeared and just as quickly dissipated into the beauty. Then, as if from nowhere, black rolling clouds formed and a storm of such violence as she had never experienced raged. At the precise moment of a striking thunderbolt she awoke to excruciating pain that eclipsed the peace she had just moments ago.

Lemvel was gone and she no longer moaned. Now her shrill scream pierced her own ears, "Oh God, please take me," she pleaded. "Sweet Jesus, I've had enough."

Lemvel picked her up in his arms. Then sitting on the edge of the bed, he began gently rocking back and forth. "No, darlin', no. Don't talk like that," he kept saying, as if he were afraid God might grant her request, a tear now escaping from his eye and running free. Still she cried for mercy, as Granny came in with her special painkiller.

"Here!" she snapped at Lemvel. "Pour this down. It should take care of it."

Taking the cup, he put it to Mary Barbara's mouth. "Drink, drink, come on," he encouraged. "Take more."

Once she had finished, he continued to rock while telling her, "It's going to be good again. I promise, I promise."

"I never heard such carryings on," the old woman blustered as she left the two of them alone.

The kerosene lamp still sitting on the chair near the foot of the bed now cast their fused, slow-moving shadow on the wall behind them. Peace, quiet, wonderful warm, soft peace now wrapped itself about her, the feeling of being lifted and floating in a caressing pool of great love was given to her. She knew everything and everyone she cared about would be all right. She could feel her spirit soar.

"Gramma?" she spoke in a hushed tone. "Hurry up, Gramma. Come on, I'll wait for you. Hurry."

Her hand reached out from Lemvel into the open space of the small room. Her body gave a small shudder, then the extended arm dropped limply.

Lemvel knew instantly he had lost her. "Mary Barbara?" he said softly. "Darlin?" He relaxed his hold a bit and her head fell back. "No!" he yelled. "No, Jesus, no, no, no . . ."

He sat there holding her close while rocking back and forth, absorbed in his anguish.

Granny was bending over trying to see between Lemvel and his now-dead wife. She tugged at his shoulder hoping to separate them. The grieving man's head shot up with such quickness that she jumped back, startled.

"Leave me be old woman! Git! Leave me be!" he shouted. His eyes were those of a wild thing that was in such pain it would be dangerous to prod him. She turned on her heels and spun out of his presence.

Lemvel sat for most of the evening holding Mary Barbara, with no one daring to separate them. The house was quiet now, except for the sounds of the group's snoring and sleeping. Lemvel gently laid Mary Barbara on the bed, covering her with the old quilt as if to keep her warm.

Backing up the short distance to the doorway, he turned and carefully picked his way through the sprawling bodies on the floor. The front door announced his departure into the night.

* * *

Orpha's ears could hear the hum of the motor and her eyes were conscious of the light finding its way to the early morning. But her mind for the most part was on her sister, and the dread of what they might find in Bald Knob. She kept hearing Mama's voice on the phone, saying, "Mary Barbara's in a bad way."

"God, if she must go, let her hang on, please, until we get there," Orpha silently prayed.

"Are you sure you're up to this long haul?" Bill asked, invading her thoughts with his concern. "It will be about a half a day's drive, including necessary stops," he went on. "I don't want you making it too tough on yourself," he stated firmly.

"Bill, don't worry," she assured him with an appreciative smile. "I would tell you. I'm not long suffering and not quiet about it. When I hurt, I want the world to know it," she said, trying hard to make light of the situation. That's one of my very few shortcomings," she scoffed.

"Good! That's just how I want you to stay. Don't change a thing," he said, patting her knee, giving it a light squeeze.

They had been on the road since five this morning, drinking coffee from a thermos and eating the snacks that Laverne had packed the night before. They stopped often, as Orpha's pregnancy, along with the coffee, brought the urgent and somewhat tiresome need to seek out gas stations with ladies rooms.

By noon they were well past the halfway mark with another two or so more hours of traveling left. It was then that wisps of steam blowing from the side of the hood caught Orpha's eye. "That's not smoke coming out from under the hood, is it, Bill?" Hoping upon hope that it might be her imagination, she willed it to stop, but the smoke instead began to thicken and pour, as from a huge black boiling kettle. Orpha's heart sank knowing precious time would now be spent on repairs that could have been used to bring her to her sister's bedside.

"Damn," Bill muttered, as he pulled to the side of the road. Climbing from the car he popped the hood. Placing the propping rod in its niche, he disappeared beneath the hood for a quick look. Orpha sat on pins and needles, waiting— hoping it wouldn't be anything too serious.

"Well, that's that," Bill said, returning to let her know what the problem was. "It's a busted water hose, sweetheart. I'll have to see if I can flag someone down who can give us a push to the nearest garage—wherever the hell that is."

Bill slammed the door shut, then stood at the edge of the road waiting for a good Samaritan.

Orpha observed him through the window as he hunched his broad shoulders while lifting his collar about his ears, then tilted his hat down over his forehead to keep the light mist that now saturated the air at bay.

"Come on! Come on!" she said out loud, looking both ways up and down the road hoping for anyone at all to stop and help. She could see a car finally coming toward them, but still at a good distance, and she watched as it began to slow down and pull to a stop across the highway from where Bill stood.

With the driver's side window cracked open, she could hear Bill yell out, "Hey, Mac, can you give a hand?"

"Sure, what's the trouble?" the man called back.

"Busted water hose. Would you mind giving a push?"

"Nah, be right with ya." The driver proceeded down the road a short way, turning around to come up behind the Lincoln, and with Bill's direction matched bumpers for the push to town.

The distance to the next town was only a couple of miles at the most but the bumping, stopping, and starting was unnerving for Orpha. She was in such a hurry and felt that everything possible was getting in the way of her reaching her destination.

They finally stopped in front of what appeared to be a large, two-car garage. It was covered with old gray tar siding and the doors seemed to be missing altogether. Junkers sat about like ornaments. After stepping from the car, Bill, with Orpha following close behind, walked to the driver's side of their benefactor's car. "Thanks pal," Bill said, giving the man a five-dollar bill and shaking his hand.

"Sure thing," he answered, and with a jaunty salute turned his car around and left.

After leaving the car with the mechanic Bill and Orpha made their way to a small, nearby diner, where they ordered hamburgers and coke.

The meal was eaten without much conversation, the silence punctuated with the exchange of an occasional brief smile. They finished eating about the same time the repairman walked in announcing, "It's ready to go!"

Pleased that it hadn't taken as much time as she thought it might, Orpha beamed a smile of gratitude and thanks.

Bill paid the mechanic, shook his hand, which left no doubt as to what he did for a living, and once again they were on the road.

It was close to two thirty when the sign on the outskirts of Bald Knob announced they had finally arrived.

"Thank God!" Orpha sighed.

The skies had cleared and the sun was shining brightly, throwing reflections of puffy white clouds on the scattered puddles about the filling station where they had stopped for directions.

The dirt road that they were told to follow ran along the now-swollen river, and was all but hidden beneath shallow water. Bill drove slowly and hung to the tall weeds lining the opposite side. The road then angled upward slightly as it moved away from the riverbank.

"That must be it there," Bill said, nodding at the house sitting a little beyond the curve ahead of them. They could see what appeared to be a large chicken coop badly in need of repair, and back from that a short distance an outhouse with the door unhinged and leaning partially against the opening. From behind the house, snakes of smoke rose slowly from a low-burning trash pile that had obviously been collecting for a long time.

The house itself looked like it had been thrown up in a hurry. It was a crude rectangular thing in which some of the holes cut for windows carried glass while others were covered with cardboard. A makeshift wooden porch with no railing ran across the front where a frail figure of a woman sat unmoved by the approaching company. She continued to push her rustic rocking chair with unbroken rhythm. Once they had pulled to a full stop she looked directly at them but did not speak nor did she budge. She kept rocking—slowly—as if in a trance.

Leaving the car Orpha and Bill walked cautiously to where the spectral figure sat by way of thin, springy wooden planks that had been thrown across deep mud puddles. While the boards helped, water still gushed over their surface and seeped into the soles of their shoes.

"Howdy, could you tell us, is this the Murphy home?" Bill asked the old woman.

No answer.

Lacking any expression she stared ahead for a moment then turned her head from them, looking in another direction.

"Granny's not talking of late," a child's voice said. The voice hesitated and then continued, "Youns looking fer Mary Barber?"

The chubby blond boy went on talking as he came around the side of the house and stood in full view now. "She's not here anymore, you know," he said, his voice heavy with sadness. His hands tucked deep into his jimmy-alls he stood quietly, swaying slightly from side to side. His large blue eyes seemed to blink back his tears. He then turned around, disappearing as quickly as he had arrived.

"Bill . . . ?" Orpha felt panic taking over and fear that maybe they were too late after all.

"Hang on, honey," he said, trying to calm her as she joined him at the front door left slightly ajar. "Anyone home?" Bill called, knocking hard enough that the door opened even further. Then suddenly it flung open.

"Yeah, what d'ya want?" snarled a tall, thin, rumpled man. He had a large lump in the side of his jaw to match the bobbing Adam's apple in his scrawny throat.

"We're looking for Mary Barbara Murphy?"

The man in the doorway softened his expression as he wiped with the back of his hand the brown spit that had escaped his lips. She's at the hardware store, waiting for her folks to come. "You them?" he asked.

"That's right. Can you tell us where this hardware store is?"

The man ignored Bill's question.

"She was a good girl. Hard worker, by golly. Never set still," he said, his head down, moving slowly from side to side in retrospection.

Orpha struggled with her emotions, the tears leaving her eyes without permission. The word—*was*—screamed her sister was dead.

He stepped back from the doorway. "Wanna come in? Lily, put a pot on!" the man yelled over his shoulder.

"Nah, thanks, we better get down there."

227

"Did you say she's at a hardware store?" Orpha broke in.

"Yup, that's as close to a funeral parlor as we can git down here."

Orpha's knees felt weak and her mind froze.

Back in the car Bill reached for her, wrapping his arms about her, kissing her on the forehead while he held her in close. "Honey, I'm sorry. I wish I could take your pain from you."

"Me too," she sobbed softly in his chest. "Me too."

A brief stillness steeped in wrenching pain filled the car.

"I'm sorry," she whispered, sitting up straight as she wiped away her tears. "We should go now. Maybe there's a phone there. I have to get hold of Mama and Arline. Why didn't these people let us know sooner? I can't believe they are so stupid that they couldn't tell when a person is dying."

Her anger at not being allowed to say goodbye to her sister took over.

"That place—from what I could see just standing in the doorway—looked like a damn tomb. She was buried before she died," Orpha said bitterly, tears welling up again.

She was remembering the bright daylight that forced its way through the dirty little window at the shack that showed its rank condition. It would have been a death trap for any sick person.

"Don't those hillbillies know what soap and water is. No excuse for filth like that. That's not being poor, that's just downright lazy. Why would they live like that?"

"Sweetheart, take it easy," Bill coaxed.

"Easy for you to say, it wasn't your sister."

No sooner had she spat it out, she could have bit her tongue.

228

"Oh God, Bill. I'm sorry. I don't mean to take it out on you. I really let Mary Barbara down. Where was I when she needed me?"

Bill took Orpha's hand, touching it to his lips.

"It's okay," he said, as he spoke softly through her fingers. "It's okay."

He held her hand gently on the seat between them as he drove from the shack back toward town.

* * *

While the heavy, red-velvet drape served well the purpose of blocking off the room, it appeared to Orpha that it might have been taken from the stage of an old theater, the gold fringe tarnished and barely hanging on to the edges of the fabric. Bill lifted the draping to one side, allowing them to pass through.

"Mama!" Orpha exclaimed in surprise. She hurried to the casket where Ruth and Arline already stood. They turned about as she approached giving forced smiles and quick embraces.

Orpha avoided looking directly at her dead sister lying before her. She was trying to ease into what she knew she must confront, but not just yet.

"How did you get here so fast," Orpha inquired, being very glad to see them.

"The first train out, a zephyr I think," Arline said softly.

The three of them stood side by side now facing the casket, and, as if on cue, they made the sign of the cross on themselves, bowing their heads together in prayer.

Orpha finished her prayers, raising her head slowly to closely observe Mary Barbara for the first time since entering the room.

She appeared to be sleeping peacefully, and Orpha detected what she thought might be a smile on her sister's face, along with a darkening by her eyes and on her forehead. The thought came to her that perhaps they were not as good at preparing the dead down here as in a large city.

"I'm sorry, Mary Barbara. I should have made a point of checking on things when we did not hear from you for so long. Maybe I could have helped you in some way."

Tears of guilt filled her eyes and she forced herself away from her sister's casket, taking a seat in the front row.

Once the service was over and they rose to leave, Orpha noticed for the first time that the room was packed. Even standing room was next to nil.

It was while they sat waiting for the last person to leave the wake that Arline informed Orpha that Mama had found out what Mary Barbara died of.

"They thought she had cancer," Arline spoke in a hushed tone, "but what it turned out to be was a severe infection caused by a botched-up abortion."

"Why didn't she call one of us or give word that she was so sick? She knew we would have come, had she only let us know," Orpha said—with a tinge of confused anger as her voice rose.

"She was probably too ashamed," Ruth said, matter of factly. "And the way you girls were raised, I dare say she should have been."

"Mama! What a thing to say for God's sake," Arline scolded.

"You know very well I'll miss my daughter," Ruth went on, "but to do something like that is not only a mortal sin, it's also asking for trouble. I don't care what anyone says."

"Did you ever?" Orpha murmured to herself, not wanting her mother to hear. For although she was feeling anger and sorrow for her dead sister, she decided this was not the time or place to argue with what appeared to be Ruth's cold detachment.

"Have either of you heard anything of Bobby?" Orpha asked.

"Well," Ruth spoke up, "whoever that person was that called to let me know Mary Barbara had died and that she would be held over until we arrived, mentioned that perhaps I might be thinking about taking him back with me. It seems his father left the night his mother died and they haven't seen or heard from him since. But, to be honest, I really don't know how I could possibly even consider that, with working and all."

Bill, who, up to this point, had been standing quietly, now broke into the conversation.

"You know, if the boy needs a home and Orpha wants him to live with us, he's more than welcome. Plenty of room out there."

Orpha smiled a loving smile.

"Thanks, Bill," she said, leaning into the side of him as she looped her arm through his.

"What a guy," Arline chimed in. "But if there's anything I can do, let me know. Maybe I can give a hand on a weekend when I have time off, but like Mama I have to work as often as I can just to keep my head above water."

"Well then it's settled. The boy will go back with us. I've got a feeling he'll fit right in," Bill said.

"Without a question," Orpha answered. "The kids will be tickled to see him again."

The funeral procession made its way to the top of a hill in what appeared to be a very old cemetery. Many small stone markers made up the uneven rows of graves, along with what could be described as rugged hand-carved crosses that varied in size.

"We stand at the mouth of this grave that now holds the remains of a young woman who—in her short years on earth—had befriended all she met. She knew no strangers and held no malice in her heart for any man or beast, and if she did it was for the injustice she felt they were committing to another. I'm told she was slow to anger and quick to forgive. Now we know Mary Barbara sinned, we all do, it's a human thing to do, but we pray that God will forgive and welcome her into his kingdom. For we know she did the best she could with what she was given. Amen."

The pastor finished his short sermon, shook the hands of the people standing about, then gave a few words of encouragement to Mama, who was polite but not impressed.

Leaving was difficult for Orpha. As she glanced back she could see a small group of colored people moving slowly toward the grave to pay their respects. She understood they had to stand back until the white folks left. Just as they had to step off the sidewalk in town to let a white person pass, she remembered Mary Barbara saying how sad it made her to see people treated that way.

The solemn gathering carried beautiful handmade wreaths and crosses densely wrapped with what was called the seven sisters rose. It grew wild and abundantly in these parts on electric poles and any other place they could attach themselves to.

Mary Barbara had written her, mentioning the wild rose, as well as a black lady friend who lived somewhere near them. She spoke of how they had visited with each other from time to time, becoming friends. But for the love of Mike, Orpha could not think of her name at the moment.

The sun now hid behind an immense, dark cloud, while strong gusts of wind blew mournfully through a scattering of large old cemetery trees. With his hand at her elbow, Bill guided Orpha over the spongy, wet ground that allowed her heels to sink in as they made their way back to the car.

Orpha looked back over her mother's and sister's heads. Through the rear window she witnessed two men shoveling dirt into the grave as Mary Barbara's black friends laid their feelings in roses beside it—after which they stood in prayer.

The drive to the railway station was one of quiet reflection. Ruth and Arline disembarked without so much as a word. Only a wave of the hand and bleak smiles were exchanged.

Bill and Orpha once again made their way along the riverbank that would lead them back to the shack in hopes of finding and taking Mary Barbara's son home with them.

The old lady's heavy chair was empty and rocking back and forth in cadence with the wind that blew across the long porch.

After stepping out from the car they could hear a Victrola being played as loud as possible. "By the sweet by and by we shall meet on that beautiful distant shore." The words were familiar. Orpha remembered Floyd singing the song often, and it fit the occasion.

Bill pounded hard on the door as he had done earlier in the day. The music stopped abruptly. A few moments later the old lady stood before them in the doorway. Once again she said nothing. She stood looking at them, her face giving no indication of feeling for what had recently transpired in her home.

"Could we see Bobby? I'm Mary Barbara's sister. We would like to talk to him."

Turning away, Granny motioned to a woman standing near. Middle-aged and attractive in an earthy kind of way, her body was long and lean and she carried herself with the sureness of a striding cat as she walked toward them barefooted. Her cotton dress clung to the curves of a body that Orpha felt sure had put in hours of strenuous work. She appeared to be a visual contradiction of Mary Barbara's description for Lemvel's kin.

"Find the boy," the withered old woman snapped. Her voice—hard and harsh—unsurprisingly, matched her manner. "Bring 'um to these here folk," she said, motioning in their direction after which she disappeared into the next room.

"Not a very pleasant person is she?" Orpha offered.

The woman was back with Bobby in hand. He stood looking at them—his face dirty and gaunt, his eyes unrecognizing. He pulled back from Orpha as she reached for him. The woman still holding his hand forced him in front of her.

"Oh Bobby, don't you remember me? I'm your Aunt Orpha. I love you and I would never hurt you."

Backing away a bit she extended her hand. "Honey, do you remember Georgy, Theresa Ruth, or Ronnie? How about Donald and Raymond?"

His eyes flickered with interest and maybe some memory of the kids, she thought. It had been well over a year since they had seen him but hopefully he would adjust quickly once he spent a few days with them.

"He's a hurtin' badly you know with his mama being gone and all, God rest her sweet soul. And then his daddy hightailing it out of here that same night."

The woman spoke softly while resting her hands on Bobby's little shoulders.

"He likes staying out under that big old tree down yonder whar his daddy last set with him. I think maybe he's a hoping that's whar he's likely to come back to git him. But weuns know he won't likely be coming back for him anymore than the man in the moon."

"Well, if no one here objects, we'd like to take him with us," Orpha smiled as she once again reached for his hand.

This time he took hold as if he felt he could now trust her. He allowed Bill to pick him up, placing him on the seat between them where he sat rigid and quiet, until he finally gave in to sleep about an hour down the road.

"We're going to have to fatten this poor kid up," Bill said as he took a quick look at the sleeping boy slumped to one side of him. "What's even more important to me is to try to make him as happy as we can. What a tough start he has had, first his mother and then his dad."

"Bill, do you think Lemvel will ever come back?"

"I don't know the man, but if he loved her so much that he ran from the pain of her death, then maybe once he gets hold of himself he might. You never know with that kind of thing, honey. He might realize that this kid is all that's left of her. It's a tough call. But until that happens we'll do what we can to fill in for them. Are you getting hungry? We haven't eaten anything since this morning."

"No, not really," she smiled weakly, but we can stop whenever you want. "He should have something, maybe soup or a hot meal of some kind."

"Soup sounds good to me," Bill agreed. "We'll stop a little farther down the road. Maybe he'll be awake by then."

The weather had gotten progressively cooler as they left Arkansas. The jackets they wore when they left home and had shed once they arrived were put on once again as they went from the car to the restaurant. Picking up Bobby, Bill held him close to his chest, wrapping the coat that he was wearing about the small boy's frame in order to share his body heat as well his garment. Bobby did not resist and once inside ate whatever Orpha put in front of him. Still, he remained quiet and watchful, only shaking his head yes or no when prodded for an answer.

"Ahh, that's better," Bill said after finishing his last bite. "How about you, young man? Do you feel better now that you ate all that soup?"

Still holding his spoon Bobby looked up without raising his head and like a ray of sunshine his faint smile tickled them both.

"Oh, he does feel better!" Orpha gushed, as she gave his shoulders a quick hug.

The ride home seemed like it might never end. Orpha's discomfort was apparent and acute.

235

"Why don't you try to get a little shut eye?" Bill recommended. "He's sleeping, so don't worry about him," he said, nodding at the small boy curled up between them with his head resting on Orpha's lap. The quiet drone of the car was relaxing and hypnotic and she drifted off to sleep.

It seemed just a short time after that that Bill was gently calling to her.

"Orpha, wake up, we're here."

Laverne had left the front porch light burning for them along with the upstairs bathroom light for the kids. It was a sight that Orpha greatly appreciated at this moment.

"Oh, thank God," she groaned as she straightened up in the seat.

"Here, I'll get him," Bill said, scooping up the sleeping boy. "Gonna make it?" he asked.

"I'm fine," Orpha answered, still finding his constant concern a little strange, but appreciated.

She awoke the next morning as the daylight was streaming through the lacy sheers that hung from the large double windows. The agony of trying to escape into sleep the night before came rushing back followed by that empty feeling that set hard in the pit of her stomach. She remembered lying there it seemed for hours last night, seeing her sister's face every time she closed her eyes. Keeping them open didn't help much, for then Mary Barbara's image appeared everywhere in the moonlit room—on the wall, the ceiling, and even on the doorknobs.

She felt a tear escape. She touched it with her fingertip, saying, "I'm sorry. I'm very sorry. I'll miss you." She then spread the wet out from under her eye across her cheek.

Throwing back the covers she reached for her robe that lay nearby. Pulling it on she left the room and made her way carefully down the stairway. She could hear the children's voices coming from the playroom and once at the doorway she peered in. She found her two boys playing cars while Bobby, who had been bathed and dressed in some of Ronald's clothing, obviously a couple of sizes too large, sat on the floor nearby watching.

George called out to him. "Come on, Bobby, you can have one of my cars. Come on, don't you want to play?"

Orpha watched as he hesitated, then got up and went directly to where George was sitting and sat down next to him. Her oldest son, pushing a small toy car into Bobby's hand, told him, "You can have this. It can be yours, okay?" Bobby smiled and shook his head yes. He sat looking at his gift then leaned over and joined the play, pushing his toy about the floor.

Orpha was pleased with what she had witnessed and left them to play.

"Good morning, Laverne," she said upon entering the kitchen. "I'm sorry about sleeping so late. I really didn't mean to."

"That's no problem for me. I'm up anyhow and I'm certainly not seven months pregnant. And with what's been going on, you needed that sleep. How about some breakfast?"

"No, thanks, not right now. But I will have some coffee if there's any."

"Coming right up," Laverne said brightly.

"No, I can get it. You don't—"

"Sit," the older women interrupted, waving her down into her chair. "I'm right here. I can get it," Laverne assured Orpha as she poured the hot steaming liquid.

"Thank you," Orpha said putting the cup to her lips. She took a cautious sip, then placed it back on the table. After letting a few seconds of silence pass she declared, "You know, Laverne, that was the second worst day of my life. The first of course being the day I felt I had no choice but to put the children in the homes. I just had no idea how my sister was living. If only I had known. Oh, I knew they had lived in a barn for a short time but I was under the impression that things had gotten better after she went back."

"Orpha, don't beat yourself up. I don't know if I should say this but, my feeling is, there's a reason for everything that happens in each of our lives and it is for the most part out of our control. We are who we are and what we are because of where we have come from. What happens because of it is the end result and therefore fate. It's not always our decisions that affect us the most. So, caring about others sometimes brings great pain. But without taking a chance on loving others, life could be very empty."

Laverne's face now flushed a bit at her attempt to philosophize, in hopes of making the younger woman feel better about her bitter experience.

"Now let me get off of my soapbox and fix you some kind of food. You're eating for two, you know," she teased.

"Well, maybe just some juice and toast," Orpha said, giving in to Laverne's insistence that she must eat something.

"Were the kids any problem this morning?"

"Not at all. They were surprised to find their little cousin, but just the same they were pleased. He seems to be as frightened as a little rabbit, poor baby."

"Well, I don't know how much Bill had a chance to tell you before he left this morning, but Bobby's father fled after my sister died and no one has heard from him since. I can't make up my mind if I should be mad at him or feel sorry for him."

"What a shame. Maybe he'll come looking for his son in time."

"I don't know, Laverne, they live so different down there. They don't seem to have any gumption or desire to do any better than what they have, and that's a four-room shack with no furniture at all from what I could see in the living room. A huge pile of dirty clothes built up high on the wall in a corner. The filth and stench you would find hard to believe. Now I know Mary Barbara was not too fussy about her appearance but I also know without a doubt she would never live in a place like that without trying to clean it up. She had to be sick for a long spell and didn't want to call us, until finally things got really bad for her, but by then, of course it was too late."

A short silence followed. Orpha broke it with, "You know, I'm so pleased with Bill. It was his idea to bring Bobby back with us. It's not enough that he has my three but now he has my sister's son, too."

"He's a good man, tenderhearted. No question about it," Laverne praised as she joined Orpha in a cup of coffee. "He now has that family he has always wanted, maybe not expecting them in such a lump, but nonetheless he seems to like it. This morning before he left he said a goodbye to each and every one of them kids, letting them know he would be seeing them later and to be good. He wanted me to tell you he would give you a call later today."

"Good, what time did he leave? I didn't hear a thing."

"Well, he didn't appear to be in any rush, took his time. I'd say around eight. The kids were up long before."

Orpha said nothing more about Mary Barbara that morning. She felt miserable enough without talking about and rehashing her pain. Being a cry baby is not how she wanted Laverne to think of her.

Lunchtime had come and gone before the telephone finally rang. "I'll get it," Orpha called out as she hurried to answer what she knew was Bill's promised call.

"Hello?"

"Say kid, how ya doin'?" The voice was one she hadn't heard for some time.

"Floyd, what do you want?"

239

"Wait, hold on. I just heard—"

"You just heard what?" Orpha said sharply, her irritation rising quickly to the surface.

"About Mary Barbara. Hey, I don't want any trouble. Just called to say I'm sorry to hear the news. We fought a lot, me and her. Almost as much as the two of us." His laugh sounded nervous and unsure. "But she was a good gal."

A tense moment passed. "Kids okay?" he asked, trying to make conversation.

"When did you start caring?" It was out before she could catch it.

"Hey, I do, but now you went and married yourself a sugar daddy and I don't have to worry do I?"

"Floyd, I've got to go. The kids are just fine." She dropped the receiver back into its cradle. Turning to leave, the phone rang again. "Damn him," she said to herself as she once again grabbed the telephone. "What?" she snapped into the mouthpiece.

"I'm in the doghouse without a clue. Where did I go wrong?"

"Bill? Oh jeez, that wasn't for you. I just hung up on Floyd. He called because he heard about Mary Barbara dying, and we got into it. I don't know why I let him get to me. He caught me by surprise."

"Well, are you ready for a little good news?" Bill asked, avoiding any conversation about his predecessor.

"I sure could use some," Orpha said, smiling now in anticipation. "What?"

"Well, everything is ready for the grand opening. I've set it up for New Year's Eve. We'll run a large ad in the papers plus hang a huge banner over the front entrance. What d'ya think?"

"Oh, Bill, it sounds exciting! The baby should be here by then, so maybe I'll be able to go with you."

"My intentions exactly," he confirmed, cheerfully. "So be prepared to dress to the teeth and stay out until sunrise. I'm looking forward to having you all to myself that night."

"It's a date. I can't wait! You won't change your mind, will you?" she teased.

"Not on your life, sweetheart. Well, better get going. See you when I get there."

"Bye, Bill. Thanks."

"For what?"

"Just for being there when I need you."

"That's what I want, angel, always to be there. Goodbye."

Fall merged with winter, and the frosted paintings on the windows throughout the house were a sign that the holidays were not far ahead.

Orpha could feel the baby stretching and kicking and growing stronger with every passing day.

Although this baby did not appear, from the size of her, anywhere as large as Ronnie, it was large enough to her liking. She was now in that familiar situation at night of trying to find a comfortable sleeping position, while the baby it seemed, chose that time to ball up or extend itself as far as possible across the entire width of her stomach.

She didn't really care at this point whether the baby was a boy or a girl, just that he or she was healthy and arrived as early as possible.

Thanksgiving dinner invitations had been extended via telephone and accepted by all. Mama and her new boyfriend, whom Orpha and Bill would be meeting for the first time, and, of course, Arline and her boys would be there.

The selection and preparation of the ill-fated turkey took place early the morning before Thanksgiving day, as Laverne sat with one leg on either side of a kitchen chair that had been pulled up to a galvanized wash tub, half full

241

of scalding water. She tugged at the feathers in between short dousings letting the feathers fall into the tub once freed from the large bird. Wide-eyed and full of questions, the four children watched with great interest.

"Can I help?" George asked.

"Sure," Laverne answered with a smile.

"Can I?" the others asked one after the other.

"Oh boy, what did I start?" Laverne said, laughing out loud. "I'll tell you what, Georgy, you can help pull feathers. But, mind you, watch out for the hot water. Ronnie you and Bobby can pick up the feathers that miss the tub, okay?"

"Okay!"

They accepted their job with glee.

"Theresa Ruth, you can keep an eye on the boys to make sure they don't miss any. How's that?"

"Okay!" the little girl responded seriously, as she placed one hand on each hip. "I'll watch them good."

Laverne let the feathers fly in all directions and the children worked hard at trying to keep up with their designated jobs, giggling and shouting as Theresa Ruth could be heard saying over and over again, "There's one, there's one."

After the last pinfeather was yanked, Laverne announced that now she must cut the turkey open and take out his insides.

Pushing her chair back she carried the naked fowl over to the sink and started running cold water over it. Without wasting a minute the boys quickly pulled up chairs to stand and watch the operation. They looked at Laverne, then at the huge knife she took from the drawer next to the sink.

Not a sound was heard until she cut into the bird. Then a small voice asked, "Does that hurt him?"

"No, it can't hurt him, silly, he's dead," George informed his younger sister.

The three boys remained watching but the little girl called out, "Ugh!" With the first handful of entrails that were pulled out, she promptly left the kitchen.

"What's that? What's that?"

The questions were asked repeatedly and answered directly.

"Gosh, there's lots of stuff in a turkey, huh?" George observantly remarked.

"Yes, there is," Laverne answered patiently, and some of these things we can use, like this here gizzard and liver and heart. We'll put that into the dressing."

"You gonna dress him up?" Ronnie asked. "No, honey, I'm going to make stuffing with bread and the parts that I just showed you, then I'll put it in here," she motioned to the cavity.

"In his butt," George grinned.

"Georgy!" Laverne scolded, then finished explaining to the other two. "And that's called dressing the bird."

Once the turkey had been readied short of the stuffing, it was covered with a clean, wet dishtowel and put into the icebox until time to roast it the following day.

"All right, boys, skedaddel!"

After helping them down from their perches on the chairs, Laverne shooed them out with the back of her hands.

"I've got to clean up now, so off with you until supper. Then tomorrow you can have all of that turkey you want," she called after them.

Very early the following morning, Orpha woke to an appetizing mixture of savory smells wafting through the house.

Everything had been scrubbed, polished, pressed, or waxed, and she was looking forward to the day that lay ahead. Her spirits high, she slipped quietly from her side of the bed so as not to wake Bill. He had his back to her but appeared to be sleeping soundly. She stood momentarily looking down at him, realizing this was something she didn't see often.

He had told her weeks before that he had made arrangements at both restaurants for them to run smoothly without him on the two holidays of the year that he felt should be spent with his family. Being a man of his word, there he was. She smiled at him as she put her robe on then left the room.

Holding on to the handrail she descended the staircase slowly, then made her way to the kitchen where Laverne had filled every available space with her wonderful pies, cakes, breads, and cookies.

"Hi, I see you're up to your old tricks again, not waking me just to keep me out of your way," Orpha teased as she entered the warm kitchen, basking in the spirit of the holiday. "What can I do to help?"

"Nothing right now, everything is under control."

"I wouldn't expect anything else. You're such a godsend," Orpha said, giving the woman a hug about the shoulders.

"Well, I don't know about that, but coffee's ready and so is one of those loaves of bread fresh from the oven."

"Oh boy! What a way to start the day! Your hot bread, with butter oozing into it. Just what a fat lady needs. Let me at it!" she laughed.

Sitting herself down she lingered over her freshly baked bread, not being in any big hurry at the moment. The kids didn't usually get up until somewhere between seven and eight o'clock and since it was only coming on six she figured she had a little time to visit and wake up slowly.

"You know," Orpha mused out loud as she sipped her coffee, "Bobby appears to be adjusting to everything pretty well aside from asking about his daddy come bed time. It just breaks my heart to have to keep telling him that someday he will come back. I know that's probably wrong but I can't take his hope from him too, with everything else he's lost."

"Well, you do what you can, and hope for the best, I guess," Laverne commented sympathetically. "He's such a cutie pie, with those big brown eyes and that sad little face. How could anyone not want him?" she asked as she bent over, opening the oven door, allowing a rush of heat and a savory whiff of roasting turkey to escape. I'd say he's a lucky kid to have you, Bill, and the little ones," she went on, basting the bird with the drippings that had collected in the roasting pan. Shutting the oven door, Laverne turned to Orpha. "No one knows," she smiled solemnly. "Only time will tell."

"But I can tell you this much. I've got to get that cranberry sauce going right now, so it has time to chill before the crowd gets here for dinner. Should have had that made yesterday."

Taking her last bite and washing it down with the swallow of coffee left in her cup, Orpha rose to leave. "Before I go I have to tell you, you make the best dang bread, I swear! Bar none! I could get as fat as a pig if I turned myself loose, and maybe this is not a good time to say that," she laughed, holding her arms out looking down at her very pregnant body.

Laverne joined her in laughing. "There should be a better way, shouldn't there?"

"Yes, wouldn't that be great? Letting the men have every other one, how about that?"

"Oooo, how painful could that be?"

They once again laughed together at their twisted humor.

"Better go get dressed while I have a bit of time to fuss. If you need me, give a call, okay?"

"Sure, take your time. Everything's on schedule here. So far, so good."

Quietly, Orpha turned the doorknob to their bedroom. Tiptoeing in, she glanced at her husband who appeared to still be sleeping. Going to the bedside, she bent over and kissed him very softly on his forehead, and as she was about to rise, his arms snatched her, bringing her down upon him. "Gotcha now, you wily little minx. Trying to kiss a poor helpless man as he sleeps, giving him no chance to kiss you back. Come here and take what you deserve."

"Cut it out," she giggled as he went for her neck. "Get away from there!" she screamed, laughing out loud. "You know I can't take that. It tickles too much. Cut it out, damn it!" They rolled about the bed laughing and taking turns at grabbing and fighting each other off.

"Shhh, we're going to wake the kids and I'm not dressed yet."

"Well than, I guess we'll have to wrestle and be quiet at the same time," he whispered in her ear, as he held her close.

"You know I would like nothing better than to make love to you, don't you? I'm sure we can figure something out. What would you suggest?"

"No, I can wait. I don't want to take a chance on making any kind of problems."

"Bill, you can't hurt anything as long as we're careful."

"Nah, my dreams and memories of our times together will do for a few weeks, just let me hold you."

They lay together quietly, Bill pressing his lips gently to her ear. "I love you so much, but then you already know that."

"Yes, you have more than proven that," she answered, softly.

Minutes went by in silence.

"Bill, have you thought of what you might want to name this baby?"

"I thought that was your job," he chuckled.

"No, it's our job," she smiled back.

"Umm, let me think. How about Mortimer Snerd if it's a boy, Daisy Mae if it's a girl?"

"Oh my gosh, if that's the best you can do I think maybe I'll have to do it on my own," she scoffed as she pushed at him while leaving his side.

"Hey, sweetheart, just razzing you some. We have plenty of time yet to pick a name. What's the hurry?" he asked, propping himself up on his elbow, watching her scurry about getting ready. "God, you're gorgeous."

"You really think I believe that?"

"Hey, you are to me. Look in the mirror, just for a minute."

She stopped brushing her hair, looking straight ahead into her dressing table mirror, as he had requested.

"See how you glow? Such radiance," he now teased.

"You make me sound like a darn light bulb," she laughed.

As the morning progressed, everything fell into place. The kids were up dressed, fed, and playing. Laverne was busy putting the finishing touches on the meal in the kitchen as Orpha snapped the large white starched table cloth open across the dining room table.

They had never eaten in this room before. She felt its special atmosphere. Taking the two silver candlesticks from the sideboard, she placed them in the center of the table, stepping back to admire them. They were very heavy, very tall, and gleamed with a magnificent luster.

Things like these had not been in her life until now. She delighted in admiring them. The silverware came next and then the crystal and china—how beautiful they were. According to Laverne they had been in Bill's family for generations.

Orpha grew just a little nervous at the thought of the children using these family heirlooms. Maybe she should use everyday dishes for them until they were older. But after placing a cloth napkin at each setting and backing up once again to look over the table she decided it was too pretty for kitchen dishes. She promised herself she would watch the children closely.

Walking around the table she doublechecked to make sure she had not forgotten anything. Once satisfied she walked over to one of the three long, heavy-draped windows and stood peering out at the ominous gray sky that accentuated the dark filigree of the tree's barren branches moving slightly in the cold November wind. She watched as five birds sitting at the very top of one tree appeared to have been skewered by the treetops until one by one they flew away.

The quiet beauty of the downy white snow that had fallen late last night still clung in the crooks and the smallest recesses of the trees, while it spread softly on the ground and bushes alike. Just then something moving off to the left snagged her attention. Looking closer, she felt a tinge of excitement. "Oh my gosh, they're here!" she said out loud.

A car was steadily moving up the driveway, and Orpha could just barely make out her sister and mother.

"Bill, they're here!" she called into his den as she passed by the open door to the front entrance. Hearing the car doors slam, she checked her reflection in the hall mirror one last time.

Not waiting for the sound of the doorknocker Orpha pulled the front door wide open. "Happy Thanksgiving! Come on in! It's too cold out there to wait for someone to answer your knock," Orpha said, gleefully explaining her premature arrival, then stepping to the side to make room for them to enter.

"Here, let me take your coats," Bill offered, appearing just in time to assist. "You boys ready for a big turkey dinner?" he asked, putting his hand on Donald's head and rumpling his hair.

"Hey, you guys!" Georgy called as he ran to the front door followed by a small entourage of noisy children.

"Wanna play?" Ronnie asked the boys as they were still in the process of shedding their coats.

"Sure," Raymond answered.

"Come on! Let's go!" Georgy encouraged, as they all ran rambunctiously down the hallway, disappearing into the playroom.

"Bill, Orpha, this is Ed Harding. Ed, my daughter and her husband."

The men shook hands as Orpha smiled her hello.

A nice-looking man, very well dressed, but nowhere near as good-looking as the pictures she remembered seeing of her father. Orpha found herself comparing this stranger with her father whom she couldn't even clearly recall.

As dinner progressed she learned that aside from being quite religious he was charming in a salesman kind of way. Which, indeed, was exactly what he was. Nice enough, but something about him—the British accent, his flashing smile—appeared not to ring true. She had heard all kinds of stories growing up about traveling salesmen, and none were too flattering. Combined with his dark good looks, her biased opinion was not weakened any.

It was perfectly clear that Mama was nuts about him. She hung on his every word, constantly bragging on something he had done or was doing, touching him it seemed every chance she got. Arline, at one point, shot her sister a look of, can you believe this? They had never seen Ruth this caught up with a man before.

The day and dinner were a great success for Orpha. Laughing and happy chatter filled the large room. The only bad moment was during grace when Bill sadly spoke of Mary Barbara being with them in spirit. And Orpha knew in her heart this was true as she glanced down the table at her sister's small son who had followed suit with the other kids and had his little hands pressed together and his head bowed for prayer.

Christmas Day had been mentioned during mealtime, with an invitation for all to return to celebrate together.

Ed thanked them graciously, but said that he wasn't sure that he could make it but would try his best.

"Of course, he'll make it," Mama chimed in, her face beaming. "How could he not spend Christmas with me?"

"We'll see, my dear, we'll see," he chuckled as he playfully pinched her cheek.

"Anyone for dessert?" Laverne asked, breaking into the amorous display. The response from the children was exactly what she had hoped for.

"Yeah!" they all shouted loudly together, while everyone laughed at their noisy exuberance.

The lingering at the table after dinner was pleasant, lasting for some time until Ed slapped his hands together proclaiming that aside from the fact that he had been treated royally, fed like a king, it had alas come time for them to leave. "What do you say blossom? We really should head back to the city."

"Yes, I suppose you're right. It's a long ride back and already getting dark," Ruth conceded. "Arline, are you ready?"

"Well, no, Mama. But I will be as soon I get the boys together."

"Here, let me give you a hand," Orpha offered, rising from her seat, as Arline got up to retrieve Donald and Raymond from the other room.

"'Blossom'? Can you believe that?" Orpha snickered, bumping into her sister's side as they walked down the hall toward the playful noises of the children.

250

"Oops, pardon me, blossom," she mocked. "Didn't mean to bruise your petals!" The women laughed, tickled with their mother's being referred to as a flower.

"A daisy, maybe, or two-lips?" Arline punned, getting sillier as she puckered her lips forward, both of them laughing even harder.

"Come on, behave," Orpha implored, obviously still pleased with their sardonic humor.

"Okay, kids, time to go," Arline announced.

"Aww," Donald objected.

"Come on, come on, let's go! You've had all day long! Gramma and Mr. Harding are ready to leave and unless you want to walk all the way home you had better make it snappy."

"Aw, gee," Raymond echoed his brother.

"Come on! Now!" Arline said, growing impatient, clapping her hands at her sons.

"Bye, you guys," Georgy called out as his two small cousins left the room. "See you later."

"Okay, see you later," Donald called back from the hallway.

"That was a great meal. I ate way too much, but probably will be wishing in a day or two that I had eaten more," Arline told her sister as they hugged each other goodbye.

"Well, the credit belongs to Laverne. She's a great cook among many other things," Orpha confessed.

"Well, do tell her for us it was delicious," Mama added.

"Yes sir," by all means, Ed added cheerfully as he was the last one out the door.

"Bye, kids," Orpha called out as she waved to them. "Bye, Mama."

"What a nice day, don't you think so Bill?" she asked as he closed the door behind their departing company.

251

"Sweetheart, couldn't have been better, except—"

"Why, what was wrong?" she asked, looking at him with great concern.

"I never got my dessert."

"What?"

"I'm still waiting for my holiday treat," Bill said, his green eyes now twinkling.

"I've developed a large problem, something like an unrelenting itch, that needs to be scratched," he joked, as he wrapped his arms about her, laying a firm kiss on her mouth. Then pulling her into him he whispered in her ear, "I know I said it's okay, but for some reason, maybe it's just being with you all day, I would like to be even closer."

Standing on her toes, she took his face gently in her hands. "Just because I'm as big as a house does not mean I can't feel what I felt before I got this way. And I promise, just as soon as we get the kids tucked in . . . Wait for me?" she smiled.

"Sweetheart, wild horses couldn't drag me away."

Chapter Eighteen

As the days followed slowly one by one, winter really set in, with more snow than usual. Two full-blown blizzards already and hardly into the first week of December. With all but the main roads closed, Bill had decided to stay in the city for a few days, in hopes of the weather clearing. "Let's pray he gets back before the baby decides to come. It would be a dirty shame for him to miss that," Orpha said, earnestly conveying her concern while she and Laverne moved from room to room doing morning chores.

"Planning to have the baby at home?"

"Yes, I was kind of thinking along those lines."

"Don't you think the hospital would be a better place to have the child? That way if there's any problem it would be—"

"You're right, but if I have it here, I don't have to be away from the kids. And I thought that then they could see him or her sooner than if we were stuck in the hospital for so long. I did have the other three with home delivery," Orpha said, neglecting to mention the rough time she had giving birth to Ronnie.

"Well, I'll tell you what. If this kind of weather keeps up, you, me, and God will have to do the best we can if that baby does decide to come. Radar's wife, Mame, is the midwife in these parts. She knows her business, by golly. I've assisted her a few times in the past. She should have gone to medical school, which is easier said than done I understand. But if need be, and she could make her way down here, it probably would be a snap being it's not your first, aside from the pain of course," she allowed with a sheepish grin.

"Well, I kind of like that idea. I'll talk to Bill to see what he thinks. You know, it's awful quiet down there," Orpha commented on not hearing a sound as she turned her ear to the direction of the stairway.

"I'll go take a look-see," Laverne said, smiling. "No telling what those scalawags are up to." But before she could turn to leave the bedroom, chilling screams of "Mommy, Mommy" pierced their ears.

"Oh my God," Orpha said in sheer horror. She tore past Laverne, taking the stairs as fast as her pregnant body would allow, tripping halfway down and landing hard at the bottom. The children were still screaming as she, with some help from Laverne, pulled herself up. Cradling her belly with her right arm as she ran down the hall, her heart leaped at the flashing images of fire that could be seen on the wall opposite the kitchen doorway.

The two oldest stood huddled in a corner screaming in unison as the women entered the now brightly lit room. The morning's crumpled newspaper was burning like a huge torch on the surface of the cooking stove, its ashes floating upward. Laverne quickly lifted the lids, shoving the burning paper down inside with the poker. The smoke now filled the room and the hall, filtering throughout the rest of the house.

"Are you all right?" Orpha yelled above the frightened, screaming twosome, checking them over, then hugging them tightly. "What in the world made you do such a stupid thing? she scolded, shaking each of them by the arm as she led them down the hall, her fear having turned to anger mixed with relief. Letting them loose, she gave each a whack on the rear. "Now get upstairs to your rooms and don't come down until I tell you to, understand? March!"

Georgy's eyes were large with hurt and fear but his mouth was set and she could see he had made up his mind not to cry. But his sister wasn't at all shy about displaying her feelings. "I'm sorry. I'm sorry, Mommy," she lamented, as she tried to get her short little legs to take the steps quickly, stumbling just enough that her brother stopped momentarily, taking her hand and helping her the rest of the way. Once at the top, they turned to face their mother.

"Go now, both of you," she ordered in an unforgiving manner.

Letting go of Theresa Ruth's hand, Georgy walked slowly into his and Ronnie's room and closed the door quietly behind him. The little girl tore into her room, leaving the door wide open.

"She was sobbing as though she'd been beaten," Orpha commented to Laverne after returning to the kitchen. And just look at these two. A smile now crossed her face as she noticed her youngest son and his small cousin who had both found a safe, warm place in Laverne's lap. "And where were you during the fire, may I ask?"

"Being good boys, weren't you?" Laverne asked, looking down at them as they munched their cookies. "They wandered in right after you took the other two in hand. I guess they weren't quite old enough to be included in the scheme of things."

"Are you all right? You're flinching."

"I'll be fine," Orpha said. "Took a harder fall than I thought. A few small twinges but nothing to worry about," she assured Laverne as she began closing the kitchen windows that had been opened to clear the smoke away.

"Might be a good idea for you to go lie down for awhile just to be on the safe side."

"Nah, I don't think it's necessary, but I will sit for a minute. Oh boy, I think we have a problem after all."

"What? What's wrong?"

"My water just broke."

"Ronnie, Bobby, get down. Go play! Shoo! Into the playroom with you."

While leaving the room obediently, the boys looked back only for a second while clearing the kitchen doorway.

"Here comes a contraction. Oh . . . it's a strong one. I had better get upstairs."

256

"Grab hold of me. I'll give you a hand. We just might be doing this on our own. I'll try to get hold of Mame. Can't believe we were just talking about this."

"God, let everything be all right?" Orpha asked openly as they slowly made their way up the stairs.

"You're a good strong girl. No reason for any problems. The three of us will do just fine. As soon as we get you bedded down, I'll call Bill. I know he'll try moving heaven and earth to get here, but I wouldn't count on it. I'll be back in a flash," Laverne said, leaving Orpha to undress and lie down.

Now centered in the large bed, Orpha waited for the next pain that would bring her new son or daughter closer to his or her arrival. Relaxing as much as possible, she had almost dozed off, when brief spasms started, following one after the other. Then shortly thereafter she could feel a hard one coming and she let out a loud moan when it hit with full force.

"The baby's coming! It's coming now!" she called out in the midst of her pain. "Laverne, hurry," Orpha cried out, her voice muffled by the next long contraction.

She could feel the head crowning, and that enormous pressure was once again made familiar to her as she pushed with the baby.

"It's okay, I'm here. Relax when you can."

Laverne yanked the sheets from the foot of the bed, flipping them up over Orpha's knees. "Oh my gosh, the baby is here! Come on, Orpha! One big push will do it! Bring her on! One two three push!" Laverne said, loudly.

Orpha bore down with all she had, then feeling the baby leave her body she let out a long sigh of relief.

"Well, looky here what we have, a brand new beautiful baby girl." And as if on cue the baby started crying on her own.

"Is she okay? Is everything there? Fingers, toes?"

"Everything she will ever need," Laverne said, smiling as she cut and knotted the umbilical cord. Then cupping the baby in her hands, she held her in such a way that Orpha could see her.

"Let me clean her up, then you can have her. She is absolutely beautiful. Bill will be so proud. He's on his way! Won't he be tickled pink? Here you go, your brand new daughter, who looks just like her mother—dark hair and all." Laverne smiled broadly as she placed the screaming baby in her mother's arms.

"Have you decided on her name?" Laverne asked as she busied herself with sponge bathing Orpha and freshening her surroundings.

"No, I'll let him do that when he gets here," she grinned. "If he can get here."

"It may take him awhile, but I'd bet my life on it."

With a little coaxing at the breast the baby began nursing, and the room was quiet once again. Laverne left with the soiled linens and checked on the children.

"Well, let's take a good look at you, little girl." With her free hand Orpha unfolded the blanket from the infant a little at a time exposing her small, slender legs and feet. Her body was longer than expected but well nourished, and the navel had a good, tight, close knot, thanks to Laverne. Once satisfied that everything was as it should be, she once again covered her baby, gazing down at her while she vigorously nursed. She would pull with her tiny mouth for a bit then would stop as if to let things settle, then start again. The soft tugging at her nipple seemed to, as with the other children, bind them even closer. "We'll make it, won't we, sweetheart? she spoke softly. "All of us together will make a good life and love each other." Closing her eyes, Orpha fell to sleep, tired from her unexpected, though very fast delivery.

She awoke to find Bill sitting next to the bed holding the baby in his arms with a grin spread across his face.

"How's my girl?" he asked, raising the baby slightly upward in his embrace. "She's almost as beautiful as her mother," he beamed. Standing up, he leaned over, kissed Orpha on the mouth, and looking into her eyes, asked, "Are you all right?"

"I'm fine," she smiled back. "Just a bit surprised. I think my spill down the stairs got things going, but I'm fine."

"Good, glad to hear it. Sorry I didn't make it in time. The roads have cleared some but travel is still very slow. Have you named her?"

"No, I thought you might have something in mind," Orpha offered, cheerfully.

"Well, I'm not prepared for this, but the first name that comes to mind is Denise after my mother who has been gone for some time now. Or Kathleen, just because it's a good Irish name. She looks like a Katie to me," he mused as he looked down at his daughter. "Yep," he smiled, "Kathleen."

A light rapping on the bedroom door caused them to look up. The door opened slowly, after which the children were led into the room by Laverne. "We came to see our new baby girl," she announced.

Theresa Ruth hurried to Bill's side peering into the baby's face. "She's little, like a dolly. Will she get big?"

"Yeah, she's real little," George observed, standing at the side of Bill's chair.

Ronny said nothing, but cautiously put his finger on Katie's cheek, then quickly pulled it back and smiled up at Bill. Bobby stood by the foot of the bed quietly. Noticing the boy, Bill said, "Come here, son." The child moved to where he could see the tiny newcomer, and as if a light had been turned on inside, his face lit up with a big smile.

"Baby," he said softly.

"Yes," Bill answered. "She belongs to all of us, you know. But for right now we'll give Katie back to her mommy and we will all go downstairs so they can rest."

The days quickly slipped by. A normal daily routine was formed and methodically followed. Although Christmas was fast approaching, Orpha had not found the time to make preparations or think of shopping for gifts, but she promised herself next week for sure, for it was already beyond the middle of December.

That following weekend as she had hoped and at Bill's insistence they hit the stores downtown, enjoying the rush and excitement of last-minute shopping and time spent alone. They separated at one point, allowing time to purchase a gift for each other. Orpha knew exactly what she wanted for Bill. A fine white Meerschaum pipe and a humidor. She had no idea what he would be buying for her, but when he returned he was empty-handed. She noticed, but said nothing. Throughout the day trips to the car had to be made in order to unload their arms. At last they made their final trip back to their car and were ready to head for home.

Traffic was heavy leaving the city. "It looks as though everyone has gotten a late start with their Christmas shopping," Orpha commented. "Do you think they all just had babies?" she asked, laughing at her own silliness while scooting in close to her husband's side. Both fell quiet as they moved from the crowded streets to the outskirts of town and then to country roads. Orpha nodded off, thinking, "Precious things come in small packages," and then, as if the rest had to be said, "and so does poison."

"I must really be tired," she mused, closing her eyes with her head resting on Bill's upper arm.

It was Christmas Eve. Laverne's breads, pies, and dozens of Christmas cookies were on display throughout the kitchen. She had the children lined up, kneeling on chairs at the table. As she went from one to the next, helping them create their own special cookies, she appeared to enjoy it more than they did.

"She is such a help," Orpha commented to Bill. "What would we do without her?" They watched her from the doorway, patiently helping the noisy, energetic youngsters who appeared to have more of what they were doing on themselves than on the large kitchen table.

The small white plastic radio on the counter was blaring out "Jingle Bells" and it seemed to be reverberating from every room in the house as they turned to leave the scene in the kitchen to begin sorting and wrapping gifts. A loud banging at the rear door added to the holiday hubbub that already filled the air. Bill hurried to answer it, with Orpha close on his heels.

The door was wide open and framing Radar with what appeared to Orpha to be the largest Christmas tree she had ever seen.

"Oh, Radar! It's a beautiful tree! It's so big!" Orpha exclaimed. "Will it fit through the door?" she asked, laughing out loud.

The kids came running to see what was going on, with flour and cookie dough caked and clinging to their hands and faces and smeared about their clothing.

"Wow!" George said, loudly.

"Yeah, wow!" Ronnie agreed.

"Come on, kids! Out of the way, now!" Laverne said, coaxing them away from the door.

"Here, let me give a hand," Bill offered as he grabbed the trunk and led the way with everyone following. "Where do you want this monster," he inquired, looking at Orpha.

"In the front window, where else?" Orpha lightly replied.

"Where else?" George echoed, earning a look from Laverne.

Once the majestic pine was solidly anchored in place the children stood spellbound as its fragrance saturated the room.

"Wow, that's a big Christmas tree," George declared. "Isn't it, Ronnie?"

"Yeah," the younger brother answered, "the biggest."

"It will really be beautiful once we decorate it, won't it?" Laverne interjected. "But right now we had better get back to business in the kitchen. Come on, let's go! Get in line!"

Laverne spun around on her heel and the manner in which she left the room tickled and amused Orpha. For she appeared to be the pied piper of Hamelin, with the kids following behind as they sang, "Oh you better watch out, you better not pout, you better not cry I'm telling you why, Santa Claus is coming to town."

Turning to Radar, Orpha smiled, appreciatively. "We want to thank you, Radar. You have a great knack for picking the best of the trees."

"Well, it's an easy job. I pick from many, can't miss."

"Did you see the children's eyes when you brought it in? They were so excited. Just watching them during the holidays is something else. Of course, Katie is a bit young this year, but next year she too will be able to enjoy the tree."

"How is the little one? The missus was sorry she couldn't help out but sometimes things ain't meant to be. Maybe when you folks are up to it we can come meet her."

"Sure, tell your wife anytime."

"Come on over for coffee and a visit," Bill piped in. "And bring the kids. They can all get together."

"I'll do that. Got to be heading home. Christmas Eve you know is our big day and the family will be waiting for me. So, a Merry Christmas to you all."

"Hold on, just a minute," Bill directed as he hurried from the room, returning with an envelope. Handing it to Radar, he explained, "A gift to the best right-hand man anyone could have. Merry Christmas to you and yours! Thanks for all of your hard work around here!"

Radar's face brightened with appreciation. "Thank you," he said, smiling broadly and bowing a bit as he took the gift. He waved his final goodbye with a short flapping of the white envelope. "Be seeing you folks. Have a good Christmas," his voice called back as he went out the back door.

The remainder of the day was spent wrapping gifts and decorating the tree with the children, the highpoint being when Bill lifted Theresa Ruth for the placing of the star on the top of what they all agreed was the most beautiful Christmas tree they had ever seen.

"It's snowing, it's snowing!" Theresa Ruth shouted excitedly as she was being lowered from her position next to the top of the tree.

"Well, by golly, it is! Would you look at that! It looks like a white Christmas is on its way!" Bill announced enthusiastically.

Looking out, Orpha could see huge white flakes floating down as though they were feathers, searching for a place to land.

"Oh boy!" George said as he and the other two boys raced to the large window. "We can build a big snowman again."

The remaining lower half of their first creation from a couple of weeks ago could still be seen—an uneven lump sitting in the front yard with the stocking cap half embedded somewhere near the top.

"Bill? Who is that?"

"Who? I don't see anyone."

"Down at the very end of the driveway," Orpha said.

"I don't know. Can't see him too clearly. He's too far away yet. The walk's not familiar."

They all stood waiting for the man to come closer.

"What? Who is it?" Laverne asked, now joining them to try to identify the stranger. "I have no idea. Maybe it's a hobo looking for a handout? But coming all the way out here? Don't make much sense."

"Oh my God!" Orpha said in disbelief. "I think I know who it is. And if I'm right, a certain little boy is going to have a very Merry Christmas! Bill, it's Lemvel!"

He was halfway to the house now all hunched over and walking very quickly with his hands shoved down in his pockets. They all watched as he turned onto the pavement in front of the house. "That's who it is all right," Orpha confirmed for all to hear. "Oh my God!"

"Bobby, do you know who that is coming up the walk?" she asked as she scooped up the young boy in her arms, pointing to the stooped figure who by this time was almost at the front door.

Bobby stared hard at the man for a second, then looking up into Orpha's face, whispered, "Daddy?"

"Yes, it's your daddy all right! Let's go see him!" Everyone assembled in the front hall, waiting for the knocker to sound.

"I'll be damned," Bill smiled. "Couldn't ask for a better gift for Bobby."

"Saints be praised," Laverne said, softly, eyes glistening and ready to spill over.

The knock was weak, and had they not been standing close by they could not have heard it. A few seconds passed and a much stronger knock was heard.

"Come on, you three, skedaddle! You don't have to be here," Laverne declared, trying to usher Theresa Ruth and her two brothers from the entryway. "You can go play now even if you don't want to," she motioned to George, who was lagging behind, curious to see what was going on.

"Yes sir, how can I help you?" Bill asked politely upon opening the door. Lemvel peered through the doorway at his son, still in Orpha's arms.

"My name is Lemvel Murphy. Uh, that thar boy, he's my son. I come to take him home." He then nodded in Orpha's direction, wearing a strained smile across his face.

"Come on in," Bill motioned with his head, as he stepped back, closing the heavy door behind him. "My name is Bill O'Dell. I'm Orpha's husband. I don't think we have met," he said as he extended his hand in a friendly greeting. "It's not the best weather to be traveling on foot, is it?"

It was apparent to Orpha that Lemvel was forcing himself to stand tall with some rigidity. He held his crumpled hat between his large, slender hands that moved nervously about its brim.

"Orpha, I . . . best tell you . . . it was wrong of me—running like a, um, scared jack rabbit," said Lemvel, shaking.

Orpha figured it was probably being nervous but more from being bone cold. It was a long walk in this kind of weather, wherever he came from.

"Lemvel, you don't need to apologize to me," she replied with a tinge of reprimand in her voice. "Here's who you need to say you're sorry to," she said, nodding at the child in her arms.

Wide eyed, Bobby remained quiet, while not taking his gaze from his father's face. Stepping in front of his son, Lemvel opened his arms, reaching outward.

The little boy's stillness made Orpha feel a momentary tension, and some pity for this man who forgot to be a father when he was needed most, but rather dwelled on his own loss and pain.

He lowered his arms slowly, his shoulders now sagging, as he began taking a backward step. In that instant, leaning out from Orpha's arms, Bobby grabbed hold of his father's shirtsleeve.

Lemvel's face, now radiating, reached out once again, taking his small son into his arms, embracing him as he smiled at Bill and Orpha.

"I'm mighty beholden to you folks for taking care of him."

"He's family, Lemvel," Orpha spoke pointedly. "What would you expect? He's my sister's baby. There would have been no way I would have left him down there in that, pardon the expression, squalid shack with both you and Mary Barbara gone."

Her buried resentment of how her sister lived and died, and his abandonment of her son, quickly surfaced.

"How's about us going into the den for coffee," Bill broke in. "We can talk there in front of the fire. Lemvel, would you want a sandwich or something hot to drink?"

"Well, umm, sure, I could use something."

"Sweetheart, would you see about getting us all some coffee and maybe something for this man to eat?" Bill asked, as he wrapped his right arm about her shoulders, squeezing her gently, while they moved down the hall in the direction of the den.

"If that's want you want me to do," she answered dryly, still feeling a need to express herself to this man who ran off to salve his own wounds before those of his four-year-old son. She prepared ham sandwiches and fresh coffee and as she did so, she began to realize that she too was being selfish by wanting to vent her anger and harsh judgment on Lemvel. After all, wasn't he here now, with Bobby clinging to his neck, obviously, happy to see him again?

"Go from here, Orpha," she instructed herself. "You don't have to have your say. The boy's happy, nothing else is important."

She sat waiting for the coffee to finish perking, her thoughts skipping over memories of Mary Barbara, how mad she was that day with the shotgun strapped to her back as she took off toward the shed to blow away the creep that tried to rape her sister.

Orpha smiled as she remembered the time while living way out on Wild Horse Creek Road that the two of them along with Arline and all of the kids were sitting at the kitchen table late one night, waiting for Floyd to return home.

The table was built like a picnic table, making enough room for everyone to sit at one time. It had been placed along the outside wall.

A sudden loud thump sent them all scurrying across the room with the kids having been snatched up—all except one. Poor Raymond sat by himself screaming at the top of his lungs.

Orpha remembered yelling at her sister, "Arline, get Raymond."

"Oh my God," Arline had answered, running back and grabbing the frightened child from the now-deserted table. They all stood waiting as the back door slowly opened. "Floyd! You son of a bitch," Mary Barbara had cursed at him. "I ought to kick you to death, scaring all these little kids like that."

Floyd was laughing so hard he could hardly stand up straight. "Hey, I watched through the window. You were running faster than any of those kids," he taunted.

Orpha got up from her chair smiling as she shook her head and began placing everything on the huge tray she would carry into the den. Upon entering the room she witnessed a handshake between her husband and brother-in-law.

Bill explained that he had just hired a new man for the new restaurant. And being that Lemvel and Bobby would be moving in with Lemvel's aunt, who lives in St.

Louis, perhaps the boy's clothes ought to be packed, unless they would want to stay for Christmas. Lemvel hemmed and hawed a little, looking in Orpha's direction.

"Oh, why not?" she said, smiling. "That would make the kids happy, and that's what Christmas is all about. Sure, stay."

The house and all that now lay sleeping in it were peaceful and silent this Christmas Eve night.

Orpha, still awake, lay contently in her bed—the room softly illuminated by the bright moonlight streaming in through the large bedroom windows.

She could just barely make out the small package Bill had left on her nightstand with orders that it was not to be opened until the following morning. "What a tease," she thought, smiling to herself. "He knows how it drives me wild to have to wait. What could he have in such a small box?"

Her thoughts moved now to the early arrival of her mother and sister Christmas morning, to how excited the kids would be throughout the day, to the fun they would have tearing open their gifts, to the delicious holiday meal Laverne would prepare for all to share.

Orpha slid her hand over, touching Bill's sleeping form that rose and fell slowly.

"God, thank you for this good man and all of this you have chosen to give me. I'm not sure I deserve such happiness, but I will do my best to make him happy. . . . Good night, Mary Barbara, I do miss you."

It's Christmas, it's Christmas," a chorus of rowdy young voices called from the doorway. Sitting up in bed Orpha could see the excited children bumping into each other as they jumped up and down in anticipation.

Fully awake now, Bill sat up and teasingly bellowed, "Hey, can't a man get any sleep around this place?"

"It's Christmas!" the children sang out once again as they charged the bed and pounced on it. Smoothing his hair down with a swipe of his hand, Bill reached out for his trousers. Snatching them from the chair, he quickly pulled them on. Then picking Theresa Ruth up from her keeling position on the bed he gave her a peck on the cheek. "I'll tell you what," he smiled, setting her on the floor. "All of you run downstairs and we will be right behind you, in one shake of a lamb's tail. Don't go anywhere now. Wait for us by the Christmas tree."

Laverne, who by now made her way to the commotion, took the kids in hand and with some assistance from a smiling Lemvel ushered them from the room. The pandemonium of their descent faded as Bill closed the door and picked up the small package from Orpha's night table. Handing it to her, he sat on the edge of the bed, watching as she slowly took the wrapping from his gift.

"Oh Bill, it's wonderful!" Orpha exhaled softly in appreciation. "I have never seen such a gorgeous locket."

She loved the beauty of its simple lines and the rich glow of its gold emanating from the tiny box.

"The locket is not the heart of the gift," he smiled. "It's what's inside."

A little perplexed, Orpha opened the rectangular-shaped locket with its nipped corners. Inscribed on the left side was MY LOVE, on the right MY LIFE. "Thank you," Orpha said, her voice cracking with emotion as her eyes mirrored her feelings. She wrapped her arms about Bill's neck kissing him gently on his lips. "My gift is downstairs and in no way can ever measure up to this. But maybe with just you knowing and with me showing how much I do love you from day to day, that will compare."

"Couldn't ask for more," he grinned, squeezing her tightly. "Now I think we had better get going before those hooligans come storming up here for us."

"Yes, they're probably on pins and needles by now," she chuckled. Hand in hand they walked down the winding stairway, and as they entered the large main room where their family waited, a loud, exuberant "Merry Christmas" greeted them.

The children ran to greet Orpha and Bill as they entered the spacious living room. They excitedly pranced about calling the couple's attention to the mountain of gifts under the brightly lit Christmas tree.

"Oh my gosh," George said, disbelieving what he was seeing.

"Oh my gosh," Theresa Ruth called out, mimicking her brother, as she often did. "Mommy," the little girl said, "Santa must like us a lot, huh? He left all these presents for us."

"Well, yes, I guess you could say that," replied Orpha, smiling at her small daughter.

They were still jumping about in anticipation along with continuous chatter when Bill called out, "Okay, now let's quiet down and see who these gifts are for."

The kids quickly sat on the floor and a hush surrounded them.

"Let's see here," Bill said, picking up the first gift of many. "This says 'to George.' Do we know a George?"

"I do!" George yelled. "That's me," he said jumping up from the floor.

"Well, then, George, come and get your gift."

"Thank you," he said, giving Bill a quick hug.

"You're welcome, young man," Bill replied, with a large grin.

Orpha was beaming with happiness as she watched her children tear open their gifts with so much enjoyment.

"Look, Mommy, look," Theresa Ruth excitedly yelled out as she held up her Shirley Temple doll for her mother to see. "I love her forever," she squealed with joy.

"I know, she is beautiful, honey," Orpha answered.

George had already opened his gift, and was in the middle of building with his Lincoln Logs. Ronnie was quite content just pushing his large red dump truck and making his own special kind of truck noises. Bobby had opened his small Lionel train set. Lemvel seemed to be getting a big kick out of setting it up while Bobby watched intently.

The dispersing of gifts continued in lightheartedness and delight for some time followed by the huge breakfast Laverne had prepared. By the end of the day all were happy, exhausted, and well fed. Laverne had outdone herself in the kitchen once again.

"Such a great blessing she truly is," Orpha remarked to Bill as they sat finishing their after-dinner coffee at the kitchen table. "She is most likely going to need a serious vacation soon from all of us," Orpha chuckled.

"You know, that is a great idea," Bill agreed. "We will see to that right now."

"How are you going to that? Where would she go? And what would she do?"

"That would be entirely up to her. I will see to it she will not be short of money. So she can pretty much go where she chooses. How does that sound to you, my love?"

"Wonderful! God knows she has earned it."

"I'll tell you what! We can take care of this now. Do you happen to know where there might be an envelope?"

Orpha got up from the table, walking over to one of the many lower drawers in the cupboards. Pulling it open, she took a long white envelope from it and placed it in front of Bill.

"What do you plan on doing?" she smiled broadly.

"Well, let's see. We write her a big fat Christmas check and give her as much time as she needs to plan a vacation."

"Are you going to give it to her now?"

"No, I'll let you take it to her room if you don't mind and let her find it when she retires for the night. She is in the middle of preparing the children for bed so we will let her catch her breath."

Bill finished the check, slid it into the envelope, sealed it, and on the front he wrote, "For our most loved and appreciated, always-there-when-needed friend, who will forever be an important member of this family. With our LOVE and respect, Bill and Orpha."

On the front he wrote MERRY CHRISTMAS!

Orpha took the gift to Laverne's room, laying it on her bed. She then went from room to room saying her goodnights to the children with hugs and kisses. She checked on the baby who was sleeping soundly. As she walked back down the staircase, her thoughts were of how her life, as well as her children's, had changed so greatly since she met Bill. "Thank you, God," she whispered.

Orpha was making her way back to the kitchen when, from the top of the stairs, she could hear Laverne's hushed voice calling her. "Orpha, wait, wait, please!"

The envelope she carried announced the purpose of rushing to her side. "This is much too much. I cannot accept this. I know it's meant well but I feel it is way too much for what I do."

"Well, all I can tell you is that Bill and I both love you dearly and we have both said we don't know what we would do without you, so please take our gift and know, as Bill said, you are family. If you want to thank him he is in the kitchen."

Orpha waited outside the kitchen doorway until Laverne had said her thank yous to Bill. Laverne and Bill had been friends for so long that Orpha wanted to give them this private moment. As she came from the kitchen Laverne gave Orpha a big warm hug. "Thank you both so very much," and with that she continued to the stairway.

"Such a steadfast woman," Orpha thought as she watched Laverne disappear once she had reached the top of the staircase.

"Shall we sit in the living room?" Orpha asked Bill as she stood in the opening of the kitchen doorway.

"Sure," he responded, getting up from his chair as he walked to her, wrapping his arms about her. Bringing her in close, he bent down, whispering in her ear, "I love you so much, Mrs. O'Dell."

"And I love you, Bill," she said, smiling up at him. With his arm still around her waist they walked into a room that just a few hours ago held joyful energy and abundant amounts of love. Now it held a feeling of peaceful serenity. The huge Christmas tree, laden with so many sparkling colored lights stood off by itself in the corner, but its reflection was caught in the expansive window across the room. The fireplace that once held fragrant, high-burning logs of birch was now left with bright orange embers slowly turning to ash.

"Would you like more coffee?" Orpha asked.

"No, sweetheart. Enough coffee for today, thank you."

Sitting on the sofa, they began relaxing. Orpha snuggled in close to Bill as they started rehashing the day. "That was something to watch when Laverne and Lemvel had the kids outside building the snowman. All of them had such a great time. The snowball fight you know was the funniest part when Lemvel had been peppering George and the rest of them. And then lo and behold to everyone's surprise George nailed him right in the nose. Good thing it was a soft snow."

"Yeah, it's been a great day, no question," Bill nodded. Could not have been better. Well, maybe we could try," he chuckled, kissing Orpha on the top of her head.

"Fine with me," she answered with a soft laugh and then moved in closer to Bill's side.

The two of them sat quietly for a spell just at peace with the world and each other.

"Bill?" Orpha broke the silence.

"Uh-huh," Bill responded.

"I don't mean to derail our world of peace and happiness at the moment but I have been thinking of something off and on all day and it really is bothering me."

"What would that be? We will fix it if we can, sweetheart," Bill replied.

"I'm worried about Bobby moving in with Lemvel. To be honest, he just doesn't seem to be responsible enough to care for a little boy like Bobby. I'm afraid Bobby wouldn't be safe. Remember when Mary Barbara died and he took off only thinking of his own loss and pain? I'm not convinced he wouldn't do it again. I'm fearful that if he moves to St. Louis he might leave Bobby at the apartment alone while he worked. I'm just unsure of his ability or devotion. Maybe if you talk to him, you could suggest that Bobby stay here during the week and he could be with him on the weekends?"

"Tell you what, I will have a talk with him and see what we can work out. But you have to keep in mind he might not want to go along with what you think is best. But I am sure we can come to some kind of agreement in order to calm your worries and make everyone content, all right?"

"Thanks Bill, I do appreciate your offer."

Once again their contentment resumed in the hushed surroundings. Orpha knew deep inside that this man was all any woman could wish for. She was not only reassured by the warmth of his love but as well by his great strength and ability. She knew that together nothing was impossible.